PENGUIN  CLASSICS

KOKORO

NATSUME SŌSEKI (1867–1916), one of Japan's most influential modern writers, is widely considered the foremost novelist of the Meiji era (1868–1912). Born Natsume Kinnosuke in Tokyo, he graduated from Tokyo University in 1893 and then taught high school English. He went to England on a Japanese government scholarship, and when he returned to Japan, he lectured on English literature at Tokyo University and began his writing career with the novel *I Am a Cat*. In 1908 he gave up teaching and became a full-time writer. He wrote fourteen novels, including *Botchan* and *Kusamakura,* as well as haiku, poems in the Chinese style, academic papers on literary theory, essays, and autobiographical sketches. His work enjoyed wide popularity in his lifetime and secured him a permanent place in Japanese literature.

MEREDITH MCKINNEY holds a Ph.D. in medieval Japanese literature from the Australian National University in Canberra, where she teaches at the Japan Centre. She taught in Japan for twenty years and now lives near Braidwood, New South Wales. Her other translations include *Ravine and Other Stories* by Furui Yoshikichi, *The Tale of Saigyo*, and, for Penguin Classics, *The Pillow Book of Sei Shōnagon* and Natsume Sōseki's *Kusamakura.*

NATSUME SŌSEKI

Kokoro

Translated with an Introduction and Notes by
MEREDITH MCKINNEY

PENGUIN BOOKS

PENGUIN BOOKS

Published by the Penguin Group
Penguin Group (USA) Inc., 375 Hudson Street,
New York, New York 10014, U.S.A.
Penguin Group (Canada), 90 Eglinton Avenue East, Suite 700, Toronto,
Ontario, Canada M4P 2Y3 (a division of Pearson Penguin Canada Inc.)
Penguin Books Ltd, 80 Strand, London WC2R 0RL, England
Penguin Ireland, 25 St Stephen's Green, Dublin 2,
Ireland (a division of Penguin Books Ltd)
Penguin Group (Australia), 250 Camberwell Road,
Camberwell, Victoria 3124, Australia
(a division of Pearson Australia Group Pty Ltd)
Penguin Books India Pvt Ltd, 11 Community Centre,
Panchsheel Park, New Delhi–110 017, India
Penguin Group (NZ), 67 Apollo Drive, Rosedale, North Shore 0632,
New Zealand (a division of Pearson New Zealand Ltd)
Penguin Books (South Africa) (Pty) Ltd, 24 Sturdee Avenue,
Rosebank, Johannesburg 2196, South Africa

Penguin Books Ltd, Registered Offices:
80 Strand, London WC2R 0RL, England

This translation first published in Penguin Books 2010

20TH PRINTING

Translation, introduction, and notes copyright © Meredith McKinney, 2010
All rights reserved

LIBRARY OF CONGRESS CATALOGING-IN-PUBLICATION DATA
Natsume, Soseki, 1867–1916.
[Kokoro. English]
Kokoro / Natsume Soseki ; translated with an introduction and notes by Meredith McKinney.
p.   cm.—(Penguin classics)
Includes bibliographical references.
ISBN 978-0-14-310603-6
I. McKinney, Meredith, 1950–   II. Title.
PL812.A8K613   2010
895.6'342—dc22   2009041363

Printed in the United States of America
Set in Adobe Sabon

Contents

KOKORO

Introduction

Natsume Sōseki's *Kokoro* was published in 1914, two years before his death at the age of forty-eight. Sōseki, even then widely acknowledged as Japan's leading novelist, was at the peak of his writing career, and *Kokoro* is unquestionably his greatest work. Today it is considered one of Japan's great modern novels, known to every schoolchild and read by anyone serious about the nation's literature.

The reasons for *Kokoro*'s importance lie not in its literary quality alone. Sōseki was a superb chronicler of his time, and *Kokoro* cannot be fully understood without some knowledge of the world from which it sprang.

Japan's Meiji period (which ended with the emperor Meiji's death in 1912) began in 1868 with the tumultuous overthrow of the old Tokugawa shogunate, which had ruled Japan unopposed for 250 years. The shift signaled far more than a change of power. Japan under the Tokugawas had been rigidly feudal and isolationist, a Confucian society cut off from the changes that were rapidly overtaking much of the rest of the world. Pressure from Western nations eager to expand their sphere of trade finally proved irresistible in 1853, when the commander of a U.S. squadron, Matthew Perry, anchored his "black ships" threateningly offshore and sent an ultimatum to Japan's ruling powers. The subsequent internal upheaval resulted in a new government that opened Japan's doors to the West and embraced the introduction of Western culture and technology. In the next four decades Japan was utterly transformed. The Meiji period is synonymous with the fundamental transformation that set Japan on the road to becoming all that it is today.

Such rapid change inevitably comes at a psychological cost, and this is what Sōseki acutely documented in his finest novels. The dilemmas that he portrayed were deeply felt. Natsume Kinnosuke (Sōseki was his *nom de plume*) was born in 1867, the year before the Meiji era began, in what was still known as Edo (now Tokyo). The old Japan was his inheritance in more than birth. He was educated in the Chinese and Japanese classics and in the Confucian moral code, which Western concepts of individualism and individual rights were only just beginning to undermine. *Kokoro*'s central character, the man referred to as Sensei, is of an age with Sōseki, and his references to the importance of his old-fashioned moral education clearly reflect Sōseki's own experience. For both, the Meiji period's embrace of Western individualism provoked irreconcilable inner conflicts that haunted them through life.

Kokoro's Sensei shares other characteristics with Sōseki as well. Family difficulties and alienation, a recurrent theme in many of Sōseki's novels, played their part in his own early life. A late child of a large family, Sōseki as an infant was formally adopted by a childless couple; his real family took him back only grudgingly when the couple divorced nine years later. Adoption, which plays an important part in the story of Sensei's friend K in *Kokoro*, was common at the time—continuing the family name was more important than maintaining blood ties. Sōseki's own adoption was a sorry failure on every level, leaving him feeling unloved, isolated, and bitter.

Like *Kokoro*'s Sensei, Sōseki, a bright student, attended the new university in Tokyo, where he specialized in English literature. Meiji-era Japan believed that foreign literature held the key to understanding the Western culture that it was then avidly embracing, and Sōseki was part of the earliest generation to be trained in this important field. His education gave him elite status, and in 1900 the Japanese government selected him to spend two years studying in London; the intention was that he would increase the nation's cultural capital by bringing back a deeper understanding of the West. But Sōseki was miserable in England, isolated and alienated from everything around him, which seems to have brought him close to nervous collapse.

After his return to Japan, he took up prestigious teaching posts at the First National College and in the English literature department at Tokyo's Imperial University. To all appearances, he was set to rise to the top of his elite profession. But Sōseki could revel in neither his status nor his success. Like *Kokoro*'s Sensei, he was an essentially introverted and retiring person; his nervous sensibility shrank from exposure to the everyday world, and the strain of teaching told badly on his nerves. Partly to soothe and entertain himself, he decided to try his hand at a light, humorous novel (*I Am a Cat*, 1905). To his surprise, upon publication it achieved instant fame. A year later came two more novels: the immensely popular *Botchan* (1906) as well as the beautiful haiku-style *Kusamakura*. At the age of forty, encouraged by the *Asahi* newspaper's guarantee to serialize any future work, Sōseki took the audacious step of resigning from his teaching posts and devoting himself to his writing.

His novels had moved from gently humorous anecdotes and observations of life to the more philosophical and experimental approach of *Kusamakura*, which maintains a delightful lightness of touch even as it engages thoughtfully and critically with Meiji Japan's transformations and its fraught relationship to Japan's past. But the mature works that now began to flow from his pen struck a new, more inward note. Sōseki became increasingly focused on his contemporaries' quintessential experience, one that he himself felt acutely: the necessity to evolve a modern, individual sense of self and to cope with the new Meiji self's resultant problems: isolation, alienation, egotism, and profound dislocation from its cultural and moral inheritance. Sōseki increasingly sought to portray for his readers not only the upheavals of their rapidly changing world but the dilemmas and suffering of the contemporary psyche.

These themes achieved their ultimate statement in the late novel *Kokoro*. It was both written and set in the first days of the new Taishō period, which began in 1912 with Meiji's death and the accession of the new emperor. The moment of transition registered profoundly throughout Japan. The unnamed protagonist in the novel's long first section, "Sensei and I," is a naive and earnest young man on the point of graduating from the Imperial University; he is one of the new generation's elite who will inherit the coming era. The focus of this section is his difficult and intense relationship with the older man he calls Sensei, whom we see through his puzzled and intrigued young eyes.

Sōseki himself would have known well the disconcerting role of *sensei* to the worshipful young. Usually translated as "teacher," *sensei* is essentially a term of deep respect for one who knows; it implies a position of authority in relation to oneself that comes close to that of master and disciple. In strongly hierarchical Meiji society, Sōseki, with his established position as a leading writer, naturally attracted a flock of eager young followers (many of whom would go on to become key literary figures of the Taishō period and beyond). We may all too easily imagine Sōseki, holding court in his role as *sensei*, registering private misgivings at the intensity of some of his disciples' devotion to him, and doubts about his suitability as role model for them. However, where Sōseki was a successful man, at least in public terms, *Kokoro*'s Sensei is essentially a failure, both in his own eyes and in those of the world. The puzzle that the first section presents is: What are the causes of this failure?

The novel's short middle section balances the unnamed young man's yearning and unfulfilled relationship with the evasive Sensei against that with his own dying father. Like Sensei, the father in some ways embodies the Meiji era, which at that moment is in its own death throes. Themes of betrayal and a failure of moral nerve, which sound through much of Sōseki's work and are fundamental to *Kokoro*, are also set to haunt the young man's own future at the end of this section as he opens the long letter he has received from Sensei and begins to read.

That letter constitutes the final section of the novel and is in many ways its real tour de force. In fact, Sōseki conceived it first and originally intended it to stand alone as a complete work. It takes us back to the world of Sensei's youth, to his own student days. The letter's painfully honest confession will finally reveal to the young man what he has longed to know—the mysterious secret that cast its long shadow over Sensei's life. But it is more than a simple confession. Writing this letter as he faces his own despairing death, Sensei attempts to redeem himself, if nothing else than in the role of Sensei that he unwillingly accepted late in life, by passing on his story for the edification of his young follower and friend. Ironically, his letter becomes the unwitting cause of the young man's own crucial act of moral failure.

The man called K, the young Sensei's friend, who precipitates the crisis with which the novel culminates, in many ways embodies the old world's strict code of values and ethics, which was coming into such painful conflict with the new Western concepts of individual rights and the primacy of the ego. K's self-elected death foreshadows the ultimate death of that old world, a world Sōseki himself had inherited and whose unattainable and rapidly vanishing certainties preoccupied him. K's death by his own hand, shocking and pointless from the perspective of the new values, is nevertheless a crucial moral victory that haunts Sensei's life. Another, later death also reverberates, both for the dying father and, crucially, for Sensei himself—the ritual suicide of General Nogi. This anachronistic gesture of ethical atonement and expression of desire to follow one's master (here the Meiji emperor) to the grave stunned Japan. The news impels Sensei, the morally paralyzed inheritor of Meiji Japan's dual worlds, finally to act. His suicide is not only an act of personal despair but is expressed half-seriously as "following to the grave ì . . . the spirit of the Meiji era itself," a final gesture of loyalty to that era's difficult dualities that, he guesses, his young friend will find incomprehensible.

Kokoro is beautifully constructed to express Meiji Japan's spiritual dilemmas. But it does much more: Sōseki is a masterful portrayer of human relations, and in fact the novel's wider historical dimensions are usually little more than flickers at the edge of the reader's consciousness. As well as being a compelling portrait of Sensei in maturity and youth, *Kokoro* tells the story of three young men whose hearts are "restless with love" and of their emotional entanglements not only with the opposite sex but variously with one another. Homosexuality is not, needless to say, at issue, although a young man's intellectually erotic attraction to an older man is beautifully evoked. The novel's women, particularly Sensei's wife, are portrayed sympathetically, but it is the men who take center stage—another, although no doubt unwitting, expression of the Meiji ethos. Their very different relationships with and reactions to one another form the core of the story and weave its suspenseful and carefully constructed plot.

In their dilemmas and responses, the characters of *Kokoro,* although in many ways specific to their time, are fundamentally immensely human. It is the human condition itself that is Sōseki's primary interest, here and elsewhere in his work. In *Kokoro* he achieved his finest expression of this great theme.

ABOUT THE TITLE

Kokoro, the novel's title, is a complex and important word that can perhaps best be explained as "the thinking and feeling heart," as distinguished from the workings of the pure intellect, devoid of human feeling. Because one's *kokoro* thinks as well as feels, "heart" is at times an inadequate translation. Nevertheless, as the concept of *kokoro* is a pervasive motif throughout the novel, I have chosen to express it with the single word "heart" and to preserve its presence in the translation wherever possible. For the title, it seemed best to retain the original word.

MEREDITH McKINNEY

Acknowledgments

I am grateful to the Japan Centre at the Australian National University, under whose auspices I completed this translation while a visiting fellow.

My warm thanks also go to two friends. Nobuo Sakai of Tezukayama Gakuin Daigaku meticulously checked the translation against the original, and Elizabeth Lawson, as always, generously spared her time to read the final draft and make invaluable suggestions.

Suggestions for Further Reading

OTHER WORKS BY NATSUME SŌSEKI

Brodey, Inger Sigrun, Ikuo Tsunematsu, and Sammy I. Tsunematsu, trans. *My Individualism and the Philosophical Foundations of Literature*. Tokyo: Tuttle Publishing, 2005.

Cohn, Joel, trans. *Botchan*. Tokyo: Kodansha International, 2007.

Ito, Aiko, and Graeme Wilson, trans. *I Am a Cat*. Tokyo: Tuttle Publishing, 2002.

McClellan, Edwin, trans. *Grass on the Wayside*. Tokyo: Tuttle Publishing, 1971.

Rubin, Jay, trans. *Sanshirō*. New York: Penguin Classics, 2010.

WORKS ON *KOKORO*

Fukuchi, Isamu. "*Kokoro* and ëthe Spirit of Meiji." *Monumenta Nipponica* 48:468–88.

McClellan, Edwin. "The Implications of Sōseki's *Kokoro*." *Monumenta Nipponica* 14:356–70.

Pollack, David. "Framing the Self: The Philosophical Dimensions of Human Nature in *Kokoro*." *Monumenta Nipponica* 43:417–27.

WORKS ON NATSUME SŌSEKI

Beangcheon, Yul. *Natsume Sōseki*. London: Macmillan, 1984.

Brodey, Inger Sigrun. "Natsume Sōseki and Laurence Sterne: Cross-

Cultural Discourse on Literary Linearity." *Comparative Literature* 50, no. 3 (Summer 1998): 193–219.

Brodey, Inger Sigrun, and Sammy I. Tsunematsu. *Rediscovering Natsume Sōseki*. Folkestone: Global Books Ltd., 2001.

Iijima, Takehisa, and James M. Vardaman Jr., eds. *The World of Natsume Sōseki*. Tokyo: Kinseido Ltd., 1987.

McClellan, Edwin. *Two Japanese Novelists: Sōseki and Toson*. Tuttle Publishing, 2004.

Miyoshi, Masao. *Accomplices of Silence: The Modern Japanese Novel*. Berkeley: University of California Press, 1974.

Rubin, Jay. "The Evil and the Ordinary in Sōseki's Fiction." *Harvard Journal of Asiatic Studies* 46, no. 2 (December 1986): 333–52.

Turney, Alan. "Sōseki's Development as a Novelist Until 1907; With Special Reference to the Genesis, Nature and Position in His Work of *Kusa Makura*." *Monumenta Nipponica* 41, no. 4 (Winter 1986): 497–99.

Viglielmo, Valdo H. "An Introduction to the Later Novels of Natsume Sōseki." *Monumenta Nipponica* 19, no. 1, 1–36.

Yiu, Angela. *Chaos and Order in the Works of Natsume Sōseki*. Honolulu: University of Hawaii Press, 1998.

PART I

SENSEI AND I

CHAPTER 1

I always called him Sensei, and so I shall do in these pages, rather than reveal his name. It is not that I wish to shield him from public scrutiny—simply that it feels more natural. "Sensei" springs to my lips whenever I summon memories of this man, and I write of him now with the same reverence and respect. It would also feel wrong to use some conventional initial to substitute for his name and thereby distance him.

I first met Sensei in Kamakura,[1] in the days when I was still a young student. A friend had gone there during summer vacation for sea bathing and urged me to join him, so I set about organizing enough money to cover the trip. This took me two or three days. Less than three days after I arrived, my friend received a sudden telegram from home demanding that he return. His mother was ill, it seemed.

He did not believe it. For some time his parents had been trying to force him into an unwanted marriage. By present-day standards he was far too young for marriage, and besides he did not care for the girl in question. That was why he had chosen not to return home for the vacation, as he normally would have, but to go off to a local seaside resort to enjoy himself.

He showed me the telegram and asked what I thought he should do. I did not know what to advise. But if his mother really was ill, he clearly should go home, so in the end he decided to leave. Having come to Kamakura to be with my friend, I now found myself alone.

I could stay or go as I pleased, since some time still remained before classes began again, so I decided to stay where I was for the moment. My friend, who was from a prosperous family in the Chūgoku region, did not lack for money. But he was a student, and young, so in fact his standard of living was actually much like my own, and I was spared the trouble of having to find a cheaper inn for myself after he left.

The inn he had chosen was somewhere in an out-of-the-way district of Kamakura. To get to any of the fashionable spots—the billiard rooms and ice cream parlors and such things—I had to take a lengthy walk through the rice fields. A rickshaw ride would cost me a full twenty *sen*. Still, a number of new summer houses stood in the area, and it was right next to the beach, making it wonderfully handy for sea bathing.

Each day I went down to the shore for a swim, making my way among soot-blackened old thatched country houses. An astonishing number of men and women always thronged the beach, city folk down from Tokyo to escape the summer heat. Sometimes the crowd was so thick that the water was a tightly packed mass of black heads, as in some public bathhouse. Knowing no one, I enjoyed my time alone amid this merry scene, lying on the sand and leaping about up to my knees in the waves.

It was here in this throng of people that I first came upon Sensei. In those days two little stalls on the beach provided drinks and changing rooms, and for no particular reason I took to frequenting one of them. Unlike the owners of the grand summer houses in the Hasé area, we users of this beach had no private bathing huts, so communal changing rooms were essential. People drank tea and relaxed here, or left their hats and sun umbrellas in safekeeping; after they bathed, they would wash themselves down at the stall, and attendants would rinse their bathing suits for them. I owned no bathing clothes, but I left my belongings at the stall whenever I went into the water, to avoid having anything stolen.

CHAPTER 2

When I first set eyes on Sensei there, he had just taken off his clothes and was about to go in for a swim, while I had just emerged from the water and was drying off in the sea breeze. A number of black heads were moving around between us, obstructing my view of him, and under normal circumstances I probably would not have noticed him. But he instantly caught my attention, despite the crowd and my own distracted state of mind, because he was with a Westerner.

The Westerner's marvelously white skin had struck me as soon as I came in. He had casually tossed his kimono robe onto the nearby bench and then, clad only in a pair of drawers such as we Japanese wear, stood gazing out toward the sea, arms folded.

This intrigued me. Two days earlier I had gone up to Yuigahama beach and spent a long time watching the Westerners bathing. I had settled myself on a low dune very close to the rear entrance of a hotel frequented by foreigners, and seen a number of men emerge to bathe. Unlike this Westerner, however, they all wore clothing that covered their torso, arms, and legs. The women were even more modest. Most wore red or blue rubber caps that bobbed prettily about among the waves.

Because I had so recently observed all that, the sight of this Westerner standing there in front of everyone wearing only a pair of trunks struck me as quite remarkable.

He turned and spoke a few words to the Japanese man beside him, who had bent over to pick up a small towel that had fallen on the sand. His companion then wrapped the towel about his head and set off toward the sea. This man was Sensei.

Out of nothing more than curiosity, my eyes followed the
two figures as they walked side by side down to the water. Step-
ping straight into the waves, they made their way through the
boisterous crowd gathered in the shallows close to shore, and
when they reached a relatively open stretch of water, both
began to swim. They swam on out to sea until their heads
looked small in the distance. Then they turned around and
swam straight back to the beach. Returning to the stall, they
toweled themselves down without rinsing at the well, put on
their clothes, and promptly headed off together for some unknown destination.

After they left, I sat down on the bench and smoked a cigarette. I wondered idly about Sensei. I felt sure I had seen his face
before somewhere, but for the life of me I could not recall
where or when.

I was at loose ends and needing to amuse myself, so the following day I went back to the stall at the hour when I had seen
Sensei. Sure enough, there he was again. This time he came
along wearing a straw hat, and the Westerner was not with him.
He removed his spectacles and set them on the bench, then
wrapped a small towel around his head and set off briskly
down the beach.

As I watched him make his way through the crowd at the
edge and start to swim, I had a sudden urge to follow him. In
I strode, the water splashing high around me, and when I
reached a reasonable depth, I set my sights on him and began
to swim. I did not reach him, however. Rather than return the
way he had come, as he did the previous day, Sensei had swum
in an arc back to the beach.

I too swam back, and as I emerged from the water and entered the stall, shaking the drops from my hands, he passed me
on his way out, already neatly dressed.

CHAPTER 3

The next day I went to the beach at the same hour yet again, and again I saw Sensei there. I did the same the day after, but never found an opportunity to speak to him or even to greet him. Besides, Sensei's demeanor was rather forbidding. He would arrive at the same time each day, with an unapproachable air, and depart just as punctually and aloofly. He seemed quite indifferent to the noisy throng that surrounded him. The Westerner who had been with him that first day never reappeared. Sensei was always alone.

Finally my chance came. Sensei had as usual come striding back from his swim. He was about to don the kimono that lay as usual on the bench, when he found that it had somehow gotten covered in sand. As he turned away and quickly shook it out, I saw his spectacles, which had been lying on the bench beneath it, slip through a crack between the boards and fall to the ground. Sensei put on the robe and wrapped the sash around his waist. Then, evidently noticing that his spectacles were missing, he quickly began to search for them. In a moment I had ducked down, thrust my hand under the bench, and retrieved them from the ground.

"Thank you," he said as he took them.

The next day I followed Sensei into the sea and swam after him. I had gone about two hundred yards when he suddenly stopped swimming and turned to speak to me. We two were the only beings afloat on that blue expanse of water for a considerable distance. As far as the eye could see, strong sunlight blazed down upon sea and mountains.

As I danced wildly in place there in the water, I felt my muscles

flood with a sensation of freedom and delight. Sensei, meanwhile, ceased to move and lay floating tranquilly on his back.
I followed his example and felt the sky's azure strike me full in
the face, as if plunging its glittering shafts of color deep behind
my eyes.

"Isn't this good!" I cried.

After a little while Sensei righted himself in the water and
suggested we go back. Being physically quite strong, I would
have liked to stay longer, but I instantly and happily agreed.
The two of us swam back to the beach the way we had come.

From this point on, Sensei and I were friends. Yet I still had no
idea where he was staying. On the afternoon of the third day
since our swim, he suddenly turned to me when we met at the
stall. "Are you planning to stay here a while longer?" he asked.

I had not thought about it and had no ready answer. "I don't
really know," I responded simply.

But the grin on Sensei's face made me suddenly awkward,
and I found myself asking, "What about you, Sensei?" This was
when I first began to call him by that name.

That evening I called on him at his lodgings. I say "lodgings,"
but I discovered it was no ordinary place—he was staying in a
villa in the spacious grounds of a temple. Those who shared the
place, I also discovered, were not related to him.

Noticing how he grimaced wryly when I persisted in calling
him "Sensei," I excused myself with the explanation that this
was a habit of mine when addressing my elders. I asked him
about the Westerner he had been with. The man was quite eccentric, he said, adding that he was no longer in Kamakura. He
told me a lot of other things about him, then remarked that it
was odd that he, who had few social contacts even with his fellow Japanese, should have become friends with such a person.

At the end of our conversation I told him that I felt I knew
him from somewhere but could not remember where. Young as
I was, I hoped that he might share my feeling and was anticipating his answer. But after a thoughtful pause, he said, "I can't
say I recall your face. Perhaps you're remembering somebody
else." His words produced in me a strange disappointment.

CHAPTER 4

At the end of the month I returned to Tokyo. Sensei had left the summer resort long since. When we parted, I had asked him, "Would you mind if I visited you from time to time?" "Yes, do," he replied simply. By this time I felt we were on quite familiar terms, and had expected a warmer response. This unsatisfactory reply rather wounded my self-confidence.

Sensei frequently disappointed me in this way. He seemed at times to realize it and at other times to be quite oblivious. Despite all the fleeting shocks of disappointment, however, I felt no desire to part ways with him. On the contrary, whenever some unexpected terseness of his shook me, my impulse was to press forward with the friendship. It seemed to me that if I did so, my yearning for the possibilities of all he had to offer would someday be fulfilled. Certainly I was young. Yet the youthful candor that drew me to him was not evident in my other relationships.

I had no idea why I should feel this way toward Sensei alone. Now, when he is dead, I understand at last. He had never disliked me, and the occasional curt greetings and aloofness were not expressions of displeasure intended to keep me at bay. I pity him now, for I realize that he was in fact sending a warning, to someone who was attempting to grow close to him, signaling that he was unworthy of such intimacy. For all his unresponsiveness to others' affection, I now see, it was not them he despised but himself.

Needless to say, I returned to Tokyo fully intending to visit Sensei. Classes would not resume for another two weeks, so I planned to visit him during that time. However, within two or

three days of my arrival in Tokyo, my feelings began to shift
and blur. The city's vibrant atmosphere, reviving as it did all my
stimulating memories, swept away thoughts of Kamakura. Seeing my fellow students in the street gave me a thrill of excited
anticipation for the coming academic year. For a while I forgot
about Sensei.

Classes started, and a month or so later I slumped back into
normalcy. I wandered the streets in vague discontentment, or
cast my eyes around my room, aware of some indefinable lack.
The thought of Sensei came into my mind once more. I wanted
to see him again, I realized.

The first time I went to his house, he was not home. The
second time was the following Sunday, I remember. It was a
beautiful day, with the sort of sky that feels as if it is penetrating
your very soul. Once again Sensei was out. I distinctly remembered him saying in Kamakura that he was almost always at
home. In fact, he had said, he quite disliked going out. Having
now found him absent both times I called, I remembered these
words, and somewhere inside me an inexplicable resentment
registered.

Instead of turning to go, I lingered at the front door, gazing
at the maid who had delivered the message. She recognized me
and remembered giving Sensei my card last time, so she left me
waiting while she retreated inside.

Then a lady whom I took to be Sensei's wife appeared. I was
struck by her beauty.

She courteously explained where Sensei had gone. On this
day every month, she told me, his habit was to visit the cemetery at Zōshigaya and offer flowers at one of the graves. "He
only went out a bare ten minutes or so ago," she added sympathetically.

I thanked her and left. I walked a hundred yards or so toward
the bustling town, then felt a sudden urge to take a detour by
way of Zōshigaya myself. I might even come across Sensei
there, I thought. I swung around and set off.

CHAPTER 5

I passed a field of rice seedlings on my right, then turned into the graveyard. I was walking down its broad maple-lined central avenue when I saw someone who could be Sensei emerging from the teahouse at the far end. I went on toward the figure until I could make out the sunlight flashing on the rim of his spectacles. "Sensei!" I called abruptly.

He halted and stared at me.

"How . . . ? How . . . ?"

The repeated word hung strangely in the hushed midday air. I found myself suddenly unable to reply.

"Did you follow me here? How . . . ?"

He seemed quite calm. His voice was quiet. But a shadow seemed to cloud his face.

I explained how I came to be there.

"Did my wife tell you whose grave I've come to visit?"

"No, she didn't mention that."

"I see. Yes, she wouldn't have any reason to, after all. She had only just met you. There'd be no need to tell you anything."

He seemed finally satisfied, but I was puzzled by what he had said.

Sensei and I walked together among the graves to the exit. One of the tombstones was inscribed with a foreign name, "Isabella So-and-so." Another, evidently belonging to a Christian, read "Rogin, Servant of God." Next to it stood a stupa with a quotation from the sutras: "Buddhahood is innate to all beings." Another gravestone bore the title "Minister Plenipotentiary." I paused at one small grave whose name I could make no sense of and asked Sensei about it. "I think that's intended to spell the name Andrei," he replied with a wry little smile.

I found humor and irony in this great variety of humanity displayed in the names on the tombstones, but I gathered that he did not. As I chattered on about the graves, pointing out this round tombstone or that tall thin marble pillar, he listened in silence. Finally he said, "You haven't seriously thought about the reality of death yet, have you?"

I fell silent. Sensei did not speak again.

At the end of the cemetery a great ginkgo tree stood blocking the sky. "It will look lovely before long," Sensei remarked, looking up at it. "This tree turns a beautiful color in autumn. The ground is buried deep in golden leaves when they fall." Every month when he came here, I discovered, he made a point of passing under this tree.

Some distance away a man had been smoothing the rough earth of a new grave; he paused on his hoe and watched us. We turned left, and soon were back on the street.

I had nowhere in particular to go, so I continued to walk beside him. He spoke less than usual. It did not make me feel awkward, however, and I strolled along easily beside him.

"Are you going straight home?" I asked.

"Yes, there's nowhere else I need to go."

We fell silent again and walked south down the hill.

"Is your family grave there?" I asked a little later, breaking the silence.

"No."

"Whose grave is it? Is it some relation?"

"No."

Sensei said no more, and I decided not to pursue the conversation. About a hundred yards on, however, he abruptly broke the silence. "A friend of mine is buried there."

"You visit a friend's grave every month?"

"That's right."

This was all he told me that day.

CHAPTER 6

I visited Sensei quite often thereafter. He was always at home when I called. And the more I saw of him, the sooner I wanted to visit him again.

Yet Sensei's manner toward me never really changed, from the day we first exchanged words to the time when our friendship was well established. He was always quiet, sometimes almost forlorn. From the outset he seemed to me strangely unapproachable, yet I felt compelled to find a way to get close to him.

Perhaps no one else would have had this response—others might have dismissed it as folly, an impulse of youth. Yet I feel a certain happy pride in the insight I showed, for later events served to justify my intuition. Sensei was a man who could, indeed must love, yet he was unable to open his arms and accept into his heart another who sought to enter.

He was, as I have said, always quiet and composed, even serene. Yet from time to time an odd shadow would cross his face, like the sudden dark passage of a bird across a window, although it was no sooner there than gone again. The first time I noticed it was when I called out to him in the graveyard at Zōshigaya. For a strange instant the warm pulse of my blood faltered a little. It was only a momentary miss of a beat, however, and in no time my heart recovered its usual resilient pulse, and I proceeded to forget what I had seen.

One evening just at the end of autumn's warm weather, I was unexpectedly reminded of it again.

As I was talking to Sensei, I was for some reason suddenly reminded of the great ginkgo tree that he had pointed out to me. A mental calculation told me that his next visit to the grave was three days away. My classes would finish at noon that day, so I would have the afternoon free.

I turned to Sensei. "I wonder if that ginkgo tree at Zōshigaya has lost its leaves by now."

"It won't be quite bare yet, I should think." He looked at me, his eyes staying on me for a long moment.

I quickly went on. "Would you mind if I go with you next time? I'd enjoy walking around the area with you."

"I go to visit a grave, you know, not to take a walk."

"But wouldn't it be nice to go for a walk while you're about it?"

Sensei did not reply at first, then said finally, "My sole purpose in going is to visit the grave." Clearly, he wanted to impress on me the distinction between a grave visit and a mere walk. It occurred to me that he might be making an excuse not to have me along. His tone seemed oddly petulant.

I felt an urge to press my case. "Well, let me come along anyway and visit the grave too. I'll pay respects with you." In truth, I couldn't really see the distinction between visiting someone's grave and taking a walk.

Sensei's brow darkened a little, and a strange light shone in his eyes. Was it annoyance, or dislike, or fear that I saw hovering there? Instantly, I had a vivid recollection of that shadow on his face when I had called out to him at Zōshigaya. This expression was identical.

"I have," Sensei began. "I have a particular reason that I cannot explain to you for wanting to visit that grave alone. I never even take my wife."

CHAPTER 7

It all struck me as very odd. But my intention in visiting him was not to study or analyze Sensei, so I let it pass. In retrospect, I particularly treasure my memory of that response to Sensei. Because of it, I think, I was able to achieve the real human intimacy with him that I later did. If I had chosen to turn the cool and analytical eye of curiosity on Sensei's heart, it would inexorably have snapped the bond of sympathy between us. At the time, of course, I was too young to be aware of any of this. Perhaps that is precisely where its true value lies. If I had made the mistake of responding less than guilelessly, who knows what might have befallen our relationship? I shudder to think of it. The scrutiny of an analytical eye was something Sensei always particularly dreaded.

It became my established habit to call on Sensei twice or even three times a month. One day he unexpectedly turned to me and asked, "What makes you come to see someone like me so often?"

"Well, no particular reason, really. Am I a nuisance, Sensei?"

"I wouldn't say that."

Indeed my visits didn't seem to annoy him. I was aware that he had a very narrow range of social contacts. He had also mentioned that only two or three of his old school friends were living in Tokyo. Occasionally, a fellow student from his hometown would be there when I called, but none of them seemed to me as close to him as I.

"I'm a lonely man," Sensei said, "so I'm happy that you come to visit. That's why I asked why you come so often."

"Why are you lonely?" I asked in return.

Sensei did not reply. He just looked at me and said, "How old are you?"

I could make no sense of this exchange and went home that day puzzled. Four days later, however, I was back at his house again.

He burst out laughing as soon as he emerged and saw me. "You're here again, eh?"

"Yes," I said, laughing too.

If anyone else had said this to me, I would surely have felt offended. But coming from Sensei, the words made me positively happy.

"I'm a lonely man," he repeated that evening. "I'm lonely, but I'm guessing you may be a lonely man yourself. I'm older, so I can withstand loneliness without needing to take action, but for you it's different—you're young. I sense that you have the urge to do, to act. You want to pit yourself against something . . ."

"I'm not at all lonely."

"No time is as lonely as youth. Why else should you visit me so often?"

Here was the same question again.

"But even when you're with me," he went on, "you probably still feel somehow lonely. I don't have the strength, you see, to really take on your loneliness and eradicate it for you. In time, you'll need to reach out toward someone else. Sooner or later your feet will no longer feel inclined to take you here."

Sensei smiled forlornly as he spoke.

CHAPTER 8

Fortunately Sensei's prophecy was not fulfilled. Inexperienced as I was, I could not grasp even the most obvious significance of his words, and continued to visit as usual. Before long I found myself occasionally dining there, which naturally put me in the position of talking to his wife.

Like other men, I was not indifferent to women. Being young, however, I had so far had little opportunity to have much to do with girls. Perhaps for this reason, my response to the opposite sex was limited to a keen interest in the unknown women I passed in the street. When I first saw Sensei's wife at the door, she had struck me as beautiful, and every time we met thereafter I thought so again. Otherwise I found nothing really to say about her.

That is not to say that she wasn't special in any way. Rather, she had had no opportunity to reveal her particular qualities to me. I treated her as a kind of appendage to Sensei, and she welcomed me as the young student who visited her husband. Sensei was our sole connection. That is why her beauty is the single impression I remember of her from those early days.

One day when I visited, I was given sake. His wife emerged to serve it to me. Sensei was more jovial than usual. "You must have a cup too," he pressed her, offering the little sake cup from which he had drunk.

"Oh no, I . . . ," she began, then rather unwillingly accepted the cup. I half-filled it for her, and she lifted it to her lips, a pretty frown creasing her forehead.

The following conversation then took place between them.

"This is most unusual," she remarked. "You almost never encourage me to drink."

"That's because you don't enjoy it. But it's good to have the occasional drink, you know. It puts you in good spirits."

"It doesn't at all. All it does is make me feel terrible. But a bit of sake seems to make you wonderfully cheerful."

"Sometimes it does, yes. But not always."

"What about this evening?"

"This evening I feel fine."

"You should have a little every evening from now on."

"I don't think that's a very good idea."

"Go on, do. Then you won't feel so melancholy."

The two of them lived there with only a maid for company, and I generally found the house hushed and silent when I arrived. I never heard loud laughter or raised voices. It sometimes felt as if Sensei and I were the only people in the house.

"It would be nice if we had children, you know," she said, turning to me.

"Yes, I'm sure," I replied. But I felt no stir of sympathy at her words. I was too young to have children of my own and regarded them as no more than noisy pests.

"Shall I adopt one for you?" said Sensei.

"Oh dear me, an adopted child . . . ," she said, turning to me again.

"We'll never have one, you know," Sensei said.

She was silent, so I spoke instead. "Why not?"

"Divine punishment," he answered, and gave a loud laugh.

CHAPTER 9

Sensei and his wife had a good relationship, as far as I could tell. I was not really in a position to judge, of course, since I had never lived under the same roof with them. Still, if he happened to need something while we were in the living room together, it was often his wife rather than the maid whom he asked to fetch it. "Hey, Shizu!" he would call, turning toward the door and calling her by name. The words had a gentle ring, I thought. And on those occasions when I stayed for a meal and she joined us, I gained a clearer picture of their relationship.

Sensei would sometimes take her out to a concert or the theater. I also recall two or three occasions when they went off for a week's vacation together. I still have a postcard they sent from the hot springs resort at Hakoné, and I received a letter from their visit to Nikko, with an autumn leaf enclosed.

Such was my general impression of them as a couple. Only one incident disturbed it. One day when I arrived at the house and was on the point of announcing myself at the door as was my custom, I overheard voices coming from the living room. As I listened, it became evident that this was no normal conversation but an argument. The living room was right next to the entrance hall, and I was close enough to get a clear sense of the general tone, if not the words. I soon understood that the male voice that rose from time to time was Sensei's. The other one was lower, and it was unclear whose it was, but it felt like his wife's. She seemed to be crying. I hesitated briefly in the entrance hall, unsure what to do, then made up my mind and went home again.

Back at my lodgings, a strange anxiety gripped me. I tried

reading but found I could not concentrate. About an hour later Sensei arrived below my window and called up to me. Surprised, I opened it, and he suggested I come down for a walk. I checked the watch I had tucked into my sash when I set off earlier, and saw that it was past eight. I was still dressed in my visiting clothes, so I went straight out to meet him.

That evening we drank beer together. As a rule Sensei did not drink much. If a certain amount of alcohol failed to produce the desired effect, he was disinclined to experiment by drinking more.

"This isn't working today," he remarked with a wry smile.

"You can't cheer up?" I asked sympathetically.

I still felt disturbed by the argument I had heard. It produced a sharp pain in me, like a fishbone stuck in my throat. I couldn't decide whether to confess to Sensei that I had overheard it, and my indecision made me unusually fidgety.

Sensei was the first to speak about the matter. "You're not yourself tonight, are you?" he said. "I'm feeling rather out of sorts too, actually. You noticed that?"

I could not reply.

"As a matter of fact, I had a bit of a quarrel with my wife earlier. I got stupidly upset by it."

"Why . . . ?" I could not bring myself to say the word "quarrel."

"My wife misunderstands me. I tell her so, but she won't believe me. I'm afraid I lost my temper with her."

"How does she misunderstand you?"

Sensei made no attempt to respond to this. "If I was the sort of person she thinks I am," he said, "I wouldn't be suffering like this."

But I was unable to imagine how Sensei was suffering.

CHAPTER 10

We walked back in silence. Then after quite some time, Sensei spoke.

"I've done wrong. I left home angry, and my wife will be worrying about me. Women are to be pitied, you know. My wife has not a soul except me to turn to."

He paused, and then seeming to expect no response from me, he went on. "But putting it that way makes her husband sound like the strong one, which is rather a joke. You, now—how do you see me, I wonder. Do I strike you as strong or as weak?"

"Somewhere in between," I replied.

Sensei seemed a little startled. He fell silent again, and walked on without speaking further.

The route back to Sensei's house passed very near my lodgings. But when we reached that point, it did not feel right to part with him. "Shall I see you to your house?" I asked.

He raised a quick defensive hand. "It's late. Off you go. I must be off too, for my wife's sake."

"For my wife's sake"—these words warmed my heart. Thanks to them, I slept in peace that night, and they stayed with me for a long time to come.

They told me that the trouble between Sensei and his wife was nothing serious. And I felt it safe to conclude, from my subsequent constant comings and goings at the house, that such quarrels were actually rare.

Indeed, Sensei once confided to me, "I have only ever known one woman in my life. No one besides my wife has really ever appealed to me as a woman. And likewise for her, I am the only man. Given this, we should be the happiest of couples."

I no longer remember the context in which he said this, so I cannot really explain why he should have made such a confession, and to me. But I do remember that he spoke earnestly and seemed calm. The only thing that struck me as strange was that final phrase, *we should be the happiest of couples*. Why did he say "should be"? Why not say simply that they were? This alone disturbed me.

Even more puzzling was the somehow forceful tone in which he spoke the words. Sensei had every reason to be happy, but was he in fact? I wondered. I could not repress my doubt. But it lasted only a moment, then was buried.

Sometime later I stopped by when Sensei happened to be out, and I had a chance to talk directly with his wife. Sensei had gone to Shinbashi station to see off a friend who was sailing abroad that day from Yokohama. Customarily, those taking a ship from Yokohama would set off on the boat-train from Shinbashi at eight-thirty in the morning. I had arranged with Sensei to stop by that morning at nine, as I wanted his opinion on a certain book. Once there, I learned of his last-minute decision to see off his friend, as a gesture of thanks for the trouble he had taken to pay Sensei a special farewell visit the day before. Sensei had left instructions that he would soon be back, so I was to stay there and await his return. And so it came about that, as I waited in the living room, his wife and I talked.

CHAPTER 11

By this time I was a university student, and felt myself to be far more adult than when I had first begun to visit Sensei. I was also quite friendly with his wife and now chatted easily and unself-consciously with her about this and that. This conversation was light and incidental, containing nothing remarkable, and I have forgotten what we spoke of. Just one thing struck me, but before I proceed I should explain a little.

I had known from the beginning that Sensei was a university graduate, but only after I returned to Tokyo had I discovered that he had no occupation, that he lived what could be called an idle life. How he could do it was a puzzle to me.

Sensei's name was quite unknown in the world. I seemed to be the only person who was in a position to really respect him for his learning and ideas. This fact always troubled me. He would never discuss the matter, simply saying, "There's no point in someone like me opening his mouth in public." This struck me as ridiculously humble.

I also sensed behind his words a contemptuous attitude to the world at large. Indeed, Sensei would occasionally make a surprisingly harsh remark, dismissing some old school friend who was now in a prominent position. I didn't hesitate to point out how inconsistent he was being. I was not just being contrary—I genuinely regretted the way the world ignored this admirable man.

At such times Sensei would respond leadenly, "It can't be helped, I'm afraid. I simply don't have any right to put myself forward." As he spoke, an indefinable expression—whether it was despair, or bitterness, or grief I could not tell—was vividly

etched on his features. Whatever it may have been, it was strong
enough to dumbfound me. I lost all courage to speak further.

As his wife and I talked that morning, the topic shifted naturally from Sensei to this question. "Why is it that Sensei always
sits at home, studying and thinking, instead of finding a worthy
position in the world?" I asked.

"It's no use—he hates that sort of thing."

"You mean he realizes how trivial it is?"

"Realizes . . . well, I'm a woman, so I don't really know
about such things, but that doesn't seem to be it to me. I think
he wants to do something, but somehow he just can't manage
to. It makes me sad for him."

"But he's perfectly healthy, isn't he?"

"He's fine, yes. There's nothing the matter with him."

"So why doesn't he do something?"

"I don't understand it either. If I understood, I wouldn't worry
about him as I do. As it is, all I can do is feel sorry for him."

Her tone was deeply sympathetic, yet a little smile played at
the corners of her mouth.

To an observer, I would have appeared to be more concerned
than she. I sat silently, my face troubled.

Then she spoke again, as if suddenly recalling something.
"He wasn't at all like this when he was young, you know. He
was very different. He's changed completely."

"What do you mean by 'when he was young'?" I asked.

"When he was a student."

"Have you known him since his student days, then?"

She blushed slightly.

CHAPTER 12

Sensei's wife was a Tokyo woman. Both she and he had told me so. "Actually," she added half-jokingly, "I'm not a pure-blood." Her mother had been born in Tokyo's Ichigaya district, back when the city was still called Edo, but her father had come from the provinces, Tottori or somewhere of the sort. Sensei, for his part, came from a very different part of Japan, Niigata Prefecture. Clearly, if she had known him in his student days it was not because they shared a hometown. But since she blushed at my question and seemed disinclined to say more, I did not press the subject further.

Between our first meeting and his death, I came to know Sensei's ideas and feelings on all sorts of subjects, but I learned almost nothing about the circumstances surrounding his marriage. Sometimes I interpreted this reticence charitably, choosing to believe that Sensei, as an older man, would prefer to be discreet on a private matter of the heart. At other times, however, I saw the question in a less positive light, and felt that Sensei and his wife shared the older generation's timorous aversion to open, honest discussion of these delicate subjects. Both of my interpretations were of course mere speculations, and both were premised on the assumption that a splendid romance lay behind their marriage.

This assumption was not far wrong, but I was able to imagine only part of the story of their love. I could not know that behind the beautiful romance lay a terrible tragedy. Moreover, Sensei's wife had absolutely no way of understanding how devastating this tragedy had been for him. To this day she knows nothing of it. Sensei died without revealing anything to her.

He chose to destroy his life before her happiness could be destroyed.

I will say nothing of that tragedy yet. As for their romance, which was in a sense born of this dreadful thing, neither of them told me anything. In her case, it was simply discretion. Sensei had deeper reasons for his silence.

One memory stands out for me. One spring day when the cherries were in full bloom, Sensei and I went to see the blossoms in Ueno. Amid the crowd were a lovely young couple, snuggled close together as they walked under the flowering trees. In this public place, such a sight tended to attract more attention than the blossoms.

"I'd say they're a newly married couple," said Sensei.

"They look as if they get on just fine together," I remarked a little snidely.

Sensei's face remained stony, and he set off walking away from the couple. When they were hidden from our view, he spoke. "Have you ever been in love?" I had not, I replied.

"Wouldn't you like to be?"

I did not answer.

"I don't imagine that you wouldn't."

"No."

"You were mocking that couple just now. I think that mockery contained unhappiness at wanting love but not finding it."

"Is that how it sounded to you?"

"It is. A man who knows the satisfactions of love would speak of them more warmly. But, you know . . . love is also a sin. Do you understand?"

Astonished, I made no reply.

CHAPTER 13

People thronged all around us, and every face was happy. At last we made our way through them and arrived in a wooded area that had neither blossoms nor crowds, where we could resume the conversation.

"Is love really a sin?" I asked abruptly.

"Yes, most definitely," Sensei said, as forcefully as before.

"Why?"

"You'll understand soon enough. No, you must already understand it. Your heart is already restless with love, isn't it?"

I briefly searched within myself to see if this might be true, but all I could find was a blank. Nothing inside me seemed to answer his description.

"There's no object of love in my heart, Sensei. Believe me, I'm being perfectly honest with you."

"Ah, but you're restless precisely because there's no object, you see? You're driven by the feeling that if only you could find that object, you'd be at peace."

"I don't feel too restless right now."

"You came to me because of some lack you sensed, didn't you?"

"That may be so. But that isn't love."

"It's a step in the direction of love. You had the impulse to find someone of the same sex as the first step toward embracing someone of the opposite sex."

"I think the two things are completely different in nature."

"No, they're the same. But I'm a man, so I can't really fill your need. Besides, certain things make it impossible for me to be all you want me to be. I feel for you, actually. I accept that your restless urge will one day carry you elsewhere. Indeed I hope for your sake that that will happen. And yet . . ."

I felt strangely sad. "If you really believe I'll grow apart from you, Sensei, then what can I say? But I've never felt the slightest urge."

He wasn't listening. ". . . you must be careful," he went on, "because love is a sin. My friendship can never really satisfy you, but at least there's no danger here. Tell me, do you know the feeling of being held fast by a woman's long black hair?"

I knew it well enough in my fantasies, but not from reality. But my mind was on another matter. Sensei's use of the word *sin* made no sense to me. And I was feeling a little upset.

"Sensei, please explain more carefully what you mean by sin. Otherwise, I'd prefer not to pursue this conversation until I've discovered for myself what you really mean."

"I apologize. I was trying to speak truthfully, but I've only succeeded in irritating you. It was wrong of me."

We walked on quietly past the back of the museum and headed toward Uguisudani. Through gaps in the hedge we caught glimpses of the spacious gardens, crowded thick with dwarf bamboo, secluded and mysterious.

"Do you know why I go every month to visit my friend's grave in Zōshigaya?"

Sensei's question came out of the blue. He knew perfectly well, what's more, that I did not. I made no reply.

There was a pause, then something seemed to dawn on him. "I've said something wrong again," he said contritely. "I planned to explain, because it was wrong of me to upset you like that, but my attempt at explanation has only irritated you further. It's no use. Let's drop the subject. Just remember that love is a sin. And it is also sacred."

These words made even less sense to me. But it was the last time Sensei spoke to me of love.

CHAPTER 14

Being young, I was prone to blind enthusiasms—or so Sensei apparently saw me. But conversing with him seemed to me more beneficial than attending classes. His ideas inspired me more than the opinions of my professors. All in all Sensei, who spoke little and kept to himself, seemed a greater man than those great men who sought to guide me from behind the lectern.

"You mustn't be so hot-headed," Sensei warned me.

"On the contrary, being coolheaded is what's led me to draw these conclusions," I replied confidently.

Sensei would not accept that. "You're being carried along by passion. Once the fever passes, you'll feel disillusioned. All this admiration is distressing enough, heaven knows, but it's even more painful to foresee the change that will take place in you sooner or later."

"Do you really think me so fickle? Do you distrust me so much?"

"It's just that I'm sorry for you."

"You can have sympathy for me but not trust, is that it?"

Sensei turned to look out at the garden, apparently annoyed. The camellia flowers that had until recently studded the garden with their dense, heavy crimson were gone. Sensei had been in the habit of sitting in his living room and gazing out at them.

"It's not you in particular I don't trust. I don't trust humanity."

From beyond the hedge came the cry of a passing goldfish seller. Otherwise all was silent. This winding little back lane, two blocks away from the main road, was surprisingly quiet. The house was hushed as always. I knew that his wife was in the next room, and could hear my voice as she sat sewing. But for the moment this had slipped my mind.

"Do you mean you don't even trust your wife?" I asked.

Sensei looked rather uneasy, and avoided answering directly. "I don't even trust myself. It's because I can't trust myself that I can't trust others. I can only curse myself for it."

"Once you start to think that way, then surely no one's entirely reliable."

"It's not thinking that's led me here. It's doing. I once did something that shocked me, then terrified me."

I wanted to pursue the subject further, but just then Sensei's wife called him gently from the next room.

"What is it?" Sensei replied when she called again.

"Could you come here a moment?" she said, and he went in. Before I had time to wonder why she needed him, Sensei returned.

"In any event, you mustn't trust me too much," he went on. "You'll regret it if you do. And once you feel you've been deceived, you will wreak a cruel revenge."

"What do you mean?"

"The memory of having sat at someone's feet will later make you want to trample him underfoot. I'm trying to fend off your admiration for me, you see, in order to save myself from your future contempt. I prefer to put up with my present state of loneliness rather than suffer more loneliness later. We who are born into this age of freedom and independence and the self must undergo this loneliness. It's the price we pay for these times of ours."

Sensei's mind was made up, I could see, and I found no words to answer his conviction.

CHAPTER 15

The conversation preyed on my mind later, every time I saw his wife. Was distrust Sensei's prevailing attitude toward her as well? And if so, how did she feel about it?

On the face of it, I could not tell whether she was content. I was not in close enough contact with her to judge. Besides, when we met, she always appeared perfectly normal, and I almost never saw her without Sensei.

Another question disturbed me too. What, I wondered, lay behind Sensei's deep distrust of humanity? Had he arrived at it simply by observing his own heart and the contemporary world around him with a cool, dispassionate eye? He was by nature inclined to sit and ponder things, and a mind such as his perhaps naturally reached such conclusions.

But I did not think that that was all there was to it. His conviction struck me as more than just a lifeless theory, or the cold ruins from some long-dead fire. Sensei was indeed a philosopher, it seemed to me, but a potent reality seemed woven into the fabric of his philosophy. Nor was his thinking grounded in anything remote from himself, observed only in others. No, behind his convictions lay some keenly felt personal experience, something great enough to heat his blood, and to halt his heart.

All this was hardly speculation—Sensei had admitted as much to me. His confession hung in the air, heavy and obscure, oppressing me like a terrifying and nameless cloud. Why this unknown thing should so frighten me I could not tell, but it unquestionably shook me.

I tried imagining that a passionate love affair was in some way the basis for Sensei's mistrust of humankind. (It would, of

course, have been between Sensei and his wife.) His earlier
statement that love was a sin certainly fit this theory. But he had
told me unequivocally that he loved his wife. In that case, their
love could hardly have produced this state of near loathing of
humanity. *The memory of having sat at someone's feet will later
make you want to trample him underfoot,* he had said—but
this could refer to anyone in the modern world, except perhaps
Sensei's wife.

The grave of the unknown friend at Zōshigaya also stirred in
my memory from time to time. Sensei clearly felt some profound connection with this grave. But as close as I had drawn
to him, further closeness eluded me, and in my efforts to know
him I internalized in my own mind this fragment of his inner
life. The grave was dead for me, however. It offered no key to
open the living door that stood between us. Rather, it barred
the way like some evil apparition.

My mind was mulling all this over when I found another
chance to talk to Sensei's wife. It was during that chilly time of
autumn, when you are suddenly aware of everyone hurrying
against the shortening days. In the past week there had been a
series of burglaries in Sensei's neighborhood, all in the early
evening. Nothing really valuable had been stolen, but something had been taken from each house, and Sensei's wife was
uneasy. One day, she was facing an evening alone in the house.
Sensei was obliged to go off to a restaurant with two or three
others, to attend a dinner for a friend from his hometown who
had a post in a provincial hospital and had come up to Tokyo.
He explained the situation to me and asked me to stay in the
house with his wife until he returned. I immediately agreed.

CHAPTER 16

I arrived at dusk, about the time the lights are beginning to be lit. Sensei, ever punctilious, had already left. "He didn't want to be late, so he set out just a moment ago," his wife told me as she led me to the study.

The room held a Western-style desk and a few chairs, as well as a large collection of books in glass-fronted cases; the rows of beautiful leather-bound spines glinted in the electric light. She settled me onto a cushion before the charcoal brazier. "Feel free to dip into any book you like," she said as she left.

I sat there stiffly, smoking, feeling awkward as a guest left to while away the time until the master of the house returns. Down the corridor in the parlor, I could hear Sensei's wife talking to the maid. The study where I sat was at the end of the corridor, in a far quieter and more secluded part of the house than the sitting room where Sensei and I normally met. After a while her voice ceased, and a hush fell on the house. I sat still and alert, half-expecting a burglar to appear at any moment.

About half an hour later Sensei's wife popped her head around the door to bring me a cup of tea. "Good heavens!" she exclaimed, startled to find me sitting bolt upright, with the formality of a guest. She regarded me with amusement. "You don't look very comfortable sitting like that."

"I'm quite comfortable, thank you."

"But you must be bored, surely."

"No, I'm too tense at the thought of burglars to feel bored."

She laughed as she stood there, the teacup still in her hand.

"It's a bit pointless for me to stand guard in this remote corner of the house, you know," I went on.

"Well, then, do please come on into the parlor. I brought a cup of tea thinking you might be bored here, but you can have it there if you'd rather."

I followed her out of the study. In the parlor an iron kettle was singing on a fine big brazier. I was served Western tea and cakes, but Sensei's wife declined to have any tea herself, saying it would make her sleepless.

"Does Sensei often go off to gatherings like this?" I asked.

"No, hardly ever. He seems less and less inclined to see people recently."

She seemed unworried, so I grew bolder. "You are the only exception, I suppose."

"Oh, no. He feels that way about me too."

"That's not true," I declared. "You must know perfectly well it's not true."

"Why?"

"Personally, I think he's come to dislike the rest of the world because of his love for you."

"You have a fine scholar's way with words, I must say. You're good at empty reasoning. Surely you could equally say that because he dislikes the world, he's come to dislike me as well. That's using precisely the same argument."

"You could say both, true, but in this case I'm the one who's right."

"I don't like argumentation. You men do it a lot, don't you? You seem to enjoy it. I'm always amazed at how men can go on and on, happily passing around the empty cup of some futile discussion."

Her words struck me as rather severe, although not particularly offensive. She was not one of those modern women who takes a certain pride in calling attention to the fact that she is intelligent. She seemed to value far more the heart that lies deep within us.

CHAPTER 17

There was more I wanted to say, but I held my tongue, for fear of seeming to be one of those argumentative types. Seeing me gazing silently into my empty teacup, she offered to pour me another, as if to soothe any possible hurt feelings. I passed her my cup.

"How many?" she asked, grasping a sugar cube with a strange-looking implement and lifting it coquettishly to show me. "One? Two?" Though not exactly flirting with me, she was striving to be charming, so as to erase her earlier strong words.

I sipped my tea in silence, and remained mute once the tea was drunk.

"You've gone terribly quiet," she remarked.

"That's because I feel as if whatever I might say, you'd accuse me of being argumentative," I replied.

"Oh, come now," she protested.

This remark provided us with a way back into the conversation. Once more its subject was the one interest we had in common, Sensei.

"Could I elaborate a little more on what I was saying earlier?" I asked. "You may find it empty reasoning, but I'm in earnest."

"Do speak then."

"If you were suddenly to die, could Sensei go on living as he does now?"

"Now how could I know the answer to that? You'd have to ask the man himself, surely. That's not a question for me to answer."

"But I'm serious. Please don't be evasive. You must give me an honest answer."

"But I have. Honestly, I have no idea."

"Well, then, how much do you love Sensei? This is something to ask you rather than him, surely."

"Come now, why confront me with such a question?"

"You mean there's no point in it? The answer is obvious?"

"Yes, I suppose that's what I mean."

"Well, then, if Sensei were suddenly to lose such a loyal and loving wife, what would he do? He's disillusioned with the world as it is—what would he do without you? I'm not asking for his opinion, I'm asking for yours. Do you feel he'd be happy?"

"I know the answer from my own point of view, though I'm not sure whether he would see it the same way. Put simply, if Sensei and I were separated, he'd be miserable. He might well be unable to go on living. This sounds conceited of me, I know, but I do my best to make him happy. I even dare to believe no one else could make him as happy as I can. This belief comforts me."

"Well, I think that conviction would reveal itself in Sensei's heart as well."

"That's another matter altogether."

"You're claiming that Sensei dislikes you?"

"I don't think he dislikes me personally. He has no reason to. But he dislikes the world in general, you see. In fact, these days perhaps he dislikes the human race. In that sense, given that I'm human, he must feel the same way about me."

At last I understood what she had been saying about his feelings for her.

CHAPTER 18

Her perspicacity impressed me. It also intrigued me to observe how her approach to things was unlike that of a traditional Japanese woman, although she almost never used the currently fashionable language.

In those days I was just a foolish youth, with no real experience with the opposite sex. Instinctively I dreamed about women as objects of desire, but these were merely vague fantasies with all the substance of a yearning for the fleeting clouds of spring. When I came face-to-face with a real woman, however, my feelings sometimes veered to the opposite pole—rather than feeling attracted to her, I would be seized by a strange repulsion.

But I had no such reaction to Sensei's wife. I was not even much aware of the usual differences between the way men and women think. In fact, I forgot she was a woman. She was simply someone who could judge Sensei honestly and who sympathized with him.

"Last time you said something," I began, "when I asked why Sensei doesn't put himself forward more in the world. You said he never used to be like that."

"I did. And it's true—he was different once."

"So what was he like?"

"He was the sort of strong, dependable person you and I would both like him to be."

"Why did he suddenly change, then?"

"The change wasn't sudden—it came over him gradually."

"And you were with him all the time it was happening?"

"Naturally. We were married."

"Then surely you must have a good idea of what brought about the change."

"But that's just the problem. It's painful to hear you say this, because I've racked my brains, but I just don't know. I don't know how many times I've begged him to talk about it."

"And what does he say?"

"He says there's nothing to talk about, and nothing to worry about, it's simply that this is how he's turned out. That's all he'll say."

I did not speak. Sensei's wife also fell silent. There was no sound from the maid's room. All thoughts of burglars had vanished from my mind.

Then she broke the silence. "Perhaps you think it's my fault?"

"Not at all."

"Don't feel you have to hide anything, please. It would be like a knife in the heart to have such a thing thought of me," she continued. "I'm doing all I can for him. I'm doing my very best."

"Please don't worry. Sensei knows that. Believe me. I give you my word."

She took up the fire tongs and sat smoothing the ash in the brazier. Then she poured water from the jug into the iron kettle, immediately quieting its singing.

"I finally couldn't stand it anymore and said to him, 'If there's any fault in me, then please tell me honestly. If I can correct it, I will.' And he replied, 'You don't have any fault. The fault is in me.' When I heard that, it made me unbearably sad. It made me cry. And I longed more than ever to know how I might be to blame."

Tears brimmed in her eyes.

CHAPTER 19

At first I had thought of Sensei's wife as a perspicacious woman. But as we talked, she gradually changed before my eyes; then my heart, rather than my mind, began to respond to her.

Nothing, it seemed, troubled her relationship with her husband—indeed, what could?—and yet something was wrong. But try as she might to learn what the problem might be, she could find nothing. Precisely this made her suffer.

At first she had thought that since Sensei viewed the world through jaundiced eyes, he must view her in that way too. But that answer failed to convince her. In fact, she thought the opposite must be true—that his dislike of her had set him against the world at large. Search as she might, however, she could find nothing that really confirmed this hypothesis. Sensei was in every way a model husband, kind and tender. So she lived with this kernel of doubt sown away in her, below the daily warmth that flowed between them.

That evening she brought out her misgivings and laid them before me. "What do you think?" she asked. "Do you think he's become like this because of me, or is it because of what you call his outlook on life or some such thing? Tell me honestly."

I had no intention of being dishonest with her. But I sensed that the root of her problem was something I could not know, and so no answer that I gave could possibly satisfy her. "I really don't know," I replied.

Her face briefly registered the unhappiness of one whose hopes have been dashed.

I quickly went on. "But I can guarantee that Sensei doesn't

dislike you. I'm only telling you what I heard from his own lips. He's not a man to lie, is he?"

She made no reply at first, then said, "Actually, I've thought of something . . ."

"You mean something to do with why he's become like this?"

"Yes. If it really is the cause, then I can cease to feel responsible, and that in itself would be such a relief . . ."

"What is it?"

She hesitated, fixing her gaze on the hands in her lap. "I'll tell you, and you must be the judge, please."

"I will if it's within my power to do so, certainly."

"I can't tell you everything. He'd be angry if I did. I'll just tell you the part that wouldn't make him angry."

I swallowed tensely.

"When Sensei was a university student, he had a very close friend. This friend died just as they were about to graduate. It was very sudden." She lowered her voice to a whisper. "Actually, it wasn't from natural causes."

Her tone provoked me to ask how he had died.

"This is as much as I can say. But that's when it began. After that Sensei's personality slowly changed. I don't know why his friend died, and I don't think Sensei does either. But seeing how he began to change afterward, somehow I can't help feeling that perhaps he may have known something after all."

"Is it this friend's grave in Zōshigaya?"

"I'm not to speak of that either. But tell me, can someone change so much with the loss of a single friend? That's what I so long to know. What do you think?"

On the whole, I tended to think not.

CHAPTER 20

I tried to comfort Sensei's wife as much as my understanding of the facts allowed, and she in turn seemed to try to be comforted. We continued to mull over the question of Sensei together. But I was unable to grasp the real source of the problem. Her distress grew out of vague perplexity and doubts. She didn't know much about what had happened, and what she did know she could not reveal to me fully. Thus were comforter and comforted equally at sea, adrift on shifting waves. Lost as she was, she clung to what frail judgment I could offer.

At around ten, when Sensei's footsteps sounded in the entrance hall, she rose to her feet, all thoughts of me and our conversation seeming instantly forgotten. She was there to greet him as he slid open the lattice door, leaving me to follow her out. The maid, who must have been dozing in her room, failed to appear.

Sensei was in rather a good mood, but his wife was even more vivacious. I gazed at her, astonished at the change. Her beautiful eyes had recently shone with tears, and her fine brow had been furrowed with suffering. Surely it had not been deceit, yet one could be forgiven for wondering if her earlier conversation had been a mere feminine ploy, a toying with my feelings. I was not inclined to be critical, however. My primary feeling was relief at seeing her instantaneously brighten. After all, I decided, there was no real need to worry about her.

Sensei greeted me with a smile. "Thank you very much," he said. "I trust no burglar appeared?" Then he added, "You must have felt the exercise was a bit pointless, if no one broke in."

"I do apologize," his wife said to me as I was leaving. Her

tone made me feel this was less an apology for taking up my precious time than an almost humorous regret for the fact that there had been no burglar. She wrapped the cakes she had brought out with the tea and handed them to me.

Slipping the package into my kimono sleeve, I set off, winding hurriedly through the chilly, largely unpeopled lanes toward the bright and lively town.

I have drawn the events of that night from deep in my memory because their details are necessary to my story now. At the time, however, as I headed for home with her cakes tucked into my sleeve, I was not inclined to think much about the conversation that had taken place that evening.

The next day after morning classes, when I returned to my lodgings for lunch, my eyes fell on the little parcel of cakes lying on my desk. I immediately unwrapped it, picked up a piece of chocolate-coated sponge cake, and popped it into my mouth. And as my tongue registered the taste, I felt a conviction that, when all was said and done, the couple who had given me this cake was happy.

Autumn ended uneventfully, and winter arrived. I came and went as usual from Sensei's house, and at some point I asked his wife if she could help me take care of my clothing—around this time I began to wear rather better clothes. She kindly assured me that it would be a fine opportunity to alleviate the boredom of her childless life.

She remarked that a garment I had given her to mend was of hand-woven cloth. "I've never worked with such good material before," she said, "but it does make it hard to sew, I must say. The needle just won't go through. I've broken two already."

For all her complaints, however, she did not seem to resent the work.

CHAPTER 21

That winter I was obliged to return home. A letter arrived from my mother, explaining that my father's illness had taken a turn for the worse. Although there was no immediate cause for concern, she wrote, considering his age she felt I should arrange to come back if possible.

My father had long suffered from a kidney ailment, and as is often the case with men of middle age and older, his illness was chronic. But he and the rest of the family believed that his condition would remain stable as long as he was careful—indeed, he boasted to visitors that it was entirely due to his rigorous care of his health that he had managed to live so long.

My mother told me, however, that when he was out in the garden, he had suddenly felt dizzy and fainted. The family at first mistook it for a slight stroke and treated him accordingly. Only later had the doctor concluded that the problem was related to his kidney disease.

The winter vacation would soon begin, and feeling that I could safely wait out the term, I let the matter slide from one day to the next. But as the days passed, images of my bedridden father and my anxious mother kept rising before my eyes, provoking such an ache in my heart that finally I decided I must go home. To avoid having to wait while the money was sent from home, I went to visit Sensei to borrow the amount for my fare. Besides, I wanted to bid him farewell.

Sensei was suffering from a slight cold. He did not feel inclined to come to the living room, so he asked me into his study. Soft sunlight, of a kind rarely seen in winter, was shining through the study's glass door onto the cloth draped over his desk. In this sunny room Sensei had set a metal basin containing water over the coals of a brazier, so that by inhaling the steam, he could soothe his lungs.

"Serious illness doesn't bother me, but I do hate these petty colds," he remarked with a wry smile.

Sensei had never had a real illness of any sort, so I found this amusing. "I can put up with a cold," I said, "but I wouldn't want anything worse. Surely you'd be the same, Sensei. Just try getting really ill, and you'll soon see."

"You think so? If I were to actually get sick, I'd prefer it to be fatal."

I paid this remark no particular attention but instead proceeded to tell him about my mother's letter and asked for a loan.

"I'm sorry to hear that," he said. "I have enough on hand to cover the amount, I think, so you must take it here and now." He called his wife and asked her to bring the money.

She produced it from the drawer of some cupboard in the far room and presented it to me, placed formally on a sheet of white paper. "This must be very worrying for you," she said.

"Has it happened before?" Sensei inquired.

"The letter didn't say. Is it likely to continue?"

"Yes."

This was how I first learned that his wife's mother had died of the same illness.

"It's not an easy illness," I ventured.

"Indeed not. I wish I could offer myself in his place. Does he feel any nausea?"

"I don't know. The letter didn't mention it, so I guess that's not a real problem."

"If he's not nauseous, then things are still all right," said Sensei's wife.

That evening I left Tokyo by train.

CHAPTER 22

My father's illness was not as serious as I had feared. When I arrived, he was sitting up cross-legged in bed.

"I'm staying put here just to please everyone, since they worry about me," he said. "I could perfectly well get up." Nevertheless, the next day he had my mother put away his bedding and refused to listen to her protests.

"Your father seems to have suddenly got his strength back now that you've come home," she remarked to me, as she reluctantly folded the silk quilt. And from what I could observe, he was not simply putting on a brave face.

My elder brother had a job in distant Kyushu and could not easily get away to visit his parents in any situation short of a real emergency. My sister had married someone in another part of the country, so could not be summoned home on short notice either. Of the three children, I was the one most easily called on, being still a student. The fact that I had followed my mother's wishes and left my studies early to come home pleased my father greatly.

"It's a shame you've had to leave classes early for such a trivial illness," he said. "Your mother shouldn't go exaggerating things in letters like that."

This bravado was not confined to words, for there he was, with his sickbed folded away, behaving as if his health were back to normal.

"Don't be too rash, or you'll have a relapse," I warned him, but he treated this with happy disregard.

"Come on now, I'm fine. All I have to do is take the usual care."

And he appeared to be fine. He came and went around the

house without becoming breathless or feeling dizzy. True, his color was awful, but this symptom was nothing new, so we paid it little attention.

I wrote to Sensei, thanking him for his kind loan and promising to call in and repay him when I returned to Tokyo in January. I went on to report that my father's illness was less critical than feared, that we had no immediate cause for concern, and that he had neither dizziness nor nausea. I ended by briefly asking after Sensei's cold—which was not something that I took very seriously.

I wrote this letter without any expectation that Sensei would reply. Then I told my parents about him, and as I spoke, the image of Sensei's distant study hovered before me.

"Why not take some of our dried mushrooms to him when you go back?" my mother suggested.

"Fine. But I'm not sure Sensei eats such things, actually."

"They're not first-rate ones, but I don't imagine anyone would dislike them."

It felt somehow odd to associate Sensei with dried mushrooms.

When a reply came from him, I was quite surprised, particularly because it seemed written for no special reason. I decided that he had written back out of sheer kindness. That idea made his straightforward letter delight me. Besides, it was the first letter I had ever received from him.

Although one might naturally have thought that we corresponded from time to time, in fact we never had. I received only two letters from Sensei before his death. The first was this simple reply. The second was an extremely long letter that he wrote for me shortly before he died.

My father's illness prevented him from being very active, even once he was up and about, and he seldom went outdoors. One unusually balmy day when he did venture out into the garden, I accompanied him just as a precaution. I offered my shoulder for him to lean on, but he brushed it off with a laugh.

CHAPTER 23

To keep my father from boredom, I frequently partnered him in a game of *shōgi*. Being lazy, we couldn't be bothered to set up a special board but sat as usual around the warm *kotatsu*, placing the board between us on the low table so that between moves we could keep our hands tucked under the rug. Sometimes one of us would lose a piece, and neither would notice until the next game. Once, to great hilarity, my mother had to use the fire tongs to retrieve a lost piece from the brazier's ashes.

"A *go* board is too high," my father remarked, "and it has those legs, so you can't put it on the table and play in comfort around the *kotatsu* the way you can with *shōgi*. This is a fine game for the indolent. How about another round, eh?"

He would always suggest another round whenever he had just won. Mind you, he'd say the same thing if he had just lost. In a word, he simply enjoyed sitting around the *kotatsu* playing *shōgi* regardless of the outcome.

At first I found this rare taste of the pleasures of the retired quite beguiling, but my youthful energies soon began to fret at such bland stimulation. From time to time I would yawn and stretch up my arms, waving aloft some piece I happened to be holding.

Whenever I thought about Tokyo, I felt the blood that pumped strongly through my heart pulsing to a rhythm that cried "Action! Action!" Strangely, through some subtle mechanism of the mind, this inner pulse seemed to be empowered by Sensei.

In my heart I experimentally compared the two men, my father and Sensei. Both were quiet, retiring people who, as far as the world at large was concerned, could just as well be dead. Neither received the slightest recognition. Yet playing partner to my *shōgi*-loving father and sharing his simple enjoyments gave me no satisfaction, while Sensei, to whom I had never gone for mere amusement, had influenced my mind far more deeply than would any idle entertainment. "My mind" sounds too cool and detached—let me rather say "my breast." It would have felt no exaggeration to say that Sensei's strength seemed to have entered my body, and my very blood flowed with his life force. When I pondered the fact that my father was my real father, whereas Sensei was quite unrelated to me, I felt as astonished as if I had come upon a new and important truth.

As tedium settled over me, my parents' initial delight in me as some rare and precious creature was also fading, and they began to take my presence for granted. I suppose everyone experiences this shift when they return home for a vacation—for the first week or so you are fussed over and treated as honored guest, then the family's enthusiasm wanes, and finally you are treated quite offhandedly, as if they don't really care whether you are there or not. This second phase now inevitably set in.

These days, furthermore, each time I came home from the city, I brought a new aspect of myself that was strange and incomprehensible to my parents. It was an element that was fundamentally out of harmony with both of them—rather as if, to make a historical analogy, I had introduced into a traditional Confucian household the disturbing aura of forbidden Christianity. Of course I did my best to hide it. But it was part of me, and try as I might to keep it to myself, they sooner or later noticed. Thus I grew bored and disillusioned with home life, and longed to go back to Tokyo as soon as possible.

Fortunately, my father's condition gave no sign of deteriorating further, although the state of his health continued to be fragile. Just to be sure, we called in a highly reputable doctor from some distance away, but his careful examination revealed no new problems.

I decided to leave a little before the end of the winter vacation. But when I announced this decision, human feelings being the perverse things they are, both parents were against it.

"You're going back already? It's very soon, isn't it?" said my mother.

My father joined in. "You could easily stay another four or five days, surely?"

But I held to my original plan.

CHAPTER 24

By the time I returned to Tokyo, the New Year decorations had disappeared from house fronts. In the city no sign remained of the recent New Year festivities; the streets were given over to a chill, wintry wind.

I took the first opportunity to visit Sensei and return the money I had borrowed. I also brought along the mushrooms that my mother had pressed on me. Laying them before Sensei's wife, I hastened to explain that my mother had suggested the gift. The mushrooms were carefully packed inside a new cake box. Sensei's wife thanked me politely. When she rose to leave the room, she picked up the box, then feeling its lightness asked in surprise what the cakes were. It was typical of the wonderfully childlike frankness she could display once she got to know someone well.

Both of them questioned me at length and with great concern about my father's illness. "Well, it seems from what you say of his condition that there's no cause for immediate alarm," Sensei said. "But being the illness it is, he'll need to look after himself very carefully."

I could see that he knew a great deal more than I did about kidney disease.

"It's typical of that illness that the patient feels quite well and unaware of the disease. I knew a military officer who was killed by it—he simply died overnight, quite astonishing. His death was so sudden that his own wife hadn't even realized he was ill. He just woke her in the night saying he felt bad, and the next morning he was dead. It happened so swiftly that she said she'd assumed he was sleeping."

The optimism I had been inclined to feel shifted to sudden anxiety. "I wonder if that's what will happen to my dad. There's no saying it won't."

"What does the doctor say?"

"He says there's no hope of curing it, but he also assured us there's no need to worry for the present."

"Well, then, that's fine, if that's what the doctor says. The man I just told you about wasn't aware he was ill, and besides, he was quite a rough army fellow, not the sort to notice things."

I felt somewhat comforted.

Seeing this change in me, Sensei added, "But sick or well, humans are fragile creatures, you know. There's no anticipating how and when they might die, or for what reason."

"That's how you feel yourself, is it, Sensei?"

"I'm in fine health, but yes, even I think this from time to time." A suggestion of a smile played on his lips. "You often hear of people keeling over and dying, don't you? Of natural causes. And then other people die suddenly, from some unnatural act of violence."

"What's an unnatural act of violence?"

"Well, I don't know. People who commit suicide use unnatural violence on themselves, don't they?"

"People who are murdered also die from unnatural violence."

"I wasn't thinking of murder, but now that you mention it, that's true, of course."

So the conversation ended that day.

Even later, after I returned home, my father's illness did not worry me unduly. Nor did Sensei's talk of natural and unnatural deaths leave more than a passing, vague impression on my mind. I was preoccupied with another matter, for I finally had to set to and write the graduation thesis that I had tried, so many times, to come to grips with before.

CHAPTER 25

If I were to graduate this June as expected, I had to finish the thesis in the required form by the end of April. But when I counted off the remaining days on my fingers, my heart began to fail me. The other students had all been visibly busy for some time gathering material and writing notes, while I alone had done absolutely nothing toward the paper. I had put it off with the intention of throwing myself into the task after the New Year, and in this spirit I now set about it.

But in no time I ground to a halt. The abstract idea of a grand theme was outlined in my mind, and the framework of the discussion felt more or less in place, but now I sat head in hands, despairing. So I set about reducing my theme to something more manageable. Finally I decided to bypass the trouble of systematically setting down my own ideas. Instead, I would simply present material from various books on the subject and add a suitable conclusion.

The topic I had chosen was closely related to Sensei's field of expertise, and when I ventured to ask his opinion about it, he had approved. In my present state of confusion, therefore, I naturally took myself straight off to visit Sensei and ask him to recommend some books.

He willingly told me all he knew and even offered to lend me two or three books. But he made absolutely no move to take on the task of actually advising me. "I don't read much these days, so I don't know what's new in the field. You should ask your professors."

I recalled then that his wife had said that he had once been a great reader, but for some reason his interest had waned considerably.

My thesis momentarily forgotten, I spontaneously asked, "Why aren't you as interested in books as you used to be, Sensei?"

"There's no particular reason. . . . I suppose it's because I believe you don't really become a finer person just by reading lots of books. And also . . ."

"What else?"

"Nothing else really. You see, in the old days I used to feel uncomfortable and ashamed whenever someone asked me a question I couldn't answer, or when my ignorance was exposed in public somehow. These days, though, I've come to feel that there's nothing particularly shameful about not knowing, so I don't any longer have the urge to push myself to read. I've grown old, in a word."

Sensei spoke quite serenely. His words held no hint of the bitterness of someone who has turned his back on the world, so they failed to strike me as they might have.

I went home feeling that, although he did not seem old to me, his philosophy was not very impressive.

From then on I spent my days sweating over my thesis like one possessed, my eyes bloodshot with effort and fatigue. I asked friends who had graduated a year ahead of me how they had fared in this situation. One told me how on the final day of submission, he had hired a rickshaw and rushed his thesis to the university office, barely managing to get it there before the deadline. Another said he had taken it in fifteen minutes past the five o'clock cut-off time and almost been rejected, but the department head had kindly intervened and allowed it to get through.

These tales made me feel both nervous and encouraged. Every day at my desk I pushed myself to the limits of my energy. When I wasn't seated at the desk, I was in the gloomy library, scanning its high shelves. My eyes foraged greedily among the gold-printed titles on the books' spines, like a collector avidly searching through antiques.

The plum trees bloomed, and the cold winter wind shifted to the south. Sometime later came the first rumors of cherry blossoms. Still I plowed doggedly ahead, like a blinkered workhorse, flogged mercilessly on by my thesis. Not until late April, when at last I had completed the writing, did I cross the threshold of Sensei's house once more.

CHAPTER 26

In the first days of summer, when the boughs of the late-flowering double cherries were misted with the first unfurling of green leaf, I finally achieved my freedom. Like a bird released from its cage, I spread my wings wide in delight and let my gaze roam over the world before me. I immediately went to visit Sensei. Along the way my eyes drank in the vivid sight of a citrus hedge, its white buds bursting forth from the blackened branches, and a pomegranate tree, the glistening yellowish leaves sprouting from its withered trunk and glowing softly in the sunlight. It was as if I were seeing such things for the first time.

When he saw my happy face, Sensei said, "So you've finished the thesis, have you? Well done."

"Thanks to you," I replied, "I've finally made it. There's nothing left to do."

Indeed I had the delightful feeling just then that I had completed all the work I had to do in life and could proceed to enjoy myself to my heart's content. I was well satisfied with the paper I had written and confident of its worth. I chattered happily on to Sensei about it.

As usual, Sensei listened with the occasional interjection of "I see" or "Is that so?" but made no further response. This lack of enthusiasm left me not so much dissatisfied as somehow deflated. But I was so full of energy that day that I attempted a counterattack. I invited him to come out with me into the world that was everywhere bursting into fresh green leaf.

"Let's go for a walk somewhere, Sensei. It's wonderful out there."

"Where to?"

I did not care where. All I wanted was to take him out beyond the city limits.

An hour later we had indeed left the city behind us and were walking aimlessly through a quiet neighborhood that was something between village and town. I plucked a soft young leaf from a citrus hedge, cupped it between my palms, and made it whistle as one does with a grass blade. I was good at this, having picked it up by imitating a friend of mine from Kagoshima. I gaily played as I strolled along, while Sensei walked beside me, ignoring me, face averted.

At length the little path opened out at a point below a large house shrouded by the fresh young leaves of an overgrown garden. We quickly realized that this was no private dwelling—the sign attached to the front gate bore the name of a plant nursery. Gazing at the gently sloping path, Sensei suggested we go in for a look. "Yes," I agreed, "it's a nurseryman's plantation, isn't it?"

Rounding a bend in the path, we came upon the house on our left. The sliding doors were all wide open, and there was no sign of life in the empty interior. The only movement was of the goldfish that swam about in a large tub that stood by the eave.

"All's quiet, isn't it. Do you think anyone would mind if we went farther?"

"I don't think it would matter."

On through the garden we went, still seeing no sign of anyone. Azaleas bloomed all around us like flames.

Sensei pointed to a tall bush of orange azaleas. "This one would be the sort they call *kirishima*."

A plantation of peonies extended a good thirty yards across, but the season was too early for flowers. Sensei stretched himself out on an old bench by the peony bed, while I sat at the end of the bench, smoking a cigarette. He lay there looking at the brilliantly clear blue sky. I was entranced by all the young leaves that surrounded me. Looking carefully, I discovered that the color of each was subtly different. Even on a single maple tree, no branch held two leaves of exactly the same hue. A passing breeze lifted Sensei's hat from where he had hung it, on the tip of a slender little cedar sapling, and tossed it to the ground.

CHAPTER 27

I immediately retrieved the hat. "It fell off, Sensei," I said, flicking off the red grains of earth that clung here and there.

"Thank you."

He half-raised himself to take it. Then, still propped there, he asked me something odd. "Forgive the sudden question, but is your family reasonably well off?"

"Not particularly, no."

"So how well off are you, if you'll excuse my asking?"

"Well, we own a bit of forested land and a few rice fields, but there's very little money, I think."

It was the first time Sensei had directly asked me about my family's financial situation. I, in turn, had never inquired about his circumstances. When I first met him, I had wondered how he could spend his days without having to work, and the question had remained with me ever since. I had kept it to myself, however, believing it would be discourteous to ask outright.

As I sat here now, my weary eyes steeping in the balm of the fresh spring leaves, the question naturally occurred to me again. "What about you, Sensei? How well off are you?"

"Do I look rich to you?"

In fact, Sensei generally dressed quite frugally. The house was far from big, and he only had one maid. Nevertheless, even an outsider like myself could see that he led a fairly affluent life. Although his lifestyle could hardly be termed luxurious, there was no sense of pinched frugality or straitened circumstances.

"Yes, you do," I replied.

"Well, I have a certain amount of money. But I'm far from wealthy. If I were, I'd build a larger house."

Sensei had by now sat up, and was cross-legged on the bench. He traced a circle on the ground with the tip of his bamboo cane. Once it was complete, he jabbed his cane upright into the earth.

"I used to be wealthy, in fact."

He seemed to be speaking half to himself. I missed my chance to come back with another question, and was reduced to silence.

"I used to be wealthy, you know," he said again, now addressing me, then he looked at me and smiled.

I continued to make no reply. In fact, I did not have the wit to know how to respond.

Sensei then changed the subject. "How has your father been recently?"

I had heard nothing of my father's illness since the New Year. The simple letter that arrived each month with my allowance was written in his hand as usual, but he made almost no mention of how he was feeling. His handwriting, moreover, was firm; the brushstrokes gave no hint of the tremors that affect those with his disease.

"No one's said anything, so I guess he's fine again."

"That would be a good thing—still, you have to remember what that illness is like."

"Yes, I guess he won't really recover. But he'll stay as he is for a while yet, I think. There's been no word about it."

"Is that so?"

I took his inquiries about my family's wealth and my father's illness at face value, as no more than an impulse of the moment. But behind his words loomed a large issue that connected the two topics. I had no way of realizing it, however, since I lacked the experiences that Sensei had been through.

CHAPTER 28

"It's none of my business, of course, but in my opinion, if there's anything to inherit you should make sure the matter's completely attended to before it's too late. Why not arrange things with your father now, while he's still well? When the worst happens, you know, it's inheritance that causes the biggest problems."

"Yes."

I paid no particular attention to his words. I believed that the others in our family, my parents included, were as little concerned about this issue as I was. Moreover, Sensei's uncharacteristic pragmatism somewhat startled me. My natural respect for an elder, however, made me hold my tongue.

"Please forgive me if my anticipating your father's death like this has offended you. But it's in the nature of things for people to die, you know. There's no knowing when even the healthiest of us will die." Sensei's tone held an unusual bitterness.

"It doesn't upset me in the slightest," I assured him.

"How many brothers and sisters did you say you had?" he asked.

He then inquired about the number of people in the family, what relatives I had, and details of my aunts and uncles. "Are they all good people?"

"I don't think there's anyone you'd call bad. They're country people, for the most part."

"Why shouldn't country people be bad?"

This interrogation was becoming disconcerting. But Sensei did not even give me time to consider my answer.

"Country people are actually worse, if anything, than city

folk," he went on. "Another thing. You said just now that you didn't think there was anyone among your relatives you'd call bad. But do you imagine there's a certain type of person in the world who conforms to the idea of a 'bad person'? You'll never find someone who fits that mold neatly, you know. On the whole, all people are good, or at least they're normal. The frightening thing is that they can suddenly turn bad when it comes to the crunch. That's why you have to be careful."

Sensei was in full flow. I was about to interrupt him when a dog suddenly barked behind us. We both turned in surprise.

Our bench stood at the front corner of a bed of cedar seedlings; to one side of it, a wide stand of thick dwarf bamboo stretched back, hiding the ground. In its midst we could make out the back and furiously barking head of a dog.

As we stared, a child of about ten came running over and set about scolding the animal. He then came over to where we sat and bowed to Sensei, without removing his black school cap.

"There was no one in the house when you came in, sir?" he asked.

"No one."

"But my mom and sister were in the kitchen."

"Oh, were they? I see."

"Yeah. You should've said hello and come on in, sir."

Sensei smiled wryly. He took out his purse and put a five-*sen* coin into the lad's hand. "Tell your mother, please, that we'd like to take a rest here for a little."

The boy nodded, his eyes twinkling with a knowing grin. "I'm leading the spy patrol in our game, see," he explained, and ran off down the hill through the azaleas.

The dog rushed after him, tail. aloft. And sure enough, a couple more children of about the same age soon came running past in the same direction as our spy patroller.

CHAPTER 29

Owing to the interruption, my conversation with Sensei never reached its proper conclusion, so I failed to discover what he was driving at. In those days, though, I felt none of his concerns about property and inheritance and so on. Both by nature and by circumstance, I was not inclined to bother my head over profit and gain. In retrospect, I realize that the whole question of money was still distant for me—I had never had to earn my own living, let alone personally confront the situation Sensei spoke of.

But Sensei had said one thing that I wanted to get to the bottom of—his statement that when it comes to the crunch, anyone can turn bad. I could understand the meaning of the words themselves well enough, but I wanted to find out more of what lay behind them.

Once the boy and his dog were gone, the leafy garden returned to its earlier tranquility. We remained there unmoving a while longer, two people held fast within a silence. As we sat, the beautiful sky was slowly drained of its brightness. Over the trees around us, mostly delicate maples dripping with soft green new leaves, darkness seemed to creep slowly.

The rumble of a cart reached our ears from the distant road. I imagined some villager setting off with his load of potted plants to sell at the market.

At the sound Sensei broke off his meditation and rose abruptly to his feet, like one restored to life. "We ought to be off. The days have grown a good deal longer recently, it's true, but evening's rapidly approaching while we sit here idly."

His back was covered with bits of leaf and twig from the bench. I brushed them off with both hands.

"Thank you. Is any resin stuck there?"

"Everything's off now."

"This coat was made quite recently, so my wife will be cross if I come home with it dirty. Thank you."

We set off down the gentle slope and emerged back in front of the house.

A woman was sitting on the once-empty veranda. She was busy winding yarn onto a spool with the help of her daughter, a girl of fifteen or sixteen. When we arrived beside the big tub of goldfish, we bowed and apologized for our intrusion.

"No, no, not at all," the woman politely responded, and thanked us for the boy's coin.

We went out the gate and set off for home. After a short distance I turned to Sensei.

"That thing you said earlier," I said, "about how people can suddenly turn bad when it comes to the crunch—what did you mean by that?"

"Well, nothing deep, really. I mean, it's a fact. I'm not just theorizing."

"Yes, that's all very well. But what do you mean by 'when it comes to the crunch'? What sort of situation are you talking about?"

Sensei burst into laughter. Now that his original impulse had flagged, he seemed to have no interest in providing me with a serious explanation.

"Money, my friend. The most moral of men will turn bad when they see money."

This reply struck me as tiresomely obvious. If Sensei was unwilling to take the conversation seriously, I too lost interest.

I strode coolly onward, feigning indifference. The result was that Sensei dropped somewhat behind.

"Hey there!" he called. Then: "There you are, you see?"

"What?" I turned and waited for him.

"All I had to do was say what I just said, and your mood changed." He was looking me in the eye.

CHAPTER 30

I disliked Sensei just then. Even when we resumed walking on together, I chose not to ask the questions I wanted. Whether he sensed that or not, however, he showed no signs of being disturbed by my sulk. He strode casually on in silence, as serene as always. I resented this, and found myself now wanting to say something to humiliate him.

"Sensei."

"What is it?"

"You got a little excited earlier, didn't you? When we were sitting in the nursery garden back there. I've almost never seen you excited before."

He did not reply immediately, which I interpreted to mean that I had hit my mark. But the intended barb also seemed to have somehow gone wide. I gave up and reverted to silence.

Then, without warning, Sensei moved to the side of the road, and there under the carefully clipped hedge, he drew his kimono aside and relieved himself. I waited blankly until he was finished.

"Pardon me," he said, and set off walking again.

I had lost all hope of getting the better of him. The road slowly grew more populous; houses now lined both sides, and we encountered no further signs of the earlier occasional sloping fields or patches of vacant land. Nevertheless, here and there on the corner of some block we saw a patch of garden with tendrils of bean vines twining up bamboo stakes, or chickens in a wire coop, which lent a certain serenity to the scene. Packhorses constantly passed us, heading home from town.

Always interested in such things, I set aside the problem that had been concerning me. By the time Sensei returned to our earlier conversation, I had forgotten about it.

"Did I really seem so very excited back there?"

"Well, I wouldn't say 'very,' but yes, a little."

"I don't mind you seeing me in a bad light. I do get excited, it's true. I get excited whenever I talk about the question of property. I don't know how I seem to you, but let me tell you, I'm a most vindictive man. When someone insults or harms me, I'll bear the grudge for ten years, twenty years."

Sensei seemed still more agitated now. It was not his tone that startled me, however, but the meaning of his words. For all my longing to know him better, I could never have dreamed that I would hear such a confession from his lips. I had not had the slightest inkling that tenacious rancor was a part of his nature. I had believed him a weaker man; my affection for him, indeed, was rooted in what I saw as his delicate, lofty nature. I had sought on a passing impulse to pierce his armor a little, but what I was now hearing made me shrink.

"I've been deceived by people, you see," he continued. "By people, what's more, who were blood relatives. I'll never forget it. They had seemed good folk in my father's presence, but the moment he died, they changed into unscrupulous rogues. I've borne the humiliation and harm they did to me all my life, and I imagine I'll go on nursing it until the day I die. For I won't ever be able to forget, you see. And I've still not taken my revenge. But I guess I'm doing something far more powerful than taking personal revenge—I not only hate them, I've come to hate the whole human race they typify. This is sufficient revenge for me, I think."

I was silent, unable to produce so much as a word of comfort.

CHAPTER 31

Our conversation that day went no further. Indeed, I had no desire to pursue the subject. I quailed to hear Sensei speak like that.

At the edge of town we caught an electric tramcar, but while riding along together we exchanged scarcely a word. Once we got off, our ways parted.

By now Sensei's mood had changed again. "You'll be living free and easy until you graduate in June, won't you?" he remarked in an unusually jolly tone. "It may actually be the freest time in your life, I shouldn't wonder. Make sure you really enjoy it, won't you?"

I laughed and raised my hat. Sensei's face just then made me wonder where in his heart he could be nursing a hatred of the human race. I detected not the least trace of misanthropy in that smile or those warm eyes.

I freely acknowledge that Sensei taught me much about intellectual questions, but I admit there were also times when I failed to gain what I sought from him in matters of the mind. Conversations with him could be frustratingly inconclusive. Our talk that day would haunt me as such an instance.

One day I frankly confessed as much to Sensei's face. He was smiling as he listened.

"It wouldn't bother me," I continued, "if I thought you didn't really know the answer, but the problem is, you know it—you just won't say it in so many words."

"I don't hide anything."

"Yes, you do."

"You're mixing up my ideas with my past. I'm hardly a good

thinker, but I assure you I wouldn't purposely conceal any ideas I'd arrived at. What would be the point? But if you're asking me to tell you everything about my past, well, that's a different matter."

"It doesn't seem different to me. Your ideas are important to me precisely because they're a product of your past. If the two things are separated, they become virtually worthless as far as I can see. I can't be satisfied with being offered some lifeless doll that has no breath of soul in it."

Sensei stared at me in astonishment. The hand that held his cigarette trembled a little. "You're certainly bold, aren't you?"

"I'm in earnest, that's all. I'm earnestly searching for lessons from life."

"Even if it means disclosing my past?"

The word *disclose* had a frightening ring. Suddenly the man seated before me was not the Sensei I loved and respected but a criminal. His face was pale.

"Are you truly in earnest?" Sensei asked. "My past experiences have made me suspicious of people, so I must admit I mistrust you too. But you are the sole exception; I have no desire to suspect you. You seem too straightforward and open for that. I want to have trusted even just one person before I die, you know. Can you be that person? Would you do that for me? Are you sincerely in earnest, from your heart?"

"If what I've just said is not in earnest, then my life is a lie." My voice shook.

"Good," said Sensei. "I shall speak, then. I'll tell you the story of my past and leave nothing out. And in return . . . But no, that doesn't matter. But my past may not actually be as useful for you as you expect, you know. You may be better off not hearing about it. Besides, I can't tell you right now—please wait until I can. It requires a suitable moment."

Even after I returned to my lodgings that evening, my memory of this conversation continued to oppress me.

CHAPTER 32

Apparently my teachers did not find my thesis quite as good as I thought it was. Nevertheless, I managed to pass. On the day of graduation I retrieved from the trunk my musty old formal winter wear and put it on. Up and down the rows of graduating students in the ceremony hall, every face looked heat-oppressed, and my own body, sealed tightly in thick wool impenetrable to any breeze, sweltered uncomfortably. I had been standing only a short time when the handkerchief I held was sodden with sweat.

As soon as the ceremony was over, I went back to my room, stripped off, and opened my second-floor window. Holding the tightly rolled diploma up to my eye like a telescope, I gazed through it, out over the world. Then I tossed it onto my desk and flung myself down spread-eagle in the middle of the floor. Lying there, I reviewed my past and imagined my future. This diploma stood like a boundary marker between the one and the other. It was a strange document indeed, I decided, both significant and meaningless.

That evening I was to dine at Sensei's house. We had agreed beforehand that if I managed to graduate, I would keep the evening free for a celebratory dinner at his home.

As promised, the dining table had been moved into the living room, close to the veranda. The patterned tablecloth, thick and crisply starched, glowed with a fine white purity beneath the electric light. Whenever I dined at Sensei's, the chopsticks and bowls were placed on this white linen that seemed to have come straight from some Western restaurant; the cloth was always freshly laundered.

"It's just as with collar and cuffs," Sensei remarked. "If you're going to have dirty ones, you might as well go for color in the first place. If it's white, it must be purest white."

Sensei was, in fact, a fastidious man—his study too was always meticulously tidy. Being rather careless myself, this aspect of him occasionally struck me quite forcibly.

Once I mentioned to his wife how finicky he seemed, and she replied, "But he doesn't pay much attention to the clothes he wears." Sensei, who had been sitting nearby at the time, laughed, "It's true, I'm psychologically finicky. It's a constant problem for me. What a ridiculous way to be, eh?"

I was not sure whether he meant that he was what we would call highly strung or intellectually fastidious. His wife didn't seem to grasp his meaning either.

This evening I was again seated across the table from Sensei with the white tablecloth between us. His wife sat at the end of the table, facing the garden.

"Congratulations," Sensei said to me, raising his sake cup. The gesture did not make me particularly happy, however. This was partly due to my own rather somber mood, but I also felt that Sensei's tone was not of the cheerful kind calculated to excite joy. Certainly he raised his cup and smiled, and I detected no irony in his expression, but I felt a distinct lack of any genuine pleasure at my success. His smile said, *I guess this is the kind of situation in which people usually congratulate someone.*

"Well done," his wife said to me. "Your father and mother must be very happy."

Suddenly the image of my sick father rose in my mind. I had to hurry home and show him my diploma, I decided.

"What did you do with your certificate, Sensei?" I asked.

"I wonder. Would it still be tucked away somewhere?" he asked his wife.

"Yes, I would have put it away somewhere," she replied.

Neither of them knew what had become of it, it seemed.

CHAPTER 33

In Sensei's house, when a meal with informal guests had progressed to the point where the rice was served, his wife dismissed the maid and served us herself. This was the custom. The first few times I dined there, it made me feel rather awkward, but once I grew more used to it, I had no difficulty handing her my empty bowl for refilling.

"More tea? More rice? You certainly eat, don't you?" she would say teasingly, completely unabashed at her own directness.

But that day, with the summer heat beginning, my normally large appetite deserted me.

"So that's all? You've begun eating like a bird lately."

"No, it's just that I can't eat a lot when it's hot like this."

She called the maid and had her clear the table, then ordered ice cream and fruit to be served.

"I made it myself," she explained. Sensei's wife was at such loose ends, it seemed, that she could take the time to make her own ice cream for guests. I had several helpings.

"So now that you've graduated," said Sensei, "what do you plan to do next?" He had half-turned his cushion toward the garden and was leaning back against the sliding doors at the edge of the veranda.

I was only conscious that I had graduated; I had not yet decided on any next step. Seeing me hesitate, Sensei's wife intervened. "Teaching?" she asked. When I did not reply, she tried again: "The civil service, then?"

Sensei and I both burst out laughing. "To be honest," I said, "I haven't any plan at all yet. I haven't even so much as thought about what profession to enter, actually. I can't see how I can choose, really, since I don't know what's a good profession and what's not until I try them out."

"That's true enough," she responded. "But after all, you'll inherit property, so it's natural that you'd feel relaxed about the question. Just take a look at others who aren't so fortunate. They're far from able to be so blithe."

Some of my friends had been searching for positions as middle-school teachers since well before graduation, so her words were true. I privately acknowledged that but what I said was "I may have been a bit infected by Sensei."

"Oh dear, he's not a good influence, I'm afraid."

Sensei grimaced. "I don't mind if you're influenced by me. What I'd like is for you to make sure, while your father is still alive, that you get a decent inheritance, as I said the other day. You mustn't relax until that's sorted out."

I recalled our conversation back in early May in the spacious grounds of the nursery garden among the flowering azaleas. Those forceful words, spoken with emotion as we were walking back, echoed in my mind. They were not only forceful, those words, they were terrible. Ignorant of his past as I was, I could not fully make sense of them.

"Are you very well off?" I asked Sensei's wife.

"Now why should you ask such a question?"

"Because Sensei won't tell me the answer."

She smiled and looked at Sensei. "That would be because we're not well off enough to make it worth mentioning."

"I'd like to know, so that when I go home and talk to my father, I'll have some idea of how much I'd need to live as Sensei does." Sensei was facing the garden, calmly puffing on his cigarette, so I naturally addressed his wife.

"Well, it's not really a question of how much, you know . . . I mean, we get by, one way and another . . . Anyway, that's beside the point. The point is, you really must find something to do in life. You can't just laze around like Sensei does . . ."

Sensei turned slightly. "I don't just laze around," he protested.

CHAPTER 34

That night it was after ten when I left Sensei's house. I was due to go back to my family home in two or three days, so I said my farewells as I left.

"I won't be seeing you for a while," I explained.

"You'll be back in September, won't you?" Sensei's wife asked.

Having graduated, I had in fact no reason to come back to Tokyo in September. Nor did I fancy the idea of returning to the city in August, at the height of the hot summer. In fact, since I felt no urgency to search for work, I could come back or not as I wished.

"Yes, I guess it'll be around September."

"Well, then, take good care, won't you? We may end up going somewhere ourselves over the summer. It promises to be very hot. If we do, we'll send you a postcard."

"Where do you have in mind, if you were to go somewhere?"

Sensei was grinning as he listened to this conversation. "Actually, we haven't even decided whether we're going or not."

As I rose to leave, Sensei held me back. "How is your father's illness, by the way?" he asked.

I had had very little news on the subject, I replied, so I could only assume that he was not seriously ill.

"You can't make such easy assumptions about an illness like his, you know," he reminded me. "If he develops uremia, it's all up with him."

I had never heard the term *uremia* and did not know what it meant. Such technical terms had not come up in my discussion with the local doctor back during the winter vacation.

"Do look after him well," Sensei's wife added. "If the poison goes to his brain, he's finished, you know. It's no laughing matter."

This unnerved me, but I managed to grin. "Well, there's no point in worrying, I guess, since they say it's not an illness you recover from."

"If you can approach it so matter-of-factly, no more need be said, I suppose," she replied, and looked down, subdued. I guessed she was recalling her mother, who had died of the same illness many years ago. Now I felt genuinely sad at the thought of my father's fate.

Sensei suddenly turned to her. "Do you think you'll die before me, Shizu?"

"Why?"

"No particular reason, I'm just asking. Or will I move on before you do? The general rule is that the husband goes first, and the wife is left behind."

"That's not always so, by any means. But the husband is generally the older one, isn't he?"

"You mean therefore he dies first? Well, then, I'll have to die before you do, won't I?"

"You're a special case."

"You think so?"

"Well, look at you. You're just fine. You've almost never had a day's illness. No, it's certainly going to be me first."

"You first, you think?"

"Definitely."

Sensei looked at me. I smiled.

"But just say it turns out to be me who goes first. What would you do then?"

"What would I do . . ." Sensei's wife faltered, seeming stricken by a sudden apprehension of the grief she would feel. But then she raised her face again, her mood brighter.

"Well, there'd be nothing I could do, would there? Death comes when it will, as the saying goes." She spoke jokingly, but her eyes were fixed on me.

CHAPTER 35

I had been about to leave, but once this conversation was under way, I settled back into my seat again.

Sensei turned to me. "What do you think?"

I was in no position to judge whether Sensei or his wife would be first to die, so I simply smiled and remarked, "Who can foretell allotted life spans?"

"Yes, that's what it amounts to, isn't it," Sensei's wife responded. "We each receive a given span of years, and there's nothing we can do about it. That's exactly what happened with Sensei's mother and father, you know."

"They died on the same day?"

"Oh no, not quite the same day, of course, but just about the same—one died soon after the other."

I was struck by this new piece of information. "Why did they die so close together?"

She was about to answer when Sensei broke in. "That's enough of this subject. It's pointless." He gave his fan a few boisterous flaps, then turned to his wife. "I'll give you this house when I die, Shizu."

She laughed. "And the earth under it too, if you don't mind."

"The earth belongs to someone else, so we can't do much about that. But I'll give you everything I own."

"Thank you. But I couldn't do much with those foreign books of yours, you know."

"Sell them to a secondhand dealer."

"How much would they come to?"

Instead of replying, Sensei continued to talk hypothetically about his own death. He was firmly assuming he would die before his wife.

Although she had initially treated the conversation lightly, it finally began to oppress her sensitive woman's heart. "You keep saying 'When I die, when I die.' That's enough talk about the next world, please. It's inauspicious. If you die, I'll do everything as you'd have wanted, rest assured. What more could you ask?"

Sensei looked out at the garden and smiled. But to avoid upsetting her further, he said no more on the subject.

I was overstaying my visit, so I hastily rose again to leave. Sensei and his wife saw me to the entrance hall.

"Take good care of your father," she said.

"See you in September," said Sensei.

I said my farewells and stepped out past the lattice gate. The bushy osmanthus between the entrance and the front gate spread its branches wide in the darkness as if to block my way. As I pushed the few steps past it, I imagined the scented flowers of the autumn to come, on those twigs where dark leaves now flourished. My mental image of Sensei's house had always been inseparable from this osmanthus bush.

As I paused there and turned back to look at the house, imagining the autumn day when I would cross that threshold again, the hall light that had been shining through the lattice front was suddenly extinguished. Sensei and his wife had evidently gone back inside. I made my way on alone through the darkness.

I did not go straight back to my lodgings. There were things I needed to buy before my journey, and besides, I had to ease my belly, which was crammed with fine food, so I set off to walk toward the bustling town. It was still full of the activity of early evening. Men and women were casually thronging the streets.

I ran into a friend who had just graduated with me, and he pulled me off to a bar, where I listened to his high-spirited chatter, frothy as the beer we drank. It was past midnight when I finally got home.

CHAPTER 36

The following day I went out again, braving the heat to buy the various things I had been asked to get. It had not seemed much when I received the letter with the list of purchases, but when it came to the point, it proved extremely tiresome. Wiping my sweat as I sat in the streetcar, I cursed these country folk who never spared a sympathetic thought for the time and effort to which they were putting someone else.

I did not intend to spend my summer back at home idly. I had worked out a daily program to follow and set out to gather the books I needed to pursue my plan. I had decided to spend a good half day on the second floor of Maruzen bookshop, looking through the foreign books. I located the shelves particularly relevant to my field and went through them methodically, investigating every book.

The most troublesome item on the shopping list was some ladies' kimono collars. The shop assistant produced quite a few of them for me to look at, but when the time came for me to decide which ones to purchase, I could not. Another problem was that the prices seemed quite arbitrary. A collar that looked cheap turned out to be highly expensive, while others that I had passed over as expensive-looking actually cost very little. For the life of me I could not tell what made one more valuable than another. The whole mission defeated me, and I regretted not having troubled Sensei's wife to come along and help me.

I bought a travel bag. It was, of course, only an inferior, locally made one, but its shiny metal fittings would look impressive enough to dazzle country folk. My mother had asked me in a letter to buy a travel bag, to carry all the gifts home, and

she had specifically said a new bag. I'd laughed aloud when I
read that. I appreciated her kindly intention, but the words
somehow struck me as funny.

Three days later I set off on the train for home, as I had told
Sensei and his wife I would on the night when I said my farewells. Sensei had been warning me about my father's illness
since winter, and I had every reason to be concerned about it,
but for some reason the question did not much bother me. I was
more disturbed by the problem of how my poor mother would
fare after his death.

Clearly, something in me had already accepted the fact that
he must die. In a letter to my elder brother in Kyushu I had
admitted as much, writing that our father could not possibly
recover his health. Although no doubt he was tied up with
work, I added, perhaps my brother should try to get back and
see him over the summer. I rounded it off with an emotional
plea that our two aged parents living together alone in the
country must surely be lonely, which should lie heavily on the
consciences of us children. I wrote those words simply as they
occurred to me, but once they were out, I found myself feeling
rather different.

In the train I pondered these contradictions, and I soon began
to see myself as superficial and emotionally irresponsible.
Gloomily, I thought again of Sensei and his wife and recalled
our conversation of a few evenings earlier, when I had gone
there for dinner.

I pondered the question that had arisen between them then:
Which will die first? Who could give a confident answer to that
question? I thought. And suppose the answer were clear. What
would Sensei do? What would his wife do? Surely the only
thing either could do was continue just as they were—just as I
too was helpless in the face of my father's approaching death
back at home. A sense of human fragility swept over me, of the
hopeless frailty of our innately superficial nature.

PART II

MY PARENTS AND I

CHAPTER 37

When I arrived home, I was surprised to see that my father's health seemed remarkably unchanged.

"So you're home, eh?" he greeted me. "Well, well. Still, it's a fine thing you've graduated. Wait a moment, I'll just go and wash my face."

He had been engaged in some task out in the garden, and now he went around to the well at the back of the house. As he walked, the grubby handkerchief he had fixed to the back of his old straw hat to keep off the sun flapped behind him.

I considered graduation a perfectly normal achievement, and my father's unexpected degree of pleasure in it was gratifying.

"A fine thing you've graduated"—he repeated these words again and again. In my heart, I compared my father's joy with Sensei's reaction at the dinner table after the graduation ceremony. He had said "Congratulations," but his private disdain was evident in his face. Sensei, I thought, was more cultured and admirable than my father, with his unashamed delight. In the final analysis, what I felt was displeasure at the reek of country boorishness in my father's innocence.

"There's nothing particularly fine in graduating from the university," I found myself responding testily. "Hundreds of people do it every year, you know."

My father's expression changed. "I'm not just talking about the graduation. That's a fine thing, to be sure, but what I'm saying has a bit more to it. If only you'd understand what I'm getting at . . ."

I asked him what he meant. He seemed disinclined to talk about it at first but finally said, "What I mean is, it's fine for

me personally. You know about this illness of mine. When I saw
you in the winter, at the end of last year, I had a feeling I might
not last more than three or four more months. And here I am,
still doing so well. It's wonderful. I can still get around without
any trouble. And now you've graduated as well. That's why I'm
happy, see?

"You must realize how it pleases me that this son of mine,
whom I raised with such love and care, should graduate while
I'm still alive and well to witness it. Having someone make such
a fuss about a mere graduation must seem boring to you, with
all your aspirations—I can see that. But stand in my shoes, and
you'll see it a bit differently. What I'm saying is, it's a fine thing
for me, if not for you, don't you see?"

Speechless, I hung my head, overwhelmed by shame that no
apology could express. I saw that my father had calmly been
preparing to die and had decided it would probably happen
before my graduation. I had been a complete fool not to think
of how my graduation would make him feel.

I took the diploma from my bag and spread it out carefully
for my parents to see. Something had crushed it, and it was no
longer quite the shape it had been.

My father smoothed it tenderly. "You should have carried
such a precious thing home by hand, rolled up," he said.

"You'd have done better to wrap it around something solid,"
my mother chipped in from beside him.

After gazing at it for a while, my father rose to his feet and
carried it over to the alcove, where he arranged it so that anyone who entered would immediately catch sight of it. Normally
I would have made some remonstrance, but just now I was a
very different person than usual. I felt not the slightest inclination to contradict my parents. I sat silently and let my father do
as he would.

The warp in the thick, elegant paper refused to respond to
his attempts to straighten it. No sooner had he managed to
smooth it flat and stand it where he wanted than it would
spring back of its own accord and threaten to tip over.

CHAPTER 38

I called my mother aside and asked about his health. "Is it really all right for him to be going out in the garden like this and being so active?"

"There's nothing wrong with him. He seems on the whole to have recovered."

She seemed oddly calm. Typically for a woman who had spent her life among fields and woods far from the city, she was completely innocent in such matters. Yet her calmness struck me as peculiar, considering how disconcerted and worried she had been earlier, when my father had fainted. "But back then the doctor's diagnosis was that it was a very problematic illness, wasn't it?"

"Well, it seems to me there's no knowing what the human body's capable of. The doctor sounded very grim, and yet look at your father today, still so hale and hearty. I was worried for a while and tried all I could to stop him from doing things. But that's just who he is, isn't it? He takes care of himself, but he's stubborn. Once he gets it into his head that he's well, he'll ignore me if I try to tell him otherwise."

I recalled the way my father had looked and acted on my previous visit, when he had made such an effort to be out of bed and shaved. *Your mother shouldn't go exaggerating things,* he had said, but I couldn't entirely blame her. I was about to suggest that she should at least keep an eye on him but thought better of it. I just told her everything I knew about his disease, although most of it was only what I had learned from Sensei and his wife.

My mother did not seem particularly affected as she listened.

She merely remarked, "Well, well, the same illness, eh? Poor thing. What age was she when she died?"

I gave up pursuing the matter with her any further and went directly to my father.

He listened to my warnings with more attention. "Absolutely. Just as you say," he responded. "But after all, my body's my own, you know, and naturally I know best how to look after it, with all my years of experience."

When I repeated this remark to my mother, she smiled grimly. "There you are, I told you so."

"But he's thoroughly aware of the problem. That's exactly why he was so overjoyed to see me after I graduated. He told me so. He said he'd thought before that he might not be alive, so he was happy he'd survived in good health till I could bring back the diploma for him to see."

"Well, he's just saying that, you know. In his heart of hearts he's convinced he's still fine."

"You really think so?"

"He plans to live another ten or twenty years. Mind you, he does talk rather mournfully sometimes. 'I may not have much longer to go,' he'll say. 'What will you do when I die? Will you stay on here alone?'"

I found myself imagining this big old country house with my mother left alone here after my father's death. Would she be able to keep it going on her own? What would my brother do? What would she say? And in the face of this knowledge, could I turn my back on the situation and go back to my carefree life in Tokyo? Now, with my mother before me, Sensei's warning sprang into my mind—that I must make sure the property division was seen to while my father was still well.

"But there you are," she continued. "People can carry on about dying and never show any sign of actually doing it, you know. That's how your father is; he'll talk of death like this, but who knows how long he'll go on living? So don't worry. There's actually more cause to worry with someone who seems healthy and never talks like that."

I listened in silence to these trite sentiments, unsure whether they sprang from mere speculation or hard facts.

CHAPTER 39

My parents discussed together the idea of inviting guests over for a special celebratory meal in my honor. I had had a gloomy premonition that this might happen ever since I arrived.

I was quick to reject the idea, begging them not to go making an unnecessary fuss.

I disliked the kind of guests you got in the provinces. They came over with the sole intention of eating and drinking, happy for any excuse to get together. Since childhood I had suffered at having to be present at the table with these people—I could well imagine how much more painful it would be if I was the cause of the gathering. But I couldn't very well tell my parents not to invite such vulgar people over for a noisy get-together, so I contented myself with stressing that I didn't want all this fuss about nothing.

"But it's far from nothing," my mother responded. "It's a once-in-a-lifetime event. It's only natural that we should have a party to celebrate. Don't be so modest." She seemed to be taking my graduation as seriously as she would a marriage.

"We don't have to invite them," my father put in, "but if we don't, there'll be talk." He was concerned about what would be said behind his back. And true enough, these people were inclined to gossip and criticize at the slightest provocation if things weren't done as they believed they should be in such situations.

"It's not like Tokyo, you know," he went on. "Here in the country people make demands."

"Your father's reputation is at stake too," my mother added.

I couldn't press my own position. I decided simply to go along with whatever suited them.

"I was just asking you not to do it for my sake. If you feel there'd be unpleasant talk behind your back, that's a different matter. There's no point in insisting on having my way if it's going to cause problems for you."

"You're making things difficult with that argument," my father said unhappily.

"Your father wasn't saying he's doing it for your sake," my mother broke in. "But surely you must be aware yourself of your social obligations." Woman that she was, my mother's reasoning grew rather incoherent at such times, though when it came to talking, she could easily outdo my father and me combined.

All my father said was "It's a shame that an education just gives people the means to chop logic." But in this simple comment I read all my father's dissatisfaction with me. Unaware of my own stiff and chilly tone, I thought only of how unfairly he was seeing me.

His mood improved that evening, and he asked me when it would suit me to invite the guests. No time was more suitable than any other for me, since I was just hanging around the old house doing nothing but sleeping and waking, so I took this as an indication that my father was being conciliatory. Seeing him so mild and gentle, I could only bow my head in acquiescence. We discussed the question and came up with a date for the invitations.

But before the day arrived, something important occurred: it was announced that Emperor Meiji was ill. The word spread quickly around Japan via the newspapers.

The plans for the celebratory party had already upset our provincial household. Now, just when the matter seemed settled, this news came to scatter those plans like so much dust upon the wind.

"Under the circumstances I think we'd better call it off." So said my father as he sat, bespectacled, reading the newspaper. He seemed to be silently thinking also of his own illness.

For my part, I recalled the sight of the emperor when he had so recently come to the university, as was the custom, for our graduation ceremony.

CHAPTER 40

A hush fell over our big old echoing house and its few inhabitants. I unpacked my wicker trunk and tried to read, but for some reason I felt restless. I had been far more happily focused and able to study back in my second-floor room in hectic Tokyo, turning the pages as the distant streetcars rattled in my ears.

Now as I read, I was inclined to drop my head onto the desk and nap; sometimes I brought out a pillow and indulged in a real sleep. I would awaken to the pounding song of cicadas. That sound, which seemed like a continuation of my dreams, suddenly tormented my ears with painful intensity. As I lay motionless, listening, sad thoughts would sometimes settle over me.

Abandoning reading for my writing brush, I wrote brief postcards or long letters to various friends. Some had stayed on in Tokyo, while others had returned to distant homes. Some replied; from others I heard nothing. Needless to say, I did not neglect Sensei—I sent him three closely written pages describing all that had happened since my return. As I sealed the envelope, I wondered whether he was still in Tokyo.

Customarily, whenever Sensei and his wife went away, a woman in her fifties with a plain widow's haircut came and looked after the house. I once asked him what relation she was to them, to which he replied, "What do you think?" I had had the mistaken impression that she was a relative of his. "I have no relatives," he responded, when I told him this. He had absolutely no communication with anyone related to him back in his hometown. The woman who looked after the house turned out to be someone from his wife's family.

As I slipped my letter into the post, an image of this woman, her narrow *obi* informally knotted at her back, rose unbidden in my mind. If this letter arrived after Sensei and his wife had left for their summer retreat, would she have the good sense and kindness to send it straight on to him? I wondered. I was well aware that the letter did not contain anything of real importance; it was just that I was lonely and anticipating his reply. But nothing came.

My father was not as keen on playing *shōgi* as he had been the previous winter. The dust-covered *shōgi* board had been set aside in a corner of the alcove. Since the news of the emperor's illness reached us, he had grown thoughtful and preoccupied. He waited each day for the newspaper to be delivered and was the first to read it. Once done he would bring its pages over for me, wherever I happened to be.

"Here, look at this. More details on His Majesty's condition." This was how he always referred to the emperor. "It's a presumptuous thing to say, but His Majesty's illness is a little like my own."

My father's expression was clouded with apprehension. At his words, I felt a sudden flicker of anxiety that he might die at any time.

"But I'm sure it will be all right," he went on. "Mere nobody that I am, *I'm* still doing fine, after all." Even as he was congratulating himself on his state of health, he seemed to anticipate the danger that threatened to descend at any moment.

"Father is actually afraid of his illness, you know," I told my mother. "He's not really determined to live another ten or twenty years as you say he is."

Bewilderment and distress appeared on her face. "Try to interest him a bit in playing *shōgi* again, will you?" she said.

I retrieved the *shōgi* board from the alcove and wiped off the dust.

CHAPTER 41

Slowly my father's health and spirits declined. His big straw hat with its handkerchief, the one that had taken me by surprise when I first arrived, now lay neglected. Whenever I caught sight of it on the soot-blackened shelf I was filled with pity for him. While he still managed to be up and about with ease, I anxiously cautioned him to take things more carefully. Now, seeing him sitting pensive and silent, I realized he had indeed been relatively well before.

My mother and I had many discussions about it.

"It's his state of mind that's doing it," she maintained, connecting his illness with that of the emperor.

But I felt it was not so simple. "I don't think it's just his state of mind; I think he's actually gone downhill physically. It's his health that's the problem, not his mood."

As I spoke, I began to feel it would be wise to call in a good doctor from somewhere else to have a look at him.

"You're having a very boring summer, aren't you?" my mother remarked. "We can't celebrate this fine graduation of yours, and your father so unwell. And then there's His Majesty's illness—we really should have had that party as soon as you got home."

I had returned on the fifth or sixth of July, and my parents had begun to talk about the celebration a week later. The date that had finally been chosen was over a week after this. This leisurely country approach, free of any sense of urgency, had spared me the social occasion I so disliked. But my uncomprehending mother seemed unaware of my relief.

The day word of the emperor's death arrived, my father

groaned aloud, newspaper in hand. "His Majesty has passed away! And I too . . ." He said no more.

I went into the town to buy some black mourning cloth. We wrapped it around the shiny metal ball on the tip of our flagpole, hung a long three-inch-wide strip from the top of the pole, and propped it at our front gate, pointing at an angle into the street. The flag and the black mourning strip hung listlessly in the windless air. The little roof over our old gate was thatch; long exposure to rain and wind had discolored it to a pale gray, and the surface was visibly pitted. I stepped out into the street to examine the effect, taking in the combination of black strip of cloth and white muslin flag with its red rising sun symbol dyed in the center, and the look of this flag against the dingy thatch of the roof. Sensei had once asked me what sort of street front our house had. "I imagine it looks very different from the gate at the house where I grew up," he'd said. I would have liked to show Sensei this old house I was born in, but the idea also made me embarrassed.

Back inside, I sat alone at my desk, reading the newspaper and imagining the scenes in distant Tokyo. The images in my mind coalesced into a scene of the vast city stirring everywhere with movement in the midst of a great darkness; I saw Sensei's house, a single point of light in the seething, anxious throng that struggled blindly through the blackness.

I could not know that even then the little light was being drawn irresistibly into the great soundless whirl of darkness, and that I was watching a light that was destined soon to blink out and disappear.

I reached for my writing brush, thinking I would write to Sensei about the emperor's death, but having written about ten lines, I stopped. I tore the page into shreds and threw it in the bin—it seemed pointless to write these things to Sensei, and besides, judging from previous experience, I would receive no reply. I was lonely. This was why I wrote letters: I hoped for a response.

CHAPTER 42

In mid-August I received a letter from one of my friends, saying that a certain middle school in the provinces had an opening for a teacher and asking me if I would like to take it. This friend was himself actively searching for such a position, from financial necessity. The offer had originally been directed to him, but he had found a position in a better part of the country, so he'd kindly offered it to me. I quickly sent back a refusal, saying that a number of other people we knew were doing their best to find teaching positions, and he should offer it to one of them.

After I sent the letter, I told my parents about it. Neither seemed to object to the fact that I had declined the offer. "There'll be other good jobs. You don't need to go off to a place like that," they both said.

Behind these words I read their exaggerated expectations for my future. Unthinkingly, they seemed to assume I would be able to find a position and salary far above what I could hope for as someone freshly graduated.

"It's actually very difficult to find a decent position these days, you know. I'm in a different field from my brother, remember, and we're different generations. Please don't go assuming it will be the same for me as for him."

"But you must at least get yourself some independent means now that you're graduated, or it makes things awkward for us too," my father said. "How do you think I'd feel if people asked, 'What's your son doing now that he's through university?' and I couldn't reply?" He frowned unhappily.

His view of life was firmly confined to the little world where he'd spent his life. Inquisitive locals had been asking him how much salary a graduate could expect to earn, guessing at princely sums of around a hundred yen a month. That made him uncomfortable, and he very much wanted to get me settled into a position that would save his face.

My own point of view, based as it was on the great cosmopolitan world of Tokyo, made me seem to my parents as bizarre as someone who walked upside down. Even I found myself on occasion considering myself this way. My parents were so many light-years from my own position that I couldn't begin to confess what I really thought, so I held my tongue.

"Why don't you go to this Sensei you keep talking about and ask for his assistance?" my mother suggested. "This is surely the very moment he could help."

These were the only terms in which she could comprehend Sensei. But this was the man who had urged me, when I got home, to ensure that I got my share of the property before my father's death. He was hardly likely to try to find me a position.

"What does your Sensei do for a living?" my father inquired.

"He doesn't do anything." I thought I had told them this long ago. Surely my father remembered.

"So why doesn't he do anything, eh? I'd have thought someone you respect so much would be in a profession." My father was gently taunting me. To his way of thinking, useful people must be out in the world, engaged in something suitably impressive. *There you are,* he was insinuating, *the fellow's worthless, that's why he's lazing about doing nothing.* "Look at me, now. I don't get a salary, but I'm far from idle, you know."

I remained silent.

"If he's as fine a person as you say, he'll surely find you a position," my mother said. "Have you tried asking?"

"No," I replied.

"Well, what's the good of that? Why won't you ask? Go on, just write a letter at least."

"Mmm," I replied vaguely, and stood up.

CHAPTER 43

My father was clearly afraid of his illness, yet he wasn't the type to plague the doctor with difficult questions when he came to visit. For his part, the doctor kept his opinions to himself and made no pronouncements.

My father was apparently giving some thought to what would happen once he died, or at any rate he was imagining the posthumous household.

"Giving your children an education has its good and bad points, I must say. You go to the trouble of training them, and then they don't come home again. It seems to me an education is the easy way to split up a family."

Thanks to my brother's education, he was living far away, and my own education had resulted in my decision to live in Tokyo. My father's grumblings were perfectly understandable. He must certainly have been feeling forlorn at the thought of my mother left all alone in this big old country house they'd lived in so long together.

My father was of the firm belief that there could be no change in the house, and that my mother would remain there until the day she died. The thought of leaving her to live out her lonely existence in this echoing shell of a place filled him with anxiety, and yet he was insisting I find a job in Tokyo. I found this contradiction rather funny, but it also pleased me, since it meant I could go back to live in the city.

In their company I was forced to pretend that I was doing my very best to look for a job. I wrote to Sensei, explaining the situation at home in great detail. I asked if he could recommend me for any position, and I assured him that I'd be happy to do whatever was in my power. As I wrote, I was aware that he was unlikely to take any notice of my request, and that even if he wished to help me, he lacked the contacts to be able to do so. But I did think that the letter would at least elicit a response from him.

Before I sealed it, I said to my mother, "I've written to Sensei, just as you wanted. Here, have a look."

As I'd anticipated, she didn't read it. "Have you? Well, then, be quick and send it off. You should have done this long ago, without having to be told."

She still thought of me as a child, and indeed I still felt like one. "But a letter by itself isn't enough," I said. "Nothing will happen unless I'm there in person. I really ought to go back to Tokyo around September."

"That may well be true, but you never know what fine offer may come up in the meantime, so it's best to put in an early request."

"Yes," I replied. "Anyway, I'll tell you more when Sensei's answer comes. He'll certainly reply." I was in no doubt that he would. Sensei was a meticulous man.

I waited expectantly for a letter from him. But I had assumed wrongly. A week passed, and still nothing arrived.

"He must have gone off somewhere to escape the summer heat," I told my mother, forced to defend him with some explanation. This justification was intended not only for her but for myself. I needed a hypothesis that would somehow justify Sensei's silence, to spare myself a growing unease.

From time to time I forgot my father's illness and felt inclined to escape back to Tokyo early. My father himself forgot that he was ill, in fact. Anxious though he was about the future, he made no moves to deal with the problem. Time passed, and I found no opportunity to bring up the matter of the division of property with him as Sensei had advised.

CHAPTER 44

When September arrived, I was impatient to return to Tokyo. I asked my father if he would continue to send money for a while, as he had for my studies.

"While I'm here, you see, I can't find myself the position you say I should," I said. This was my explanation to him for returning to Tokyo. Of course, I added, he need only send the money until I found myself a job.

Privately, I felt that such a thing was unlikely to actually come my way. My father, on the other hand, knew nothing of actual circumstances and firmly believed the opposite.

"Well, then, it's only for a short while, so I'll see what I can do. But not for long, you understand. You have to get yourself some good work and become independent, you know. You really should not have to rely on anyone from the day you graduate. Young people these days seem just to know how to spend money and never think of how to make it."

He had various other things to say on the subject as well, including, "In the old days children fed their parents, but these days they devour them."

I heard him out in silence. When his lecturing seemed to have run its course, I stood quietly to leave.

He asked me when I was planning to go. The sooner the better, as far as I was concerned.

"Ask your mother to find an auspicious day in her almanac," he said.

"I will."

I was extraordinarily meek with him. I hoped to be able to leave without having to stand up to him, but he held me back.

"We'll be lonely when you're gone, with just the two of us here. It would be fine if I were well, but as things stand, there's no knowing what might happen when."

I did my best to console him and returned to my desk. Sitting among my jumble of books, I thoughtfully turned over in my mind my father's unhappy words and what lay behind them. As I did so, I heard again the cicada's song. This time it wasn't a continuous shrill but the intermittent call of the cicada known as *tsutsukubōshi,* which sings toward the end of summer. In past summers when I had been home, I had often tasted a strange sadness as I sat quietly in the midst of the seething cicada song. This sorrow seemed to pierce deep into my heart along with the piercing insect cry. Always at such times I would sit alone and still, gazing into myself.

Since returning home this time the sadness had undergone a gradual change. As the summer cicada's strident song gradually gave way to the more hesitant call of the *tsutsukubōshi,* the fates of those around me also seemed to be slowly turning through the great karmic wheel. As I pondered my father's lonely words and feelings, I thought of Sensei, from whom I had received no reply. Since Sensei and my father seemed exactly opposite types, they easily came to mind as a pair, through both association and comparison.

I knew almost everything about my father. When we parted, the emotional bond between parent and child would be all that remained. Of Sensei, on the other hand, I still knew very little. I had had no chance to hear from him the promised story of his past. Sensei was, in a word, still opaque to me. I could not rest until I had moved beyond this state and entered a place of clarity. Any break in relations with him would cause me anguish.

I asked my mother to consult the almanac and fixed on a date for my return to Tokyo.

CHAPTER 45

It was almost time for me to leave—it must have been my second-to-last evening at home—when my father had another fall. I was tying up the wicker trunk packed with my books and clothes. My father had just gone into the bathroom. My mother went in to wash his back, then cried out to me. When I rushed in, my naked father was slumped over, supported from behind by my mother. By the time we brought him back into his room, however, he was declaring that he was all right. Nevertheless, I sat by his pillow cooling his forehead with a damp towel until nine o'clock, when I finally got up to eat a light supper.

The next day my father was in better shape than expected and insisted on getting up to go to the toilet himself, despite our protests.

"I'm fine again," he announced, repeating the words he had spoken to me the previous winter, after he had had the first fall. At that time he had indeed been more or less fine, and I hoped that the same would prove to be the case this time. But the doctor just cautioned us to be careful, and even when we pressed him, he would say nothing more definite.

Because of this fresh anxiety, when the day of my departure arrived, I no longer felt inclined to go. "Should I stay a bit longer, just to see how it goes?" I said to my mother.

"Yes, please do," she begged me.

My mother, who had been unconcerned as long as my father could still go out into the garden or the backyard, now over-reacted in the opposite direction and was consumed with worry.

"Wasn't this the day you were going back to Tokyo?" my father inquired.

"Yes, but I've put it off for a while," I told him.

"Is it because of me?" he asked.

I hesitated. If I said it was, it would only confirm that he was seriously ill. I didn't want to unnerve him.

But he must have read what was in my heart, for he said, "That's a shame for you," and turned away to face the garden.

I went back to my room and looked at the wicker trunk abandoned there. It was securely fastened, ready to leave at a moment's notice. I stood vacantly before it, wondering whether to untie the straps.

I spent three or four days in a state of awkward suspension, like one half-risen from his seat to leave. Then my father had another fall. The doctor ordered absolute rest.

"What will we do?" my mother murmured to me, in a voice hushed so that my father would not hear. She looked miserable.

I got ready to send telegrams to my brother and sister. But my father was experiencing almost no pain. The way he talked, he might have been in bed with no more than a cold. And he had an even better appetite than usual. He was disinclined to listen to warnings from those around him.

"Since I'm going to die, I intend to die eating tasty food."

These words struck me as both comic and tragic. After all, he was not in the city, where really tasty food was actually to be had. In the evening he asked for strips of persimmon-flavored rice cake, which he munched on with relish.

"Why should he hanker so? He must surely still have quite a strong spirit," said my mother, groping in her despair for anything positive. Interestingly, to refer to his desire for food, she was using an old expression that was once specifically associated with illness.

My uncle paid my father a visit, and as he rose to leave, my father held him back, loath to let him go home. He said it was because he was lonely, but he also seemed to want to complain to someone about how my mother and I weren't giving him enough to eat.

CHAPTER 46

My father's condition remained unchanged for over a week. During that time I sent a long letter to my brother in Kyushu and asked my mother to write to my sister. I had a strong feeling that these would probably be the last letters detailing to them my father's state of health. Our letters included the information that we would telegram when the time came, so they should stand ready to come at short notice.

My brother was in a busy line of work. My sister was pregnant. Neither was in a position to be called until my father was in evident danger. On the other hand, it would be awful if they were asked to make the journey only to arrive too late. I felt a private weight of responsibility about exactly when the telegrams should be sent.

"I couldn't give you a precise answer on that, but you must understand that the danger can arise at any time," said the doctor, who had come from the nearby railway station. I talked it over with my mother, and we asked him to arrange for a nurse from the hospital to be hired. When my father laid eyes on this woman, who arrived at his bedside in a white uniform to greet him, he had a peculiar expression on his face.

My father had long known that he was mortally ill. Nevertheless, he was unaware that death was now fast approaching.

"When I'm well again, I might take another trip to Tokyo," he remarked. "Who knows when you'll die? You have to do all the things you want while you're alive to do them."

My mother could only respond with "I hope you'll take me along when you go."

But sometimes he grew deeply dejected. "Do make sure to take good care of your mother when I die," he said to me.

His "when I die" evoked a certain memory. That evening after my graduation, when I was preparing to leave Tokyo, Sensei had used this same phrase several times in the conversation with his wife. I remembered Sensei's smiling face as he spoke, and his wife blocking her ears against the inauspicious words. The words had been merely hypothetical then, but now they rang with the certainty that sometime soon they would be fulfilled.

I could not emulate Sensei's wife's response, but I did need to find a way of distracting my father from his thoughts.

"Let's hear you talking a bit more optimistically. Didn't you say you'd take a trip to Tokyo when you were well again?" I asked. "With Mother. You'll be amazed when you see it next, at how it's changed. The streetcars, for instance—there are all sorts of new routes now. And once streetcars go into a neighborhood, of course, the whole look of the area changes. And the city divisions were recently revised—there's not a moment day or night when Tokyo stands still." My tongue went prattling on out of control, while he listened contentedly.

The presence of an invalid meant that there were a lot more comings and goings at the house. Every few days one or another of the relatives called to visit my father. Among them were some who lived farther away and were normally not in close contact. One remarked as he left, "I was wondering how he'd be, but he seems quite well. He talks without effort, and I must say, to look at his face, he hasn't lost a bit of weight." The household, almost too quiet for comfort when I first arrived, was now filled with increasing bustle and activity.

My father's illness was the one thing that stood still in the midst of all this coming and going, and it was slowly growing worse. After consulting with my mother and uncle, I finally sent off the telegrams I had prepared. My brother replied that he would soon be there, and my sister's husband replied similarly— her previous pregnancy had ended in a miscarriage, and her husband had already intimated that they were taking particular care that it wouldn't become the pattern, so he would probably come in her place.

CHAPTER 47

Amid all this unrest, I nevertheless found time to sit quietly. Occasionally I even managed to open a book and read ten pages or so before I was distracted. The trunk I had packed and closed had been reopened, and I retrieved things from it as the need arose. I reviewed the schedule of study I had set up for myself back in Tokyo. I had not achieved even a third of what I'd hoped to do. The same depressing thing had happened numerous times before, it's true, but rarely had my study gone less according to plan than this summer. I tried telling myself that this was probably simply the way it goes, but nevertheless my sense of failure oppressed me.

Huddled unhappily in self-castigations, I also thought of my father's illness. I tried to imagine how things would be after his death. And this thought brought another, the thought of Sensei. At both ends of the spectrum of my misery were poised the images of these two men, so opposite in social standing, education, and character.

Once when I left my father's bedside and went back to my room, my mother looked in and found me sitting alone, arms folded, amid my jumble of books.

"Why not take a nap?" she suggested. "You must be a bit exhausted."

She had no comprehension of how I felt. Nor was I childish enough to really expect her to. I simply thanked her. However, she continued standing in the doorway.

"How's Father?" I asked.

"He's having a good sleep," she replied.

Suddenly she stepped into the room and came and sat beside me.

"Has anything come from Sensei yet?"

She had believed me when I assured her there would be a reply. But even when I was writing to him, I had had no expectation that he would send the kind of reply they were hoping for. In effect, I had knowingly deceived her.

"Write to him again, will you?" she urged.

I was not inclined to begrudge the effort of writing any number of useless letters if it would comfort my mother, but having to press Sensei on this matter was painful. I dreaded earning his scorn far more than being scolded by my father or hurting my mother. I already suspected that his lack of response to my previous letter bespoke precisely that reaction from him.

"It's easy enough to write a letter," I said, "but this isn't the sort of matter that gets solved through the mail. I have to go to Tokyo and present myself in person."

"But with your father the way he is, there's no knowing when you can go to Tokyo."

"Exactly. And I'll be staying here till we know what the story is, whether he gets better or not."

"That goes without saying. Who on earth would leave someone as ill as he is and take off to Tokyo, after all?"

My first reaction was pity for my innocent mother. But I couldn't understand why she would choose this hectic moment to bring up the problem. Was there something in her makeup that was equivalent to the oddly casual way I could forget my father's illness and sit calmly reading, something that allowed her to temporarily forget the invalid in her care and concern herself like this with other matters?

As this thought was crossing my mind, my mother spoke. "Actually," she said, "actually, it's my belief it would be a great comfort to your father if you could find yourself a position before he died. The way things are going, it may be too late, but really, the way he talks shows he's still quite aware of things. You should be a good son and make him happy while you still can."

Alas, the situation prevented me from being a good son, and I wrote no more to Sensei.

CHAPTER 48

When my brother arrived, my father was lying in bed reading the newspaper. My father had always made a special point of looking through the newspaper every day, and since he had taken to his bed, boredom had exacerbated this urge. My mother and I held our tongues, determined to indulge him in any way he wanted.

"It's wonderful to find you looking so well," said my brother cheerfully as he sat talking with him. "I came expecting you to be in a pretty bad way, but you seem absolutely fine." His boisterous high spirits struck me as rather out of keeping with the situation.

When he left my father's side and came to talk to me, however, he was much more somber. "Isn't it a bad idea to let him read the newspaper?"

"I think so too, but he won't take no for an answer, so what can we do?"

My brother listened in silence to my justifications, then asked, "How well does he understand it, I wonder?" He had apparently concluded that my father's illness had affected his grasp of things.

"He understands just fine," chimed in my sister's husband, who had arrived at about the same time. "I spent twenty minutes or so at his bedside talking about this and that, and there was no sign of a problem. He may well last a while yet, to judge from how he seems." He was far more optimistic than we were.

My father had asked him a number of questions about my sister. "You mustn't let her rock about in trains, in her condition," he had told him. "It would only be a worry for me if she endangered herself by coming to see me." And he added, "Don't worry, I'll be better in no time, and then I'll take the trip up there myself for a change and meet the baby."

When General Nogi committed ritual suicide soon after the emperor's funeral, stating that he was following his lord into death, my father was the first to learn of it from the newspaper.

"Oh no, this is dreadful!" he exclaimed.

We, of course, knew nothing of what had prompted these words, and they gave us quite a shock. "I really thought he'd turned a bit odd," my brother said later to me. "It sent a cold shiver down my spine." My sister's husband agreed that he'd been alarmed as well.

Just then the paper was filled daily with news that made us country folk eager to read every issue. I would sit beside my father going carefully through its pages, and if I didn't have enough time, I quietly carried it off to my room, where I read it cover to cover. The photograph of General Nogi in his military uniform, and his wife, who had died with him, dressed in what looked like the clothing of an imperial lady-in-waiting, stayed with me vividly for a long time.

These tragic winds were penetrating even our distant corner of the land, shaking summer's sleepy trees and grasses, when suddenly I received a telegram from Sensei. In this backwater, where the mere sight of someone dressed in the Western style would set the dogs barking, even a telegram was a major event.

My startled mother was the one to accept its delivery at the door, and she called me over to hand it to me in private.

"What is it?" she said, standing expectantly beside me as I opened the envelope.

The telegram simply stated that he wanted to see me and asked if I could come. I cocked my head in puzzlement.

"It's bound to be about a position he's found for you," declared my mother, leaping to conclusions.

Perhaps she was right, but if so, it seemed a bit strange. At any rate, having called my brother and brother-in-law to come because the end was near, I certainly couldn't turn my back on my father's illness and run off to Tokyo.

I talked it over with my mother and decided to send a telegram replying that I was unable to go. I appended a very brief explanation that my father's illness was becoming critical, but that was not enough to satisfy me. "Letter follows," I added, and the same day I sent off a letter detailing the situation.

"It's such a shame it's come at such a bad time," my mother said ruefully, still convinced the summons had to do with some position he had found for me.

CHAPTER 49

The letter I wrote to Sensei was a fairly long one, and both my mother and I assumed that this time he would answer. Then two days later another telegram arrived for me. All it said was that I need not come. I showed it to my mother.

"He must plan on sending a letter about it," she said, still insisting on interpreting things in terms of the position that Sensei was helping me procure. I wondered if she might be right, though it did not fit the Sensei I knew. The proposition that "Sensei would find a position for me" struck me as out of the question.

"Anyway, my letter won't have reached him yet," I said firmly. "He clearly sent this telegram before he read it."

"That's true," said my mother solemnly, appearing to ponder the matter, although the mere fact that he had sent the telegram before he read the letter could have given her no fresh information.

That day the doctor was coming with the hospital's head physician, so we had no more opportunity to discuss the subject. The two talked about my father and gave him an enema, then left.

Ever since the doctor had ordered total rest, my father had needed help to urinate and defecate. Fastidious man that he was, at first he loathed the process, but his physical incapacity meant he had no option but to resort to a bedpan. Then perhaps his illness slowly dulled his reactions, for he gradually ceased to be concerned by excretion difficulties. Occasionally he would soil the bedclothes, but although this distressed those around him, he seemed unperturbed by it. The nature of his illness, of course, meant that the amount of urine lessened dramatically. This worried the doctor. His appetite too was gradually fading. If he occasionally wanted to eat something, it was only to taste it—he actually ate very little. He even lost the strength to take up his accustomed newspaper. The glasses by his bedside lay untouched in their black case.

When he received a visit from Saku-san, a friend since childhood who now lived about two miles distant, my father merely turned glazed eyes in his direction. "Ah, Saku-san, is it?" he said. "Thanks for coming. I wish I was well like you. It's all over for me."

"You're the lucky one," Saku-san responded. "Here you are with two sons graduated—a little illness is nothing to complain about. Look at me, now. Wife dead, and no children. The best you can say for me is I'm alive. What pleasure's mere good health, eh?"

A few days after Saku-san's visit, my father was given the enema. He was delighted and grateful at how much better the doctor had made him feel, and his mood improved. He seemed to regain some of his will to live.

Perhaps swayed by this improvement, or hoping to boost him further, my mother proceeded to tell him about Sensei's telegram, quite as if a position had already been found for me in Tokyo as my father wished. It made me cringe to sit there listening to her, but I couldn't contradict her, so I held my peace.

My father looked happy.

"That's excellent," my brother-in-law remarked.

"Do you know yet what the position is?" asked my brother.

Now things had gone so far, I lost the courage to deny the story. I prevaricated with some vague reply, incomprehensible even to myself, and left the room.

CHAPTER 50

My father's condition deteriorated to the point where the fatal blow seemed imminent, only to hover there precariously. Each night the family would go to sleep feeling that tomorrow might well be the day of reckoning.

He was completely free of the kind of pain that is a torture for others to witness—in this way at least, he was easy to nurse. We took care to ensure that someone was always taking his turn by the bedside, but the rest of us could usually settle down to sleep at a reasonable hour.

Once when I couldn't get to sleep for some reason, I mistakenly thought I heard my father faintly groaning. I slipped out of bed in the middle of the night and went to check on him. That evening it was my mother's turn to stay up with him. I found her asleep beside him, her head resting on her crooked arm. My father lay peacefully at her side, like one laid gently down inside a deep sleep. I tiptoed back to bed again.

I shared a bed under a mosquito net with my brother, while my sister's husband, who was treated more as a guest, slept alone in a separate room.

"Poor Seki," my brother said. Seki was our brother-in-law's family name. "He's caught here day after day, when he ought to be getting back."

"But he can't really be so busy, if he can stay on like this," I said. "You're the one who must be finding it difficult to stay so long."

"There's no help for it, is there? This isn't an everyday matter, after all."

So our conversation went as we lay there side by side. My

brother believed, as did I, that our father was doomed, and this being so, we longed for it all to be over. Essentially we were awaiting our father's death, but we were reluctant to express it that way. Yet each of us was well aware of what the other was thinking.

"He seems to be still hoping he'll recover, doesn't he?" my brother remarked.

This idea was not entirely unjustified. When neighbors came to visit him, my father always insisted on seeing them. He would then proceed to apologize that he hadn't been able to invite them to my graduation celebration, sometimes adding that he'd make amends once he was better.

"It's a good thing your celebration party was canceled, you know," my brother remarked to me. "Mine was dreadful, remember?" His words prodded my memory, and I smiled wryly, thinking of that event's alcohol-inflamed disorder. I had painful memories of the way my father had gone around forcing food and drink on everyone.

We two brothers were not terribly close. When we were little, we had fought a lot, and being the younger, I was constantly reduced to tears. In school our different choices of field of study clearly reflected our different characters. While I was at the university, and especially once I had come in contact with Sensei, I came to look on my distant brother as rather an animal. We had not met for a long time and lived very far apart, so both time and distance separated us.

But circumstances had at last brought us together again, and a brotherly affection sprang up naturally between us. The nature of the situation played a large part. There at the bedside of our dying father, my brother and I were reconciled.

"What do you plan to do now?" my brother asked me.

I responded with a question of a completely different order. "What's the situation with the household property?"

"I've no idea. Father hasn't said a thing about it yet. But as far as actual money goes, it won't amount to much, I'm sure."

As for my mother, she continued to fret over the awaited letter from Sensei, badgering me with reminders about it.

CHAPTER 51

"Who is this Sensei you keep talking about?" my brother asked.

"I told you about him the other day, remember?" I replied crossly, annoyed that he could so easily forget the answer to a question he himself had asked.

"Yes, I know what you said then." He was implying that what I'd said didn't explain it.

Personally, I felt no need to bother trying to explain Sensei to my brother. But I was angry. *That's just like him,* I thought.

My brother was assuming that since I so evidently respected this man I honored with the name Sensei, he must be someone of distinction in the world, at the very least a professor at the university. What could be impressive about someone who had made no name for himself and did nothing?

This instinct of my brother was in complete accord with my father's. But while my father had jumped to the conclusion that Sensei was living an idle life because he was incapable of doing anything, my brother spoke in terms that dismissed him as hopelessly lazing about despite his abilities.

"Egoists are worthless types. It's sheer brazen laziness to spend your life doing nothing. A man's talent amounts to nothing if he won't set it to work and do all he can with it."

I felt like retorting that my brother didn't seem to understand the meaning of the word *egoist,* which he was bandying about.

"Still," he added as an afterthought, "if this fellow can find you a position, it's a fine thing. Father's delighted at the prospect as well, you know."

As for me, I couldn't believe Sensei could do such a thing until he gave me a clear answer; nor did I have the courage to claim otherwise. But thanks to my mother's announcement of her hasty conclusions, I could not suddenly turn around and deny it. My longing for a letter from Sensei needed no urging from her, and I prayed that when it came, it might somehow fulfill everyone's hopes with word of a position that would make me a living. Faced with the expectations of my father, so close to death, my mother with her urgent desire that he should be somehow reassured, and my brother and his statements that a man wasn't fully human unless he worked, and indeed all the other relatives, I found myself tormented by an issue that I privately cared nothing about.

Not long afterward my father vomited a strange yellow substance, and I recalled the danger that Sensei and his wife had spoken of.

"His stomach must be upset from being bedridden for so long," my mother concluded. Tears came to my eyes to see how little she understood.

When my brother and I met in the sitting room, he said, "Did you hear?" He was referring to something the doctor had said to him as he was leaving.

I needed no explanation to understand its import.

My brother looked at me over his shoulder. "Would you like to come back home and manage the place?"

I could make no reply.

"Mother won't be able to cope with it on her own," he went on. Apparently he was perfectly happy to let me rot here in the dank and dreary countryside. "You can do all the reading you like in the country, and you wouldn't have to work. It'd suit you down to the ground."

"The elder son's the one who ought to come back," I said.

"How could I do that?" he said, curtly dismissing the suggestion. He was driven by the powerful urge to work in the wider world. "If you don't want to do it, I suppose we could ask our uncle to help out, but someone will have to take Mother in."

"The first big question is whether she'd be willing to leave here or not."

Even while our father still lived, we were talking at cross-purposes about what would happen after his death.

CHAPTER 52

In his delirium my father sometimes spoke aloud.

"General Nogi fills me with shame," he mumbled from time to time. "Mortified to think of it—no, I'll be following His Majesty very soon too."

These words disturbed my mother. She did her best to gather everyone at his bedside. That seemed to be what my father wanted, as whenever he was fully conscious, he constantly complained of loneliness.

He was particularly upset if he looked around and found no sign of my mother. "Where's Omitsu?" he would ask, and even when he did not speak the question, it was evident in his eyes. I would often stand and go to call her. She would leave what she had begun to do and come to the sickroom, saying, "Is there anything I can do?" but sometimes he would simply gaze wordlessly at her. At other times he would talk about something quite irrelevant. Or he would surprise her by saying gently, "You've been very good to me, Omitsu." At this my mother's eyes would always fill with tears. Then, however, she would remember his earlier, healthy self and remark, "He sounds so tender now, but he was quite a tyrant in the old days, you know."

She told the tale of how he had beaten her on the back with a broomstick. My brother and I had heard the story many times before, but now we listened with very different feelings, hearing in her words a precious recollection of one, as it were, already dead.

Though the dark shadow of death hovered before his eyes, my father still did not speak of how he wished his estate to be managed after death.

"Don't you think we should ask while there's still time?" my brother said, looking anxiously at me.

"Yes, I guess so," I replied. I could see arguments both for and against bringing up the subject when he was so ill.

We decided in the end to take the question to our uncle before making a final decision, but he too scratched his head over the problem. "It would be a great pity if he died leaving things he wanted to say unsaid, but on the other hand, it doesn't seem right to press things from our side."

The question ended up bogged down in indecision. And then my father slipped into unconsciousness. My mother, as innocent as ever, mistook it for sleep, and was quite pleased. "It's a relief for everyone around if he can sleep as well as this," she said.

Occasionally my father would suddenly open his eyes and ask after one or another of us, always someone who had only just left his bedside. He seemed to have dark and light areas of consciousness, and the light part wove its way through the darkness like a discontinuous white thread, now there, now gone again. It was natural enough that my mother should confuse his comatose state for sleep.

Then his words grew tangled. Sentences he began would end in confusion, so that often his speech made no sense. Yet when he first began to speak, it was in a voice so strong it seemed incredible that it emerged from one on his deathbed. Meanwhile whenever we spoke to him, we had to raise our voices and bring our lips close to his ear.

"Does that feel good, when I cool your head?"

"Mm."

The nurse and I changed his water pillow, then laid a fresh ice pack on his head, pressing it gently to the bald area above his forehead, until the sharp little fragments of chopped ice inside the bag settled with a harsh rustle.

Just then my brother came in from the corridor and silently handed me a postal item. My right hand on the ice pack, I took it with my left, and as my hand received the weight, I registered puzzled surprise.

It was considerably heavier than the usual letter. It wasn't in a normal-size envelope; indeed, it was too bulky to fit in one.

The package was wrapped in a piece of white writing paper, carefully pasted down. As soon as I took it from my brother, I realized it had been sent by registered mail. Turning it over, I saw Sensei's name, written in a careful hand. Busy as I was just then, I couldn't open the letter right away, so I slipped it into the breast of my kimono.

CHAPTER 53

That day my father's condition seemed particularly bad. At one point, when I left the room to go to the toilet, I ran into my brother in the corridor.

"Where are you off to?" he asked sharply, challenging me almost like a watch guard. "We must try to be constantly with him. He seems in bad shape."

I thought so too and returned to the sickroom without touching the letter I had tucked away.

My father opened his eyes and asked my mother to tell him who was present. She carefully named us one by one, and at each name he nodded. If he failed to nod, she raised her voice and repeated the name, asking if he understood.

"Thank you all very much," my father said with careful formality, then sank back into unconsciousness. Everyone gathered around his bed watched him in silence for a while. Finally someone got up and went into the next room. Then another left. I was the third to leave at last and go off to my room. I intended to open the letter I had earlier slipped into my breast. I could, of course, easily have done this at the bedside, but the letter was evidently so long that I couldn't have read it all then and there, so I stole some special time to myself to devote to the task.

I tore roughly at the strong, fibrous paper that wrapped it. When I got it open, what emerged was a document written in a clear hand on ruled manuscript paper that had been folded in quarters to post. I bent back the kinks of the folds to straighten the pages for ease of reading.

My astonished heart wondered what this great bulk of pages

and its inked writing might tell me. Simultaneously, I was anxious about what was happening in the sickroom. I was in no state of mind to settle down calmly and read Sensei's letter—I had a strong foreboding that if I began it, something would have happened to my father before I finished, or at the least someone would call me to his bedside. Nervously, I ran my eye over the first page. This is what it said:

"When you asked me that day about my past, I had not the courage to reply, but I believe I have now achieved the freedom to lay the story clearly before you. This freedom, however, is merely circumstantial and will be lost if I wait until your return to Tokyo, and if I do not make use of it while I may, I will have forever missed the chance to present you with the story of my past, which will then become indirectly your own experience. If this opportunity is missed, that firm promise I made to you will have come to naught. Therefore, I must relate with my pen the words I should be speaking to you."

Only when I had read this far did I fully understand why he had written this long missive. I had believed all along that he would not bother sending a letter on the trivial question of my future employment. But why should Sensei, who disliked writing, have felt the urge to write about the past at such length? Why had it been impossible for him to wait until I returned?

I am telling you because I am now free to. But that freedom will soon be lost forever. I turned the words over and over in my head, struggling to understand. Then a sudden anxiety flooded me. I returned to the letter, determined to read on, but at this moment there came a shout from my brother, calling to me from the sickroom. Startled, I jumped to my feet and ran down the corridor to join the others. I was prepared for this to be my father's end.

CHAPTER 54

The doctor had appeared in the sickroom and was giving my father another enema in an attempt to ease his discomfort. The nurse, who had stayed up with him all night, was asleep in another room. Unused to such scenes, my brother was standing there looking unnerved. "Lend us a hand here," he said when he saw me, and sat down again. I took his place by the bedside, helping out by holding the piece of oiled paper under my father's buttocks.

My father began to look a little more comfortable. The doctor stayed with him for about half an hour and checked the results of the enema, then left, saying he'd be back. As he was on his way out, he made a point of telling us we should call him at any time if something untoward occurred.

Even though something seemed likely to happen at any moment, I left the fraught atmosphere of the sickroom to make another attempt to read Sensei's letter. But I was quite unable to compose myself and give the words my attention. As soon as I was settled at my desk, I fully expected my brother to call out for me again, and my hand holding the letter shook with fear that this time it really would be the end.

I flipped abstractedly through the pages, my eyes taking in the careful script that filled the little squares of the manuscript paper but completely unable to concentrate enough to read it. I could barely even skim it for a general sense of what was written.

I went through page after page until I reached the last, then began to fold them up to leave on the desk. As I did so, a couple of lines near the close of the letter caught my eye.

"When this letter reaches your hands, I will no longer be in this world. I will be long dead."

I caught my breath. My heart, until that moment agitated and distracted, instantly froze. I ran my eyes hastily back through the letter from the end, picking up a sentence here or there on each page. My eyes attempted to pierce the flickering words passing in front of them, in a desperate attempt to gain an understanding. All I wanted was reassurance that Sensei was safe. His past, that vague past that he had promised to explain, was completely beside the point in my present state of urgent need.

At length, having run through the letter backward, I gave up and folded the pages, infuriated by this long letter that refused to give me the information I sought.

I returned to the doorway of the sickroom, to check on my father's condition. All was unusually quiet around him. I beckoned to my mother, who was sitting there looking faint from weariness, and asked how he was. "He seems unchanged for the moment," she replied.

I lowered my head to his face and asked, "How are you? Was the enema any help?"

My father nodded. "Thanks," he said in a clear voice. His mind seemed surprisingly lucid.

Retreating to my room once more, I checked the clock against the train timetable. Suddenly I stood, tightened my kimono belt, and thrust Sensei's letter into my sleeve. I went out through the backdoor. Frantically, I ran to the doctor's house—I had to ask him to tell me plainly whether my father would survive a few more days, to beg him to use injections or some means to keep him alive a little longer.

Unfortunately, the doctor was out. I had neither the time nor the patience to await his return. I climbed into a rickshaw and hurried on to the station.

Once there, I penciled a letter to my mother and brother, holding the page against the station wall. It was very brief, but I judged it was better than simply running off without apology or explanation, so I gave it to the rickshaw man and asked him to hurry and deliver it. Then, with the vigor of decision, I leaped onto the Tokyo-bound train.

Seated in the thundering third-class carriage, I retrieved Sensei's letter from my sleeve and at last read it from beginning to end.

PART III

SENSEI'S TESTAMENT

CHAPTER 55

I have had two or three letters from you this summer. I seem to remember that in the second or third you asked my aid in securing a suitable position. When I read this, I had the impulse to help in some way. At the very least I should have replied, and I felt bad that I did not. But I must confess that I made absolutely no effort in response to your request. Living, as you know, not so much in a confined social milieu as entirely cut off from the social world, I simply had no means of doing so.

But this was not my real problem. Truth to tell, I was just then struggling with the question of what to do about myself. Should I continue as I was, like a walking mummy doomed to remain in the human world, or . . . but whenever I whispered in my heart this *or*, a horror overcame me. I was like a man who rushes to the edge of a cliff and suddenly finds himself gazing down into a bottomless chasm. I was a coward, suffering precisely the agony that all cowards suffer. Sorry as I am to admit it, the simple truth is that your existence was the last thing on my mind. Indeed, to put it bluntly, the question of your work, of how you should earn a living, was utterly meaningless to me. I didn't care. It was the least of my problems. I left your letter in the letter rack, folded my arms, and returned to my thoughts. Far from feeling sympathetic, I did no more than cast a bitter glance your way—a fellow from a family with a decent amount of property, only just graduated, and already making a fuss about a job! I confess this to you now by way of explanation for my unforgivable failure to respond. I am not being intentionally rude to stir your anger. I believe that as you read on, you will fully understand. At all events, I neglected to reply as I should have done, and I now apologize for my remissness.

Afterward I sent you a telegram. In truth I rather wanted to see you just then. I wanted to tell you the story of my past, as you had asked. When you replied that you could not come to Tokyo, I sat for a long time gazing at the telegram in disappointment. You must have felt that your brief response was not enough, for you then wrote me that long letter, from which I understood the circumstances that held you at home. I have no cause to consider you rude. How could you have left your dear sick father back at home and come? Indeed, it was wrong of me to have summoned you so high-handedly, ignoring the problem of your father's health—I had forgotten about him when I sent that telegram, I must admit. This despite the fact that I was the one who so earnestly advised you to take good care of him and emphasized how dangerous his illness was. I am an inconsistent creature. Perhaps it is the pressure of my past, and not my own perverse mind, that has made me into this contradictory being. I am all too well aware of this fault in myself. You must forgive me.

When I read your letter—the last letter you wrote—I realized I had done wrong. I thought of writing to that effect, but I took up my pen, then laid it down again without writing a line. If I were to write to you, it must be this letter, you see, and the time for that had not yet quite come. That is why I sent the simple telegram saying you need not come.

CHAPTER 56

I then began to write this letter. Being unaccustomed to writing, I have agonized over the difficulty of describing my thoughts and experiences precisely as I wanted. Time and again I almost reached the point of giving up and abandoning the effort to fulfill my promise to you. But it was useless to put down the pen and decide to stop. Within an hour, the urge to write would return. You may well attribute this simply to my nature, as someone who is meticulous about promises and obligations. I don't deny it. Being, as you know, quite isolated from human intercourse, I have not a single truly binding obligation in my life. Whether intentionally or by nature, I have lived so as to keep such ties to an absolute minimum. Not that I am indifferent to obligation. No, I spend my days so passively because of my very sensitivity to such things—I lack the energy to withstand the toll they take on my nerves. And so once I make a promise, it distresses me deeply if I do not fulfill it. It is partly in order to avoid being distressed on account of you that I must keep taking up the pen.

Besides, I want to write. I want to write about my past, quite aside from the obligation involved. My past is my own experience—one might call it my personal property. And perhaps, being property, it could be thought a pity not to pass it on to someone else before I die. This is certainly more or less how I feel about it. But I would rather that my experience be buried with me than be passed to someone incapable of receiving it. In truth, if you did not exist, my past would have remained just that and would not become someone else's knowledge even at second hand. Among the many millions of

Japanese, it is to you alone that I want to tell the story of my past. Because you are sincere. You are serious in your desire to learn real lessons from life.

I will not hesitate to cast upon you the shadow thrown by the darkness of human life. But do not be afraid. Gaze steadfastly into this darkness, and find there the things that will be of use to you. The darkness of which I speak is a moral darkness. I was born a moral man and raised as one. My morality is probably very different from that of young people today. But different though it may be, it is my own. It is not some rented clothing I have borrowed to suit the moment. This is why I believe it will be of some use to you, a young man just starting out in life.

You and I have often argued over questions of modern thought, as I'm sure you remember. You well understand my own position on such things, I'm sure. I never felt outright contempt for your opinions, yet I could not bring myself to actually respect them. Nothing lay behind your ideas. You were too young to have had your own experience. Sometimes I smiled. At times I glimpsed dissatisfaction on your face. Meanwhile you were also pressing me to unroll my past before you like some painted scroll. This was the first time I actually privately respected you. You revealed a shameless determination to seize something really alive from within my very being. You were prepared to rip open my heart and drink at its warm fountain of blood. I was still alive then. I did not want to die. And so I evaded your urgings and promised to do as you asked another day. Now I will wrench open my heart and pour its blood over you. I will be satisfied if, when my own heart has ceased to beat, your breast houses new life.

CHAPTER 57

I was not yet twenty when I lost both my parents. My wife told you, I remember, that they died of the same illness. You were astonished when she said they died at virtually the same time. The fact is that my father contracted the dreaded typhoid fever, and my mother became infected through nursing him.

I was their only son. The family was quite wealthy, so I was brought up in considerable comfort. Looking back, I now think that if my parents had not died when they did—if one of them, it does not matter which, had continued to be there to support me—I would have remained as generous and easygoing as I was in those days.

Their deaths left me stunned and helpless. I had no knowledge, no experience, no wisdom. My mother had been too ill to be with my father when he died. She did not even learn of his death before she died herself. I have no idea whether she intuited it, or whether she believed what those around her told her, that he was on the road to recovery. She left everything in the hands of my uncle. I was at her bedside with him when she indicated me and begged him to look after me. I had already gained my parents' permission to go up to Tokyo, and she evidently intended to tell him so, but she had only got as far as saying "He'll go to . . ." when my uncle broke in with "Very good, you have no need to worry." He turned to me and said, "Your mother's a fine, strong woman."

Perhaps he was referring to how well she was coping with the throes of fever. Looking back on it now, though, it is hard to say whether those words of hers in fact constituted a kind of last will. She was of course aware of the identity of the terrible illness my father had contracted and knew she had also been infected by it. But did she understand that she too was dying? It is impossible to say. And no matter how lucidly and sensibly she spoke in her fevered states, she often would have no memory of it later. So perhaps . . . but I must stick to the point.

The fact is that I had already developed the habit of taking nothing at face value but analyzing and turning things over obsessively in my mind. I should explain this to you before I proceed. The following anecdote, though not particularly relevant to my story, serves as a good example of this trait, so please read it in that light. For I feel my impulse to doubt the honorable nature of others' actions and behavior probably grew from this time. This has unquestionably much exacerbated my suffering and misery, and I want you to keep that in mind.

But I must not confuse you by such digressions; let me return to my tale. It's possible I am writing this long letter to you with a calmer heart than someone else in my position might. The rumble of streetcars, which disturbs the night once the world is sleeping, has now ceased. Beyond the doors the faint, touching song of a little cricket has begun, subtly evoking the transient dews of autumn. My innocent wife is sleeping soundly and unaware in the next room. My pen moves over the page, the sound of its tip registering each word and stroke. It is with a tranquil heart that I sit here before the page. My hand may slip from lack of practice, but I do not believe my clumsy writing derives from an agitated mind.

CHAPTER 58

Left alone in the world as I was, I could only do as my mother said and throw myself on my uncle's mercy. For his part he took over all responsibilities and saw to my needs. He also arranged for me to go to Tokyo as I wished.

I came to Tokyo and entered the college here. College students in those days were far wilder and rougher than they are today. One boy I knew, for instance, got into an argument with a working man one night and struck him with his wooden clog, leaving a gash in his head. He had been drinking. As they fought, the man seized the boy's school cap and made off with it. His name, of course, was clearly printed on a white cloth patch inside the cap. This all produced such a ruckus that the police threatened to report the matter to the school, but luckily the boy's friends stepped in and managed to keep it out of the public eye. No doubt tales of this sort of wild behavior must sound utterly foolish to someone of your generation, brought up in more refined times. I find it foolish myself. But students in those days did at least have a touching simplicity that present-day students lack.

The monthly allowance my uncle sent me was far smaller than the amount you now receive from your father. Of course things were cheaper then, I suppose, yet I never felt the slightest lack. Furthermore, I was never in the unfortunate position of having to envy the financial good fortune of any other classmate. More likely they envied me, I realize now. Besides my fixed monthly allowance, I also applied to my uncle quite often for money for books (even as a student I enjoyed buying books) and other incidental expenses, and I was able to use this money just as I liked.

Innocent that I was, I trusted my uncle completely, indeed I felt grateful respect for him. He was an entrepreneur and had been a member of the prefectural government—no doubt this was behind the connection with one of the political parties that I also recall. He was my father's full brother, but they seem to have developed very different characters.

My father was a true gentleman and managed his inheritance with great diligence. He enjoyed elegant traditional pursuits such as flower arranging and ceremonial tea-making, and reading books of poetry. I believe he had quite an interest in antique books and such things as well. Our house was in the country, about five miles from town, where my uncle lived. The antiques dealer in town would sometimes come all the way out to show my father scrolls, incense holders, and so on. The English expression "a man of means" probably sums up my father; he was a country gentleman of somewhat cultivated tastes.

He and my bustling, worldly uncle were thus of very different temperaments. Yet they were oddly close. My father would often praise him as a professional man, much more capable and reliable than himself. People in his own position, who inherit their wealth, often find, he told me, that their native abilities lose their edge. His problem was, he had had no need to fight his way in the world. My father said this both to my mother and to me, but his words seemed specifically for my benefit. He fixed his gaze on me and said, "You'd better remember that." I did as I was told, and remember his words to this day. How could I have doubted my uncle's integrity, then, when my father had praised him so highly and trusted him so thoroughly? I would have been proud of him even had my parents lived. Now that they were dead and I was left entirely in his care, it was no longer simple pride I felt. My uncle had become essential for my survival.

CHAPTER 59

The first time I returned from Tokyo for the summer holidays, my uncle and aunt had moved into the house where I had suffered through the death of my parents, and were now ensconced there. This had been decided on before I left for Tokyo. It was the only thing to be done, since I was the only remaining person in our family, and no longer living there myself.

My uncle, I recall, was involved with a number of companies in the town at the time. When we were discussing how to arrange things so that I would be free to go to Tokyo, he had remarked half-jokingly that it would actually be more convenient for him to stay in his home in town to attend to his work, rather than move out to this house five miles away. My family home was an old and important one in the area, fairly well known to the local people. As you probably know, to demolish or sell an old house with a history when there is an heir who could live there is a serious matter. Nowadays I would not let such things bother me, but I was still essentially a child. The problem of leaving the house empty while I was living in Tokyo was a great worry for me.

My uncle grudgingly agreed to move into the empty house that now belonged to me. But he insisted he would need to keep his house in town and move to and fro between the two as the need arose. I was, of course, in no position to object. I was happy to accept any conditions as long as I could get to Tokyo.

Child that I still was, I looked back with a warm nostalgia on the house I had now left. I felt about it as a traveler feels about the home to which he will one day return. For all that I had longed to leave it for Tokyo, I had a strong compulsion to go back there when the summer holidays came, and I often had dreams of the house I would return to after the hard study and fun of the term were over.

I do not know just how my uncle divided his time between the two places while I was away, but when I arrived in the summer, the whole family was gathered there under a single roof. I imagine that the children were there for the holidays, although they would have lived in town for most of the year to attend school.

Everyone was delighted to see me, and I was happy to find the house so much livelier and more cheerful than it had been in my parents' day. My uncle moved his eldest son out of the room that had been mine so that I could occupy it again. There were quite enough rooms to go around, and at first I demurred, saying I didn't mind where I slept. But he would not hear of it. "It's your house," he told me.

Recollections of my dead mother and father were all that disturbed the pleasure of the summer I spent with my uncle's family before returning to Tokyo. But one event did cast a faint shadow across my heart. Although I had barely begun my college life, my uncle and aunt both urged me to consider marrying. They must have repeated it three or four times. The first time they brought up the subject, it was so unexpected that I was no more than taken aback. The second time I made my refusal clear. When they brought it up a third time, I was forced to ask their reasons for pressing marriage on me in this way. Their answer was brief and straightforward. They simply wanted me to make an early marriage so that I could come back to live in the house and become my father's heir.

Personally, all I wanted to do was to come back during vacations. I was familiar enough with country ways to understand this talk of succeeding my father and the consequent need for a wife, of course, and I was not even really against the idea. But I had only just gone to Tokyo to pursue my studies, and to me it was all in some distant future landscape, seen as it were through a telescope. I left the house without consenting to my uncle's wish.

CHAPTER 60

I forgot all about this talk of marriage. None of the young fellows around me, after all, had the air of responsible householders—all seemed their own men, individual and free of constraints. If I had penetrated below the apparent happiness, I might have found some whom family circumstance had already forced to marry, but I was too young and innocent to be aware of such things then. Besides, anyone who found himself in that kind of situation would have kept it to himself as far as possible, considering it private and quite irrelevant to a student's life. I now realize that I was already in this category myself, but in my innocence I continued to pursue my studies contentedly.

At the end of the school year I once more packed my trunk and returned to the home that held my parents' graves. Once again I found my uncle and aunt and their children in the house where my parents used to live. Nothing had changed. I breathed again the familiar scent of my home, a scent still filled with nostalgic memories. Needless to say, I also welcomed being back there as a relief from the monotony of the year's studies.

But even as I breathed this scent, so redolent of the air I had grown up in, my uncle suddenly thrust the question of marriage under my nose again. He repeated his line from my previous visit, giving the same reason as before. But while the summer before he had had no particular woman in mind, this time I was disconcerted to learn that a prospective wife had been selected for me. She was my uncle's daughter—in other words, my own cousin. Marrying her would suit both of us, he maintained, and furthermore my father had actually spoken of it before he died.

Put this way, I supposed it was a suitable enough arrangement, and I easily accepted that my father could have had that conversation with my uncle. I was certainly rather surprised, since this was the first time I had heard of it. My uncle's request seemed perfectly reasonable and comprehensible, however.

No doubt I should not have taken his words on faith. But what primarily concerned me was that I felt quite indifferent to this younger daughter of my uncle. We'd been close ever since childhood, when I had been a constant visitor at my uncle's house in town, not only on day visits but also as an overnight guest. As you will know, romantic love never develops between siblings. I may be stretching the interpretation of this well-known fact, but it seems to me that between any male and female who have been close and in continual contact, such great intimacy rules out the fresh response necessary to stimulate feelings of romantic love. Just as you can only really smell incense in the first moments after it is lit, or taste wine in that instant of the first sip, the impulse of love springs from a single, perilous moment in time, I feel. If this moment slips casually by unnoticed, intimacy may grow as the two become accustomed to each other, but the impulse to romantic love will be numbed. And so, consider it as I might, I could not find it in me to marry my cousin.

My uncle said that if I wanted, I could put off the marriage until after my graduation. "But," he went on, "we should 'seize the day,' as the saying goes, and perform the basic exchange of marriage cups as soon as possible."[1] The question of when it should happen was of no concern to me, since I felt no interest in the bride. I reiterated my refusal. My uncle looked unsatisfied, and my cousin wept. Hers were not tears of regret that she could not take her place beside me; they were the tears of a humiliated woman who has sought marriage and been rejected. I knew perfectly well that she loved me as little as I loved her. I went back to Tokyo.

CHAPTER 61

A year later, at the beginning of the following summer, I went back home for the third time. As always, I couldn't wait to finish final exams and get out of Tokyo, which indicates how much I longed for my home. I am sure you know this well too— the very color of the air in the place I was born was different, the smell of the earth was special, redolent with memories of my parents. To spend July and August nestled back inside that world, motionless as a snake in its hole, filled me with warm pleasure.

My innocent and uncomplicated mind felt no need to bother itself much over the problem of the proposed marriage to my cousin. If you didn't want to do something, you simply said no, I believed, and there would be no further repercussions. So although I had not submitted to my uncle's will, I remained unperturbed. I returned home in my usual high spirits, after a year spent unworried by the question.

But when I got home, I discovered that my uncle's attitude had changed. He did not embrace me with a welcoming smile as he had before. For the first four or five days I remained unaware of the change—my loving upbringing had not prepared me even to recognize coldness. Finally, however, some chance event finally brought it to my notice. I then realized in bewilderment that it was not only my uncle who had changed, but also my aunt. My cousin was also odd, and so was my uncle's son, who had earlier written a friendly letter asking me to investigate the Industrial College he intended to enter in Tokyo once he had graduated from middle school.

Being who I am, I puzzled over this development. Why had

my feelings changed? Or rather, why had theirs changed? Then it occurred to me that perhaps my dead parents had suddenly cleansed my dulled eyes and given me a clear vision of the world. Deep inside, you see, I felt that my parents continued to love me as in life. Even though I was already well acquainted with the real world by then, the strong superstitious beliefs of my ancestors coursed deep in my blood. No doubt they still do.

I climbed the nearby hill alone and knelt before my parents' graves, half in mourning and half in gratitude. I prayed to them to watch over me, feeling as I prayed that my future happiness lay in those hands buried beneath the cold stone. You may laugh, and no doubt I deserve it. But that is who I was.

In a flash, my whole world changed. This was not, mind you, my first such experience. When I was sixteen or seventeen, my sudden discovery of beauty in the world had stunned me. Many times I rubbed my eyes in sheer disbelief, and doubted my own eyes, while my heart exclaimed, "Ah, how beautiful!" At that age boys and girls alike attain what is commonly called sensuality. In this new state, I was for the first time able to see women as representative of the beauty that the world contains. My eyes, until then quite blind to this beauty in the opposite sex, sprang open, and from that moment my universe was transformed.

It was with precisely the same sort of shock that I became conscious of the change in my uncle's attitude to me. I was stunned by the realization, which came upon me abruptly, without any premonition. Suddenly, my uncle and his family seemed to me completely different creatures. I was haunted by the feeling that I must make some move, or who knew what might befall me?

CHAPTER 62

I decided that I owed it to my dead parents to obtain a detailed understanding of the house and property that I had until then left for my uncle to look after. My uncle presented himself as living a hectic life. He bustled endlessly between the town house and the country estate, spending perhaps one in three nights in town. Forever on the move, he made a great fuss about how busy he was. I had always taken him at his word, although I sometimes cynically suspected that he was following the modern fashion to appear busy. But now, with my newfound desire to find a time to talk through the question of property, I could only interpret this endless rush as an excuse to avoid me. I never had a chance to pin him down.

A friend from my middle-school days told me that my uncle kept a mistress in town. Knowing the sort of man he was, I had no reason to doubt that he might have a mistress, but I had no memory of such talk while my father was alive, so the rumor startled me. The friend also passed on to me various other rumors that were circulating about my uncle. Among them was the story that his business had been generally thought to be going under, but in the last two or three years it had suddenly revived and prospered. This tale heightened my own suspicions.

I finally managed to open negotiations with my uncle. Perhaps the word *negotiations* is a little harsh, but as we talked, the tenor of our relations sank to such a low level that only this word can express what took place. My uncle persisted in treating me as a child, while I viewed him through the jaundiced eyes of suspicion. Under these circumstances, the chances of a peaceful resolution were nil.

Unfortunately, my need to press on with my story prevents me from describing the details of those negotiations for you. To tell the truth, there is another, more important matter I have yet to speak of, one that I have with difficulty restrained my pen from writing all this time. I have lost forever the chance to talk quietly with you, and now I am also forced to omit some of what I would like to write—not only because I lack the skill to express myself on the page but also because time is precious to me.

You may remember I once said to you that no one is inherently bad by nature, and I warned you to be careful because most honest folk will suddenly turn bad when circumstances prompt it. You warned me I was becoming excited and upset, and you asked me what kind of circumstances provoked good people to become wicked. When I answered with the single word *money,* you looked dissatisfied. I well remember that look. I can reveal to you now that I was thinking at that moment of my uncle. I was thinking of him with hatred, as an example of an ordinary, decent person who will suddenly turn bad when he sees money, and I was thinking of the fact that no one in this world is to be trusted.

Probably my reply dissatisfied you because you were bent on seeing things in terms of philosophical questions, and you found my answer trite. But I spoke from experience. I was upset at the time, I agree. But I believe that a commonplace idea stated with passionate conviction carries more living truth than some novel observation expressed with cool indifference. It is the force of blood that drives the body, after all. Words are not just vibrations in the air, they work more powerfully than that, and on more powerful objects.

CHAPTER 63

To put it simply, my uncle cheated me out of my inheritance. He did it with ease, during the three years that I spent in Tokyo. From a worldly perspective, I was an absolute fool to have left everything in my uncle's hands without a thought. From some more elevated viewpoint, perhaps I could be admired as pure and innocent. But when I look back on that self now, I wonder why I should have been born so innocent, and that foolish credulity makes me grind my teeth. And yet I also long to be once again that person who still retained his first innate purity. Bear in mind that the Sensei you know is a man who has been sullied by the world. If we define our betters as those who have spent more years being tarnished by the dirt of the world, then I can certainly claim to be your better.

Would I have been materially better off if I had married my cousin as my uncle wanted? The answer is clear, I think. But the fact is, my uncle was scheming to force his daughter on me. He wasn't offering me this marriage out of some kindly intended idea of how well it would suit both sides of the family; no, what drove him was the baser motive of personal profit. I did not love my cousin, but nor did I dislike her. Still, thinking back on it now, I can see it gave me a certain degree of pleasure to refuse her. Of course my refusal did not alter the basic fact that he was cheating me, but at least as the victim I had the satisfaction of standing up for myself a little. I wasn't letting him entirely have his way. This point is so trivial, however, that it is hardly worth bothering over. To your outsider's point of view, it must seem like nothing more than foolishly stubborn pride.

Other relatives stepped in to mediate between us. They were

people I did not trust at all—indeed, I felt quite hostile toward them. Having discovered my uncle's treachery, I was convinced that others must be equally treacherous. After all, my reasoning went, if the man my father had praised so highly could behave like this, what could one expect of others?

Nevertheless, these relatives sorted out for me everything that pertained to my inheritance. Its cash value came to a great deal less than I had anticipated. I had only two options: to accept this accounting without complaint, or to take my uncle to court. I was angry, and I was confused. If I sued him, I feared the case might continue for a long time before it was settled. It also seemed to me that it would cause me added difficulties by taking precious time away from the studies I was still pursuing. After thinking it all through, I went to an old school friend in the town and arranged to have everything I had received converted to cash. My friend advised me against the plan, but I refused to listen to him. I had decided to leave my native home forever. I vowed that I would never lay eyes on my uncle again.

Before I left, I paid a final visit to my parents' graves. I have not seen it since, and now I never will.

My friend disposed of everything as I had asked. Naturally, it took some time after my return to Tokyo to finalize it all. Selling farm land in the country is no easy matter, and I had to be careful lest others take advantage of me, so in the end I settled for a lot less than the market price. To be honest, my assets amounted to the few government bonds I had in my pocket when I left home, and the money my friend subsequently sent. Sadly, the inheritance my parents had left me was greatly diminished. And it felt all the worse because it was not profligacy on my part that had reduced it. Still, the proceeds were more than enough for me to survive on as a student—indeed, I used less than half the interest from it. And it was this financial security that subsequently propelled me into an utterly unforeseen situation.

CHAPTER 64

With my new financial freedom, I began to play with the idea of quitting my noisy boardinghouse and finding myself a house to live in. I soon realized, however, that this would entail the bother of buying the necessary furniture, and employing a servant to run the household, one who was honest, so that I could leave the house unattended without worrying. One way or another, I could see that it would be no easy matter to achieve my plan.

At any rate I should look around for a suitable house, I thought, and with this aim at the back of my mind one day I happened to go west down the slope of Hongō Hill, and climb Koishikawa toward Denzūin Temple.[1] That area has changed completely since the streetcar line went in; back then the earthen wall of the Arsenal was on the left, and on the right was a large expanse of grassy vacant land, something between a hillside and an open field. I stood in the grass and gazed absentmindedly at the bluff before me. The scenery there is still quite good, but in those days that western side was far lovelier. Just to see the deep, rich green of all that foliage soothed the heart.

It suddenly occurred to me to wonder if there might not be a suitable house somewhere nearby. I immediately crossed the grassy expanse and set off north along a narrow lane. Today it is not a particularly good area, and even back then the houses were fairly ramshackle and run-down. I wandered around, ducking down lanes and into side alleys. Finally I asked a cake-seller if she knew of any little house for rent in the area.

"Hmm," she said, and cocked her head for a moment or two. "I can't think of anything offhand . . ." Seeing that she apparently had nothing to suggest, I gave up hope and was just turning for home when she asked, "Would you lodge with a family?"

That set me thinking. Taking private lodgings in someone's home would save me a lot of the trouble involved in owning my own house. I sat down at her stall and asked her to tell me the details.

It was the house of a military man, or rather of his surviving family. The cake-seller thought he had probably died in the Sino-Japanese War.[2] Until about a year before, the family had been living near the Officers' Academy in Ichigaya, but the place was too grand, with stables and outbuildings, and too big for the family, so they had sold it and moved to this area. Apparently, however, they felt lonely here, just the two of them, and had asked her if she knew of a suitable lodger. She told me the household consisted solely of the widow, her daughter, and a maid.

It sounded perfect for me, being so quiet and secluded, but I feared that if I were to turn up suddenly and offer myself, an unknown student, the widow might turn me down. Perhaps I should give up the idea then and there, I thought. But I was dressed quite respectably for a student and besides, I was wearing my school cap. You will probably scoff at the idea that this was important. But in those days, unlike today, students had quite a good reputation, and my square cap invested me with a certain confidence. And so I followed the cake-seller's directions and called in at the house unannounced.

Introducing myself to the widow, I explained the purpose of my visit. She asked me numerous questions about my background, my school, and my studies. Something in my answers must have reassured her, for she said right away that I could move in whenever I wanted. I admired her thoroughly upright, plainspoken air—a typical officer's wife, I decided. On the other hand, she also rather surprised me. Why should a woman of such apparent strength of character feel lonely?

CHAPTER 65

I moved in immediately and was given the room where our initial interview had taken place. It was the best room in the house. At that time a few better-quality student boardinghouses were springing up in the Hongō area, and I had a fair idea of the top of the range in student accommodation. The room I was now master of was far finer than anything else available. When I moved in, it seemed almost too good for a simple student like me.

It was a large room of eight tatami mats. The alcove had a pair of staggered shelves set into one side, and the wall opposite the veranda contained a long built-in cupboard. There were no windows, but the sun streamed in from the south-facing veranda.

On the day I arrived, I noted the flowers arranged in the alcove, and a *koto* propped beside them.[1] I did not care for either. I had been brought up by a father who appreciated the Chinese style of poetry, calligraphy, and tea-making, and since childhood my own tastes had also tended toward the Chinese. Perhaps for this reason I despised this sort of merely charming decorativeness.

My uncle had squandered the collection of objects that my father had accumulated during his lifetime, but some at least had survived. Before I left home, I had asked my school friend to care for most of them and carried four or five of the best scrolls away with me in my trunk. I intended to take them out as soon as I arrived and hang one in the alcove to enjoy it. But when I saw the flower arrangement and the *koto*, I lost my courage. Later I learned that these flowers had been put there especially to welcome me, and I smiled drily to myself. The *koto* had been there all along, for want of somewhere else to store it.

From this description you will no doubt have sensed the presence of a young girl somewhere in the story. I must admit, I myself had been curious about the daughter ever since I first heard of her. Perhaps because these guilty thoughts had robbed me of a natural response, or perhaps because I was still awkward with people, when I first met her I managed only a flustered greeting. She, in turn, blushed.

My imaginary idea of Ojōsan[2] had been built on hints gained from her mother's appearance and manner. This fantasized image of her, however, was far from flattering. Having decided that the mother conformed to the type of the military wife, I proceeded to assume that Ojōsan would be much the same. But one look at the girl's face overturned all my preconceptions. In their place a new and utterly unanticipated breath of Woman pervaded me. From that moment the flower arrangement in the alcove ceased to displease me; the *koto* propped beside it was no longer an annoyance.

When the flowers in the alcove inevitably began to wilt, they were replaced with a new arrangement. From time to time the *koto* was carried off to the L-shaped room diagonally opposite mine. I would sit at the desk in my room, chin propped on hands, listening to its plangent tone. I had no idea whether the playing was good or bad, but the fact that the pieces were fairly simple suggested that the player was not very skilled. No doubt her playing was of a piece with her flower-arranging skills. I knew something of flower arranging and could see that she was far from good at it.

Yet day after day flowers were unashamedly arrayed in my alcove, although the arrangement always took the same form, and the receptacle never changed. As for the music, it was odder than the flowers. She simply plucked dully away at the instrument. I never heard her really sing the accompanying songs. She did murmur the words, it's true, but in such a tiny voice that she might have been whispering secrets. And whenever the teacher scolded her, the voice ceased altogether.

But I gazed in delight at those clumsy flower arrangements, and I listened with pleasure to the *koto*'s awkward twang.

CHAPTER 66

By the time I left home, I was already thoroughly disenchanted with the world. My conviction that others could not be trusted had, you might say, penetrated me to the marrow. My despised uncle and aunt and relatives seemed representative of the whole of humanity. Even on the train I found myself glancing warily at my neighbors, and when someone occasionally spoke to me, my mistrust only deepened. I was sunk in depression. At times I felt a suffocating pressure, as if I had swallowed lead. Yet at the same time every nerve was on edge.

This state of mind was largely what had prompted my decision to leave the noisy boardinghouse, I think. True, my financial security meant I could consider living in a place of my own, but my earlier self would never have thought of going to such bother, no matter how much money might be in my pocket.

For some time after my move to Koishikawa, I continued in a highly strung state. I kept glancing furtively about, so much so that I unnerved even myself. Although my mind and eyes were abnormally active, my tongue grew less and less inclined to speak. I sat silently at my desk, observing those around me like a cat. Sometimes my keen awareness of them was so intense it shamed me to think of it. All that distinguished me from a thief was that I was stealing nothing, I thought in self-disgust.

You must find all this most peculiar—how on earth did I have energy to spare to feel attracted to Ojōsan, to delight in gazing at her clumsy flower arrangements or listen with joy to her inept playing? I can only answer that these were the facts, and as such I must lay them before you. I will leave it up to your clever mind to analyze them, and simply add one thing. I distrusted the human race where money was concerned, but not yet in the realm of love. So despite the obvious contradiction, both states of mind happily coexisted inside me.

I always called the widow by the polite title of Okusan, so I shall do the same here. Okusan apparently considered me a quiet, well-behaved person, and she was full of praise for my studious habits. She made no mention of the uneasy glances or the troubled, suspicious air. Perhaps she simply did not notice it, or maybe she was too polite to speak of it; at any event, it never seemed to bother her. Once she even admiringly told me I had a generous heart. I was honest enough to blushingly deny this, but she insisted. "You only say that because you're not aware of it yourself," she said earnestly.

The fact is, she had not originally planned on having a student as a boarder. When she had asked around the neighborhood if anyone knew of a lodger, she had thought in terms of a government official or the like. I imagine she was envisaging some underpaid fellow who couldn't afford a place of his own. Compared with her impoverished imaginary lodger, I struck her as far more generous in my ways. I guess I was in fact more liberal with my money than someone in more straitened circumstances would have been. But this was a product of circumstance rather than any natural generosity, so it was hardly an indication of what kind of person I was. In her woman's way, however, Okusan did her best to view my liberality with money as an expression of my general character.

CHAPTER 67

Okusan's warm perception of me inevitably started to influence my state of mind. After a while my glances became less mistrustful, and my heart felt more tranquil and settled within me. This new happiness I owed, in effect, to the way Okusan and the rest of the household turned a blind eye on all my wariness and shifty glances. No one reacted nervously to me, and so my own nerves grew steadily calmer.

Perhaps she did indeed find me generous and open-hearted, as she claimed, but Okusan was a wise woman, and her treatment of me may well have been intentional. Or she may simply not have noticed anything odd, since all my nervous activity was largely in my mind and may not have been evident to others.

Gradually, as my inner turmoil subsided, I grew closer to the family. I could now joke with Okusan and her daughter. Sometimes they invited me to have tea with them, and on other evenings I would bring cakes and invite them to join me in my room. My social world had suddenly expanded, I felt. I constantly found my precious study time frittered away on conversation, but oddly, this disruption never bothered me. Okusan was, of course, a lady of leisure. Ojōsan not only went to school but had her flower arranging and *koto* study, so she should by rights have been extremely busy. But to my surprise she seemed to have all the time in the world. Whenever the three of us came across one another, we would settle down for a long chat.

It was generally Ojōsan who arrived to fetch me. She would come via the veranda to stand in front of my room, or else approach through the sitting room and appear at the sliding doors that led to the room next to mine. She would always pause in front of my room. Then she would call my name and say, "Are you studying?"

I was usually sitting staring at some difficult book lying open on the desk in front of me, so no doubt I looked impressively studious. But to tell the truth, I wasn't devoting myself to my books as much as it might seem. Though my eyes were fixed on the page, I was really just waiting for her to come for me. If she failed to appear, I would have to make a move. I would rise to my feet, make my way to her room, and ask the same question—"Are you studying?"

Ojōsan occupied a six-mat room beyond the sitting room. Okusan was sometimes in the sitting room, sometimes in her daughter's. Neither had a room she considered exclusively her own. Despite the partition between them, the two rooms formed a single space, with mother and daughter moving freely between them. When I stood outside and called, it was always Okusan who answered, "Come on in." Even if Ojōsan happened to be there as well, she rarely responded herself.

In time Ojōsan developed the occasional habit of coming to my room on some errand and then settling down to talk. Whenever this happened, a strange uneasiness beset my heart. It wasn't simply a nervous response to finding myself alone face-to-face with a young woman. Her presence made me oddly fidgety and ill at ease, and this unnatural behavior distressed me as a self-betrayal. She, however, was entirely at her ease. It was difficult to believe that this unabashed girl and the girl who managed to produce only a timid whisper when practicing her *koto* singing could be the same person. On occasion she stayed so long that her mother called her from the sitting room. "Coming," she would answer, but she continued to sit there. Yet she was far from a mere child—this much my eyes told me clearly. And I could see too that she was behaving in a way that let me know as much.

CHAPTER 68

I would sigh with relief after Ojōsan left my room, but I also felt a certain dissatisfaction and regret. Perhaps there was something girlish in me. I imagine a modern youth such as you would certainly think so. But in those days this was the way most of us were.

Okusan rarely left the house, and on the few occasions when she did, she never left me alone with her daughter. I can't judge whether this was intentional. It may be out of place for me to say this, but after careful observation I could only conclude that Okusan wanted to bring us closer, yet at other times she seemed secretly guarded. I had never been in such a situation, and it often made me uncomfortable.

I needed Okusan to make her position clear. Rationally speaking, her attitudes were clearly contradictory. But with the memory of my uncle's deceitfulness still so fresh, I could not repress another suspicion—that one of her two conflicting attitudes must be fake. I was at a loss to decide which was the real one, and I could make no sense of why she behaved so strangely. At times I chose simply to lay the fault entirely at the door of womanhood itself. When it comes down to it, I told myself, she's acting this way because she's a woman, and women are stupid. Whenever my cogitations arrived at a dead end, this answer was the one I reached for.

Yet although I despised women, I could not find it in me to despise Ojōsan. Faced with her, my theorizing lost its power. I felt for her a love that was close to pious faith. You may find it odd that I use a specifically religious word to describe my feelings for a young woman, but real love, I firmly believe, is not so different from the religious impulse. Whenever I saw her face, I felt that I myself had become beautiful. At the mere thought of her, I felt elevated by contact with her nobility. If this strange phenomenon we call Love can be said to have two poles, the higher of which is a sense of holiness and the baser the impulse of sexual desire, this love of mine was undoubtedly in the grip of Love's higher realm. Being human, of course, I could not leave my fleshly self behind, yet the eyes that beheld her, the heart that treasured thoughts of her, knew nothing of the reek of the physical.

My love for the daughter grew as my antipathy toward the mother increased, and so the relationship among the three of us ceased to be the simple thing it had once been. This change was largely internal, mind you. On the surface all was the same.

Then some little thing made me begin to wonder if I had misunderstood Okusan. I now revised my idea that one of her two contradictory attitudes toward me and her daughter must be false. They did not inhabit her heart by turns, I decided—they were both there together. Despite the apparent contradiction, I realized, her careful watchfulness did not mean she had forgotten or reconsidered her urge to bring us closer. Her wariness surely sprang from the worrying possibility that we might become more intimate than she considered proper. Her anxiety seemed to me quite unnecessary, since I felt not the slightest physical urge toward her daughter, but I now ceased to think badly of Okusan's motives.

CHAPTER 69

Piecing together the various bits of evidence, it became clear to me, in a word, that the people of this household trusted me. In fact, I even found proof enough to convince me that this trust had existed from the very beginning. Having come to suspect others, I was oddly moved by this discovery. Were women so much more intuitive than men? I wondered. And did this account for women's tendency to be so easily deceived? In retrospect, these thoughts seem ironic, since I was responding just as irrationally and intuitively to Ojōsan. While swearing to myself that I would trust no one, my trust in her was absolute. And yet I found her mother's trust in me peculiar.

I did not talk much about my home and was careful to make no mention of recent events. Just recalling them filled me with distress. I spent as much of our conversations as possible listening to Okusan. But she had other ideas. She was always curious about my home and the situation there, so in the end I revealed everything. When I told her that I had decided never to return, that there was nothing left for me there except the graves of my parents, she seemed deeply moved, and her daughter actually wept. I thought then that it was good to have spoken. It made me happy.

Now that I had told her all, it was abundantly clear that Okusan felt her intuitions confirmed. She began to treat me like some young relative. This did not anger me; indeed, I was pleased by it. But in time my paranoid doubts returned.

It was a tiny thing that sparked my suspicion, but as one insignificant incident was added to another, distrust gradually took root. I began to suspect that Okusan was trying to bring her daughter and me together from the same motives as my uncle. And with this thought what had appeared to be kindness suddenly seemed the actions of a cunning strategist. I brooded on this bitter conviction.

Okusan had always stated that she had wanted a lodger to look after because the house was forlornly unpeopled. This did not seem a lie to me. Having grown close enough to become her confidant, I was now quite sure it was true. On the other hand, she was not particularly wealthy. From the point of view of her own interests, she certainly had nothing to lose by cultivating the relationship.

And so I grew wary again. Still, at times I scoffed at my own foolishness. What use was all my caution about her mother, when I still loved Ojōsan as deeply as ever? But no matter how foolish I recognized myself to be, this contradiction was hardly a source of much pain. My real anguish began when it occurred to me that Ojōsan might be as devious as her mother. The instant it occurred to me that everything was a result of plotting behind my back, I was racked with agony. This was not mere unhappiness—I was in the grip of utter despair. And yet, at the same time I continued to have unwavering faith in Ojōsan. Thus I found myself paralyzed, suspended between conviction and doubt. Both seemed to me at once the product of my imagination and the truth.

CHAPTER 70

I kept up my attendance at college, but the professors' lectures sounded distant in my ears. It was the same with my own study. My eyes took in the print on the page, yet its meaning vanished like a wisp of smoke before it really penetrated. I grew taciturn. Several friends, misinterpreting this, reported to others that I seemed as if deep in meditation. I made no attempt to correct them; in fact, I was delighted to be provided with this convenient mask. But at times some inner dissatisfaction would produce an outburst of high-spirited romping, astonishing my friends.

Not many visitors came to the house. The family seemed to have few relatives. Once in a while Ojōsan's friends stopped by, but generally they would spend the time talking in such low voices that one could scarcely tell they were in the house. For all my heightened sensitivity, I did not realize that they spoke quietly out of deference to my presence. My own friends who came calling, though hardly rowdy, were not inclined to feel constrained by the presence of others. Thus, where guests were concerned, our roles were essentially reversed—I seemed the master of the house, while Ojōsan behaved like a timorous guest.

I write this simply because it is something I recall, not because it bothered me. One thing did bother me, though: one day I heard the startling sound of a male voice coming from somewhere in the house, either the sitting room or Ojōsan's room. It was a very quiet voice, unlike that of my own visitors. I had no idea what he was saying, and the more I tried and failed to catch the words, the more it provoked my straining nerves. A strange sense of mounting frustration seized me as I sat in my room. I began by wondering whether he was a relative or only some acquaintance. Then I tried to guess if he was a young man or someone older. I had no way to tell from where I sat. Yet I could not get up and open the door to look. My nerves were not so much trembling as afflicting me with strong waves of painful tension.

Once the man left, I carefully inquired his name. They gave a simple and straightforward answer. Though I made it clear I was still not satisfied, I lacked the courage to ask further. Nor, of course, did I have the right to do so. I had been taught to maintain dignified self-respect, but a blatant greed for information undermined it; both were evident on my face. They laughed. So perturbed was my state that I was unable to judge whether their laughter was scornful or well intentioned. Even once the incident had passed, I continued to mull over the thought that they might have been jeering at me.

I was quite free—I could leave college at any time if I chose, go or live anywhere I liked, or marry any girl I wished, without having to consult anyone. Many times I had reached the decision to come right out and ask Okusan if I could marry her daughter. But each time I hesitated, and in the end said nothing. It wasn't that I was afraid of a refusal—I could not imagine how life might change for me if she turned me down, but I could at least steel myself with the thought that a refusal might give me the advantage of a new perspective on the world. No, what irked me was the suspicion that they were luring me on. The thought that I could be innocently playing into their hands filled me with resentful rage. Ever since my uncle's deception, I was determined that come what may I would never again become such easy prey.

CHAPTER 71

I spent my money on nothing but books. Okusan told me I should get some clothes, and it was true, all I had were the country-woven cotton robes that had been made for me back home. Students in those days never wore anything with silk in it. One of my friends, who came from a wealthy family of Yokohama merchants who did things extravagantly, was once sent an underrobe of fine silk. We all laughed at it. He produced all sorts of shamefaced excuses and tossed it unworn into his trunk, till we gathered around one day and bullied him into wearing it. Unfortunately, the thing became infested with lice. This was a lucky break for my friend, who bundled it up and carried it off on one of his walks, where he threw it into the large ditch in Nezu. I was with him, and I remember standing on the bridge laughing as I watched him. It never crossed my mind that this was a wasteful thing to do.

I must have been quite grown-up by then, but I still had not come to understand the need for a set of good clothes. I had the odd idea that I had no need to bother about clothes until I graduated and grew an adult mustache. So my response to Okusan was that I only needed books. Knowing just how many I bought, she asked whether I read them all. I was stuck for an answer; some were dictionaries, but there were quite a few others that I should have read but whose pages were not even cut. Books or clothing, I realized then—it made no difference if the thing went unused. Besides, I wanted to buy Ojōsan an obi or some fabric that took her fancy, on the pretext of repaying them for all the kindness I had received. I therefore relented and asked Okusan to purchase the necessary things for me.

She was not prepared to go alone. I must accompany her, she told me, and furthermore her daughter must come too. We students were brought up in a different world from today, remember, and it was not the custom in those days to go around in a girl's company. Being still very much a slave to convention, I was hesitant, but I finally gathered up my courage and we all set off together.

Ojōsan was dressed up for the occasion. She had whitened her naturally pale face with copious amounts of powder, and the effect was striking. Passersby stared at her. Then their eyes would stray to my face as I walked beside her, which I found disconcerting.

We went to Nihonbashi and bought all we wanted. The process involved a lot of dithering over choices, so it took longer than anticipated. Okusan made a point of constantly calling me over to ask my opinion. From time to time she hung a piece of fabric over Ojōsan's shoulder and asked me to step back a few paces and see what I thought. I always managed to respond convincingly, declaring that this worked or that did not.

It was dinnertime when we were finally through. Okusan offered to treat me to a meal by way of thanks, and she led us down a narrow side street where I remember there was a vaudeville theater called Kiharadana. Our restaurant was as tiny as the lane. I knew nothing of the local geography, and Okusan's familiarity with it quite surprised me.

We didn't get home until after dark. The next day was a Sunday, and I spent it shut away in my room. On Monday no sooner did I arrive at the university than a classmate asked me teasingly when I'd gotten myself a wife, and congratulated me on marrying such a beauty. He had evidently caught sight of the three of us on our Nihonbashi excursion.

CHAPTER 72

When I got home, I told this story to Okusan and Ojōsan. Okusan laughed, then looked me in the eye and added, "That must have been awkward for you." I wondered then whether this was how a woman induces a man to talk. Her look certainly gave me reason to think so. Perhaps I should have asked for Ojōsan's hand then and there. But my heart was by now deeply ingrained with distrust. I opened my mouth to speak, then stopped and deliberately shifted the direction of the conversation elsewhere.

Carefully avoiding the crucial subject of my own feelings, I probed Okusan on her intentions for her daughter's marriage. She told me frankly that there had already been two or three proposals, but as her daughter was still a young schoolgirl, there was no hurry. Though she did not say as much, she clearly set great store by her daughter's good looks. She even remarked in passing that a suitable husband could be found anytime they wished. But as her daughter was an only child, she said, she was not inclined to send her off with just anyone. I got the impression that she was of two minds about whether to adopt a son-in-law as a member of their own household, or let her daughter marry out as a bride.[1]

I felt I was gaining quite a lot of information as I listened. Effectively, however, I had forfeited my own chance to speak. I couldn't say a word on my own behalf now. At an appropriate point I broke off the conversation and returned to my room.

Ojōsan, who had been sitting with us laughing and protesting at my tale, by this time had retreated to a corner with her back turned. As I stood to leave, I turned and saw her there. It is impossible to read the heart of someone who is looking away, and I couldn't guess what she might have been thinking as she listened. She was sitting beside the half-open closet and had taken something from it and laid it on her lap. She now appeared to be gazing intently down at it. In a corner of the open closet, I caught sight of the fabric I had bought her two days before. My own new robe, I saw, lay folded there with hers.

As I was standing wordlessly to leave, Okusan suddenly grew serious. "What's your opinion?" she asked. Confused by the unexpected question, I had to ask what she meant. She wanted to know, she explained, whether I thought an early marriage was a good idea. I said I thought it wise to take things slowly. "I think so too," she replied.

It was at this point in the relationship among the three of us that another man entered the picture, one whose arrival in the household crucially affected my fate. If he had not crossed my path, I doubt that I would need to write this long letter to you now. It was as if I stood there oblivious as the devil brushed by me, unaware that he cast a shadow upon me that would darken my whole life. It was I who brought this man into the house, I must confess. Naturally, I needed Okusan's consent, so I told her his story and asked if he could move in with me. She advised against it but had no convincing argument to offer. For my part, I could see every reason why I must bring him into the household, and so I persisted in following my own judgment and did what I believed was right.

CHAPTER 73

I will call this friend of mine K. We had been friends since childhood. As you will no doubt realize from this, our native place was a bond between us. K was the son of a Pure Land Buddhist priest—but not the eldest son and heir, I should add, which is how he came to be adopted by a doctor's family. The Hongan subsect had a very powerful presence in my home district, and its priests were better off than others. If the priest had a daughter of marriageable age, for instance, one of his parishioners would help to find her a suitable match, and the wedding expenses would of course not come out of his own pocket. Pure Land temple families were thus generally quite wealthy.

K's home temple was a prosperous one. Even so, the family may not have had the funds to send him to Tokyo for his education. Did they decide to have him adopted into the other family because the other family had the means to educate him? I have no way of knowing. I only know that the doctor's family adopted him while we were still middle-school students. I still remember the surprise I felt when the teacher called the roll one day and I realized K's name had suddenly changed.

His new family was also fairly wealthy, and they paid for him to go to Tokyo for his studies. I left before he did, but he moved into the same dormitory when he arrived. K and I shared a room—in those days it was common for two or three students to study and sleep together in the one room. We lived huddled together like wild animals trapped in a cage, hugging each other and glaring out at the world. Tokyo and its inhabitants frightened us both. There in our little room, however, we spoke with contempt of the world at large.

But we were in earnest, and determined one day to become great. K's willpower was particularly strong. Son of a temple family that he was, he was in the habit of talking in terms of the Buddhist concept of dedicated self-discipline, and his behavior certainly seemed to me to epitomize this ideal. In my heart, I stood in awe of him.

Ever since our middle-school days, K had bewildered me with difficult discussions on religion and philosophy. I do not know whether his father had inspired this interest, or whether the atmosphere peculiar to temple buildings had infected him as a child. In any event, K seemed to me far more monkish than the average monk. His adoptive family had sent him to Tokyo to study medicine. In his stubborn way, however, he had decided before he arrived that he would not become a doctor. I reproached him, pointing out that he was in effect deceiving his adoptive parents, and he brashly agreed that he was. Such deception did not bother him, he said, since it was in the cause of his "chosen path." I doubt if even he understood precisely what he meant by this phrase. I certainly had no idea. But we were young, and this vague abstraction had for us a hallowed ring. Comprehension was beside the point. I could not but admire these lofty sentiments that governed and impelled him. I accepted his argument. I do not know how important my agreement may have been for K, but he would surely have gone his way, stubbornly, regardless of any protest I made.

Child though I still was, however, I was prepared to accept that by going along with him, I would bear some responsibility if problems ever arose. Even if I could not quite summon such resolve at the time, nevertheless I spoke my words of encouragement to him firm in the belief that if in later life I ever had cause to look back on this moment, I would properly acknowledge the degree of responsibility I bore.

CHAPTER 74

K and I entered the same faculty. He proceeded to pursue his chosen course of study, using the money sent to him, quite unconcerned. I could only interpret this as a mixture of complacent faith that the family would not find out, and a defiant resolve that if they did, he would not care. I was far more concerned than he over the question.

During the first summer vacation he did not go home, choosing instead to rent a room in a temple in the Komagome area[1] and study during the break. When I came back in early September, he was holed up in a shabby little temple beside the Great Kannon. He had a small room tucked in beside the main temple building, and he seemed delighted that he had been able to get on with his studies there as planned. I think it was then I realized that he was becoming more and more monastic in lifestyle. A circlet of Buddhist rosary beads adorned his wrist. I asked the reason, and in response he told off a couple of beads with his thumb. I gathered that he counted through them a number of times each day. The meaning of this escaped me. If you count off a circle of beads, you never reach an end. At what point, and with what feelings, would his fingers cease to move those beads? This may be a silly question, but it haunts me.

I also saw a Bible in his room, which rather startled me. On numerous occasions in the past he had referred to Buddhist sutras, but we had never discussed the subject of Christianity. I could not resist asking about it. There was no real reason, he replied. He thought it natural to want to read a book that brought such comfort to others. If he had the chance, he added, he would like to read the Koran as well. He seemed particularly interested in the idea of Muhammad spreading the Word "with book or sword."

In the second year he finally gave in to family pressure and went home for the summer. He apparently told them nothing about what he was studying even then, and they did not guess. Having been a student yourself, you will of course be well aware of such things, but the world at large is surprisingly ignorant about student life, school regulations, and so forth. Things that are quite routine for students mean absolutely nothing to outsiders. On the other hand, locked away in our own little world, we are far too inclined to assume that the world is thoroughly acquainted with everything great and small to do with school. K no doubt understood this ignorance better than I. He returned to college with a nonchalant air. We set off for Tokyo together, and as soon as we were in the train, I asked him how it had gone. Nothing had happened, he told me.

Our third summer vacation was the time when I decided to leave forever the land that held my parents' graves. I urged K to go home that summer, but he resisted. He said he saw no point in going back every year. He clearly planned to spend the summer in Tokyo studying again, so I resignedly set off for home without him. I have already written of the deep turmoil into which my life was thrown by those two months at home. When I met K again in September, I was in the grip of anger, misery, and loneliness.

In fact, his life had undergone an upheaval rather like my own. Unknown to me, he had written a letter to his adoptive parents confessing his deceit. He had intended all along to do so, he said. Perhaps he was hoping that they would react by grudgingly accepting the change, and decide it was too late to argue, so he could have his way. At any rate, it seemed he was not prepared to continue deceiving them once he entered university; no doubt he realized that he would not get away with it much longer.

CHAPTER 75

His adoptive father was enraged when he read K's letter and immediately sent off a forceful reply to the effect that he could not finance the education of a scoundrel who had so deceived his parents. K showed me the letter. He then showed me the one he had received from his own family, which condemned him in equally strong terms. No doubt an added sense of failed obligation to the other family reinforced their decision to refuse to support him. K was faced with the dilemma of whether to return to his own family or consent to compromise with his adoptive parents to stay on their family register. His immediate problem, however, was how to come up with the money he needed to stay at college.

I asked if he had found a solution, and he replied that he was thinking of taking work teaching at an evening school. Times were far easier back then; it was not as difficult as you might think to find part-time work of this sort. I thought it would see him through very well. But I also bore responsibility in the matter. I had been the one to agree with his decision to ignore his adoptive family's plans for him and tread a path of his own choosing, and I could not now stand idly by. I immediately offered K financial assistance. He rejected it absolutely. Given who he was, no doubt financial independence gave him far greater satisfaction than the prospect of living under a friend's protection. Now that he was a university student, he declared, he must be man enough to stand on his own two feet. I was not prepared to hurt K's feelings for the sake of satisfying my own sense of responsibility, so I let him have his way and withdrew my offer of a helping hand.

K soon found the kind of job he hoped for, but as you can well imagine for someone with his temperament, he chafed at the amount of precious time it consumed. Still, he pushed fiercely on with his studies, never slackening under the added burden. I worried about his health; iron-willed, he laughed me off and paid no heed to my warnings.

Meanwhile his relations with his adoptive family were growing increasingly difficult. His lack of time meant that he no longer had a chance to talk with me as he used to, so I never learned the details, but I was aware that more and more stood in the way of a resolution. I also knew that someone had stepped in and attempted to mediate. This person wrote to K encouraging him to return, but he refused, having made up his mind that it was absolutely out of the question. This obstinacy—or so it would have struck the other party, although he claimed that it was impossible for him to leave during the school term—seemed to exacerbate the situation. Not only was K hurting the feelings of his adoptive family, he was fueling the ire of his real family as well. Worried, I wrote a letter that attempted to soothe the situation, but it was too late by now for it to have any effect. My letter sank without a word of response. I too grew angry. The situation had always encouraged my sympathy with K, but now I was inclined to take his side regardless of the rights and wrongs of the matter.

Finally, K decided to officially return to his original family's register, which meant that they would have to repay the school fees paid by the other party. His own family, however, responded by washing their hands of him. To use an outmoded expression, they, as it were, disowned him. Perhaps it was not quite so radical as that, but that was how he understood it. K had no mother, and certain aspects of his character were perhaps the result of his being brought up by a stepmother. If his mother had not died, I feel, this distance between him and his family might never have arisen. His father, of course, was a priest, but his sternness in matters of Confucian moral obligation suggests that there was a lot of the samurai in him.

CHAPTER 76

K's crisis had begun to resolve itself a little when I received a long letter from his elder sister's husband. This man was related to the adoptive family, K told me, so his opinion had carried a lot of weight both during the attempted mediation and in the decision that K return to his original family register.

The letter asked me to let him know what had happened to K since relations were severed. I should reply as soon as possible, he added, as K's sister was worrying. K was fonder of this sister, who had married out, than he was of the elder brother who had inherited the family temple. K and his sister shared the same mother, but there was a large age gap between them, and when he was little, she must have seemed to him more of a mother than his adoptive mother.

I showed the letter to K. He said nothing in direct response, but he did tell me that he had received two or three such letters from his sister herself, and that he had replied that she need not be concerned for him. She had married into a household that did not have much money, so unfortunately she was not in a position to offer financial help, much as she sympathized with him.

I replied to her husband along similar lines and assured him firmly that if problems arose, I would help in any way I could. This was something I had long since decided. My words were intended partly as a friendly reassurance to the sister who was so worried about him, but also as a gesture of defiance toward the two families whom I felt had snubbed me.

K's adoption was annulled in his first year of university studies. From then until the middle of his second year, he supported

himself. But it was apparent that the prodigious effort this required was slowly telling on his health and nerves. No doubt the
stress of his indecision over whether to leave his adoptive family
had also played its part. He grew overly emotional. At times he
spoke as if he alone bore the weight of the world's woes on his
shoulders, and he grew agitated if I contradicted him. Or he
would fret that the light of future hope was receding before his
eyes. Everyone, of course, at the beginning of their studies is full
of fine aspirations and dreams, but one year passes and then
another, and as graduation draws near, you realize you are plod-
ding. At this point the majority inevitably lose heart, and K was
no exception. His feverish anxiety was excessive, however. My
sole concern became to somehow calm him.

I advised him to give up all unnecessary work, and added
that for the sake of that great future of his, he would be wise
to relax and enjoy himself more. I knew it would be difficult to
get this message through to my stubborn friend, but when the
time came for me to say my piece, it took even more persuasion
than I had anticipated, and I struggled to hold my ground. He
countered me by asserting that scholarship was not his primary
aim; his goal was to develop a toughness of will that would
make him strong, and to this end his circumstances must remain
as straitened as possible. From any normal point of view, this
determination was wildly eccentric. Furthermore, the situation
to which he chose to cling was doing nothing to strengthen his
will—indeed, it was rapidly driving him to nervous collapse. All
I could do was present myself as deeply sympathetic. I declared that I too intended to pursue a similar course in life. (In
fact, these were no empty words—K's power was such that
I felt myself increasingly drawn by his views.) Finally, I proposed that he and I should live together and work to im-
prove ourselves. In effect, I chose to give in to him in order to
be able to bend his will. And with this, at last, I brought him
to the house.

CHAPTER 77

From the entrance hall the only access to my room was through a little four-mat room that lay between. This anteroom, in effect a passageway, was virtually useless for practical purposes. This is where I put K. At first I re-created our previous arrangement, placing two desks side by side in my own larger room, with the idea that we would also share the small one. But K chose to make the small room exclusively his, declaring that he was happier alone no matter how cramped the space.

As I mentioned, Okusan initially opposed my plan to bring K in at all. In an ordinary lodging house, she agreed, it made sense for two to share, and still better three, but she wasn't doing this as a business, she said, and urged me to reconsider. I told her K would be no trouble. Even so, she replied, she did not like the idea of housing someone she didn't know. In that case, I pointed out, she should have objected to me as well. But she countered with the statement that she had known and trusted me from the beginning. I smiled wryly. At this point she changed her tactics. Bringing in someone like K, she said, would be bad for me. When I asked why, it was her turn to smile.

To tell the truth, there was no real necessity for me to live with K. But if I had tried to give him a monthly cash allowance, I felt sure, he would have been very reluctant to accept it. He was a fiercely independent man. Better to let him live with me, while I secretly gave Okusan money enough to feed us both. Nevertheless, I had no desire to reveal K's dire financial situation to her. I did, however, talk about his precarious state of health. If left to himself, I told her, he would only grow more perverse and eccentric. I went on to describe his strained relations with his adoptive parents and his severance from his original family. By attempting to help him, I said, I was grasping a drowning man, desperate to infuse in him my own living heat. I begged Okusan and Ojōsan to help by warmly accepting him. Okusan finally relented.

K knew nothing of this discussion, and I was satisfied that he remain ignorant. When he came stolidly into the house with his bags, I greeted him with an innocent air.

Okusan and Ojōsan kindly helped him unpack and settle in. I was delighted, interpreting each generous gesture as an expression of their friendship for me. K, however, remained his usual dour self.

When I asked what he thought of his new home, he replied with a simple "Not bad." This brief response was a wild understatement, I felt. Until then he had been living in a dank, grimy little north-facing room, where the food was of a piece with the lodging. The move to my place was, as the old saying goes, "from deep ravine to treetop high." It was partly sheer obstinacy that caused him to make light of the new place, but partly principle as well. His Buddhist upbringing had led him to think that paying attention to comfort in the basic needs of life was immoral. Brought up on tales of worthy monks and saints, he tended to consider flesh and spirit as separate entities; in fact, he may well have felt that to mortify the flesh was to exalt the soul.

I decided to do my best not to argue, however. My aim was to apply a sunny warmth that would thaw his ice. Once the melted water began to trickle, I thought, he would sooner or later come to his senses.

CHAPTER 78

Aware that under Okusan's kind treatment I myself had grown cheerful, I set about applying the same process to K. From my long acquaintance with him I was all too aware of how different we were. But just as my own nerves had relaxed considerably since I'd moved into this household, I felt surely K's heart too would eventually grow calmer here.

K's will was far steelier than mine. He studied twice as hard, and his mind was a good deal finer. I cannot speak for the later years, when we chose different areas of study, but in the middle and high school years, while we were classmates, he was consistently ahead of me. I used to feel, in fact, that K would best me in everything. But in convincing the stubborn K to move in with me, I was sure I was showing more good sense than he. He failed to understand the difference between patience and endurance, I felt.

Please listen carefully now, I am saying this for your benefit. All our capacities, both physical and mental, require external stimuli for both their development and their destruction, and in either case these stimuli must be increased by slow degrees in order to be effective. But this gradual increase creates a very real danger that not only you yourself but those around you may fail to notice any problems that might develop. Doctors tell us that a man's stomach is a thoroughly rebellious creature, inclined to misbehave. If you feed it nothing but soft gruel, it will lose the power to digest anything heavier. So they instruct us to train it by feeding it all manner of foods. I don't think this is just a matter of getting it used to the variety, however. I interpret it to mean that the stomach's resilience gradually increases as the stimuli build up over time. Now imagine what would happen if the stomach instead grew steadily weaker under this regimen. K was in just such a situation.

Now K was a greater man than I, but he failed to comprehend what was happening to him. He had decided that if he accustomed himself to hardship, then pain would sooner or later cease to register. The simple virtue of repetition of pain, he was sure, would bring him to a point where pain no longer affected him.

In order to bring about a change of heart in K, it was this above all that I would have to clarify to him. But if I spelled it out, he would doubtless resist; he would bring up the example of those stoics and saints of old in his defense, I knew, and I would then have to point out the difference between them and him. That would be worthwhile if he were of a mind to listen to me, but by nature, once an argument reached that point, he would stick to his guns. He would simply assert his own position more vehemently, and having once spoken he would feel obliged to follow through with action. In this respect he was quite intimidating. He was grand in his convictions. He would stride forward to meet his own destruction. In retrospect, the only thing that had any kind of grandeur was the resultant ruin of any hope of success. But there was certainly nothing run-of-the-mill about the process, at any rate.

Knowing his temperament as I did, therefore, I couldn't utter a word. My sense that he was close to a nervous breakdown also made me hesitate. Even if I did manage to convince him, it would only agitate him further. I didn't mind quarreling, but I remembered how poorly I had withstood my own sense of isolation, and I couldn't bear to think of placing my friend in a similar situation, let alone exacerbating it. And so, even after bringing him into the house, I held back from voicing any real criticism. I decided simply to wait calmly to see what effect his new environment would have on him.

CHAPTER 79

Behind his back, I asked Okusan and Ojōsan to talk to K as much as possible, convinced that the silence of his previous life had been the cause of his ruin. It seemed clear to me that his heart had rusted like iron from disuse.

Okusan laughed, remarking that he was rather curt and unapproachable, and Ojōsan supported this by describing an encounter she had had with him. She'd asked him if his brazier was lit, and he had told her it wasn't. She offered to bring some charcoal, but he said he didn't need any. Wasn't he cold? she asked. He replied curtly that he was but didn't want a fire, and he refused to discuss the matter further. I couldn't simply dismiss her story with a rueful smile; I felt sorry for her, and that I must somehow make up for his rudeness. It was spring, of course, so he had had no real need for a warm fire in the brazier, but I could see that they had good reason to feel that he was difficult.

I then did my best to use myself as a catalyst to bring them together. At every opportunity I encouraged K to spend time in the company of all three of us. When I was talking with him, I would call them in, or when I met up with them in one of the rooms, I'd invite him to join us. Naturally, K did not much care for this. Sometimes he would abruptly rise to his feet and walk out. At other times he ignored my calls. "What's the point of all that idle chatter?" he asked me. I just laughed, but I was well aware that he despised me for indulging in such frivolities.

In some ways I doubtless deserved his scorn. His sights were fixed on far higher things than mine, I'll not deny it. But it is surely crippling to limp along, so out of step with the lofty gaze you insist on maintaining. My most important task, I felt, was somehow to make him more human. Filling his own head with the examples of impressive men was pointless, I decided, if it did not make him impressive himself. As a first step in the task of humanizing him, I would introduce him to the company of the opposite sex. Letting the fair winds of that gentle realm blow upon him would cleanse his blood of the rust that clogged it, I hoped.

This approach gradually succeeded. The two elements, which had seemed at first so unlikely to merge, slowly came together until they were one. K apparently grew to realize that there were others in the world besides himself. One day he remarked to me that women were not after all such despicable creatures. He had at first assumed, he told me, that women had the same level of knowledge and academic ability as I had, and when he discovered that they didn't, he had been quick to despise them. He had always viewed men and women without any distinction, he said, without understanding that one could see the sexes differently. I pointed out that if we two men were to go on talking exclusively to each other forever, we would simply continue in the same straight line. Naturally, he replied.

I spoke as I did because I was by then quite in love with Ojōsan. But I did not breathe a word to him of my inner state.

This man who had constructed a defensive fortress of books to hide behind was now slowly opening up to the world, and the change in his heart delighted me. Opening him up had been my plan all along, and its success sent an irrepressible wave of joy through me. Though I said nothing of it to him, I shared my joy with Okusan and Ojōsan. They too seemed gratified.

CHAPTER 80

Although K and I were in the same faculty, our fields of study were different, which meant that we came and went at different times. If I returned home early, I could simply pass through his empty room to reach my own. If he got home before I did, I always acknowledged him briefly before going on into my room. As I came through the door, K would glance up from his book and invariably say: "Just back, are you?" Sometimes I'd nod, and sometimes I'd simply give a grunt of assent.

One day on my way home I had reason to stop in at Kanda, so I returned much later than usual. I hurried to the front gate and the lattice door clattered as I thrust it open. At that moment I heard Ojōsan's voice. I was sure it came from K's room. The sitting room and Ojōsan's room lay straight ahead through the entrance hall, while our two rooms were off to the left, and by now I had become attuned to deciphering the location of voices. Just as I hastened to close the lattice door, her voice ceased. While I was removing my shoes—I now wore fashionable Western lace-ups—not a sound emerged from K's room. This struck me as odd. Had I been mistaken?

But when I opened the sliding doors as usual to pass through K's room, I found the two of them sitting there. "Just back, are you?" said K, as always.

"Welcome home," Ojōsan said, remaining seated. For some reason, her straightforward greeting struck me as slightly stiff and formal. The tone had a somehow unnatural ring to my ears.

"Where's Okusan?" I asked her. The question had no real significance—it was just that the house seemed unusually hushed.

Okusan was out, and the maid had gone with her. K and Ojōsan therefore were alone in the house. This puzzled me. I had lived there a long time by now, but Okusan had never left me alone in the house with Ojōsan. Had she had urgent business to attend to? I inquired.

Ojōsan simply laughed. I disliked women who laugh in response that way. All young ladies do it, of course, but Ojōsan had a tendency to laugh at silly things. When she saw my face, however, her usual expression quickly returned. There had been nothing urgent, she replied. Okusan had just gone out on a small errand.

As a lodger, I had no right to press the matter further. I held my tongue.

No sooner had I changed my clothes and settled down than Okusan and the maid returned. At length, the time came for us all to face one another over the evening meal. When I had first moved in as a lodger, they had treated me much like a guest, the maid serving dinner in my room, but this formality had broken down, and these days I was invited in to eat with the family. When K arrived, I insisted that he too be brought in for meals. In return I donated to the household a light and elegant dining table of thin wood, with foldable legs. These days one can find tables like this in any household, but back then there were almost no homes where everyone sat around such a thing to eat. I had gone especially to a furniture shop in Ochanomizu and ordered it made to my specifications.

As we sat at the table that day, Okusan explained that the fish seller had failed to call at the usual hour, so she had had to go into town to buy our evening's food. Yes, I thought, that seems quite reasonable, given that she has guests to feed. Seeing my expression, Ojōsan burst out laughing, but her mother's scolding quickly put an end to it.

CHAPTER 81

A week later I again passed through the room when Ojōsan and K were talking there together. This time she laughed as soon as she caught sight of me. I should have asked then and there what she found so humorous. But I simply went past them to my own room without speaking. K thus missed his chance to come out with his usual greeting. Soon I heard Ojōsan open the sliding doors and go back to the sitting room.

That evening at dinner she remarked that I was an odd person. Once again I failed to ask the reason. I did notice, however, that Okusan sent a hard stare in Ojōsan's direction.

After dinner K and I went for a walk. We went behind Denzūin Temple and around the botanical gardens, emerging below Tomizaka. It was a long walk, but we spoke very little. K was temperamentally a man of even fewer words than I. I was not a great talker, but as we walked, I did my best to engage him in conversation. My main focus of concern was the family in whose house we were lodging. I asked him what he thought of Okusan and Ojōsan. He was quite impossible to pin down on the subject, however. He not only avoided the point, but his responses were extremely brief. He seemed far more interested in the topic of his studies than in the two ladies. Our second-year exams were almost upon us, I admit, so from any normal point of view he was behaving much more typically than I. He launched into a disquisition on Swedenborg[1] that made my uneducated mind reel.

We both passed our exams successfully, and Okusan congratulated us on entering our final year. Her own daughter, her sole pride and joy, was soon to graduate as well. K remarked to me that girls emerged from their schooling knowing nothing. Clearly he chose to completely overlook Ojōsan's extracurricular study of sewing, *koto* playing, and flower arranging. Laughing, I countered with my old argument that a woman's value did not lie in scholarly accomplishment. While he did not refute this statement outright, he did not seem willing to accept it either. That pleased me—I interpreted this casual dismissal of my ideas as an indication that his former scorn of women had not changed. Ojōsan, whom I thought the embodiment of womanly excellence, was evidently still beneath his notice. In retrospect, I see that my jealousy of K was already showing its horns.

I suggested that the two of us go away together somewhere during the summer vacation. He responded with apparent reluctance. It's true that he could not afford to go wherever he wanted, but on the other hand nothing prevented him from accepting an invitation to travel with me. I asked why he didn't want to come. He replied that there was no real reason; he simply preferred to stay at home and read. When I contended that it would be healthier to spend the summer studying in some cooler place out of the city, he suggested I go on my own.

I wasn't inclined to leave K there in the house alone, however—his growing intimacy with the two ladies was disturbing enough already. Needless to say, it was ridiculous for me to be so upset over a situation that I had gone out of my way to engineer in the first place. I was clearly being foolish.

Okusan, tired of seeing us endlessly at cross-purposes, stepped in to mediate. The result was that we decided the two of us would go off to the Bōshū Peninsula[2] together.

CHAPTER 82

K seldom took trips, and I had never been to Bōshū, so we both disembarked at the boat's first port of call in complete ignorance of the place. Its name was Hota, I remember. I don't know what it might be like today, but in those days it was a dreadful little fishing village. For one thing, the whole place stank of fish. For another, when we tried sea bathing the waves knocked us off our feet, and our arms and legs were soon covered in scratches and grazes from the fist-size rocks that were forever tumbling around in the water with us.

I soon had enough of the place. K, however, said not a word either for or against it. Judging from his expression at least, he seemed quite unperturbed, although he never emerged from a swim without a bruise or a cut.

I finally persuaded him to leave Hota and move on to Tomiura. From there we went to Nako. All that part of the coast was a popular vacation place for students in those days, and we found beaches to our liking wherever we went. K and I often sat on a rock gazing out at the sea's colors, or at the underwater world at our feet. The water below us was beautifully crystal clear. In the transparent waves we could point out to each other the brilliant flashes of little fish, whose vivid reds and blues were more spectacular than anything to be seen in the fish markets.

I frequently read while sitting on the rocks, while K spent most of his time sitting silently. Was he lost in thought, or gazing at the scene before him, or intent on some happy fantasy? I had no idea. Occasionally I glanced up and asked what he was doing. Nothing, he replied simply. I often thought how pleasant it would be if Ojōsan, rather than K, were sitting there beside me. This was all very well, but I sometimes felt a stab of suspicion that K might be thinking the same thing. Whenever this occurred to me, I found I could no longer sit calmly reading. I rose abruptly to my feet and let out a great unrestrained yell. I couldn't dispel my pent-up feelings in a civilized manner, such as blandly declaiming some poem or song. All I could do was howl like a savage. Once, I grabbed K by the scruff of the neck and demanded to know what he would do if I tossed him into the sea. K remained motionless. "Good idea. Go right ahead," he replied without turning. I quickly let go.

The state of his nerves by now seemed to have considerably improved, while my own peace of mind had disintegrated. I observed his calm demeanor with envy, and with loathing, interpreting it as indifference to me. His serenity smacked of self-confidence, and not of a kind that it pleased me to see in him. My growing suspicions now demanded clarification of just what lay behind his self-assurance. Had his optimism about his chosen goals in life suddenly revived? If so, then we had no collision of interests—indeed, it would have pleased me to think I had helped him on his way. But if his calm originated in his feelings for Ojōsan, this I could not countenance. Strangely, he seemed oblivious to the signs that I myself loved her—though needless to say, I was anything but eager to alert him to my feelings. Quite simply, he was constitutionally insensitive to such things; indeed, it had been in the faith that no such problems would arise that I had brought him into the house in the first place.

CHAPTER 83

Summoning up my courage, I decided to confess to K what was in my heart. It was not the first time I had reached this decision. It had been my plan since before our trip together, in fact, but so far I had had the skill neither to seize an appropriate moment nor to create one. It strikes me now that the people I knew back then were all a bit peculiar—no one around me ever spoke about private matters of the heart. No doubt quite a few had nothing to confide, but even those who did kept silent. This must seem most peculiar to you, in the relative freedom of your present age. I will leave it to you to judge whether it was a lingering effect from the Confucianism of an earlier time or simply a form of shyness.

On the face of it, K and I could say anything to each other. Questions of love and romance did occasionally come up, but our discussions around them always descended into abstract theory, and were in any case rare. For the most part, our conversations were confined to the subject of books and study, our future work, our aspirations, and self-improvement. As close as we were, it was difficult to break into these rigid, impersonal discussions with a personal confession. High-minded gravity was integral to our intimacy. I do not know how often I squirmed with impotent frustration at my inability to speak my heart as I had resolved to do. I longed to crack open some part of K's mind and soften him with a breath of gentler air.

To your generation, this will seem quite absurd, but for me at the time it constituted a huge difficulty. I was the same coward on vacation as I had been back home. Though constantly alert for a chance to make my confession, I could find no way to break through K's determined aloofness. His heart might as well have been sealed off with a thick coating of hard black lacquer, it seemed to me, repelling every drop of the warm-blooded feeling that I was intent on pouring upon it.

Sometimes, though, I found K's fiercely principled stance toward the world reassuring. Then I would regret ever doubting him and silently apologize for my suspicions. In this state of mind, I seemed a deeply inferior person and suddenly despised myself. But then the same old doubts would sweep back in and reassert themselves with renewed force. Since I deduced everything on the basis of suspicion, all my conclusions cast me in a disadvantageous light. It seemed to me that K was handsomer and more attractive to women than I, and that my fussiness made my personality less appealing to the opposite sex. His combination of firm manliness with something a little absurd, also struck me as superior. Nor did I feel myself a match for him in scholarly ability, although of course our fields differed. With all his advantages so constantly before my eyes, any momentary relief from my fears soon reverted to the old anxieties.

Observing my restlessness, K suggested that if I didn't like it here, we might as well go back to Tokyo, but as soon as he said this, I wanted to stay after all. What I actually wanted was to prevent him from going back himself, I think. We plodded on around the tip of the peninsula, miserably roasting in the painful rays of the hot sun and plagued by the notorious local habit of understating distances when we asked our way. I could no longer see any point in going on walking like this and said as much half-jokingly to K. "We're walking because we have legs," he replied. Whenever the heat grew too much for us, we took a dip in the sea wherever we happened to be. But when we set off again, the sun was just as fierce, and we grew limp with fatigue.

CHAPTER 84

With all this walking, the heat and weariness inevitably took their toll on us. It's not that we were actually ill; rather it was the disturbing feeling that one's soul had suddenly moved on to inhabit someone else. Though I continued to talk to K as normal, I felt anything but normal. Both our intimacy and the antagonism I felt toward him took on a special quality that was peculiar to this journey. I suppose what I am saying is that, what with the heat, the sea, and the walking, we entered a different kind of relationship. We became for the moment like nothing so much as a couple of wandering peddlers who had fallen in with each other on the road. For all our talk, we never once broached the complex intellectual topics that we usually discussed.

Eventually we arrived at Chōshi.[1] One extraordinary event on our journey I will never forget. Before leaving the peninsula, we paused at Kominato to take a look at the famous Sea Bream Inlet. It was many years ago, and besides, I was not particularly interested, so the memory is vague, but I seem to remember that this village was supposed to be the place where the famous Buddhist priest Nichiren[2] was born. On the day of his birth, two sea bream were said to have been washed up on the beach there, and the local fishermen have avoided catching bream ever since, so the sea there is thronged with them. We hired a boat and went out to see.

I was intent on the water, gazing entranced at the remarkable sight of all the purple-tinted sea bream milling below the surface. K, however, did not appear as interested. He seemed preoccupied with thoughts of Nichiren rather than fish. There was an impressive temple in the area called Tanjōji, or "Birth Temple," no doubt referring to the saint's birth, and K suddenly announced that he was going to go to this temple and talk to its head priest.

We were, I may say, very oddly dressed. K's appearance was particularly strange, since his hat had blown into the sea, and he was instead wearing a peasant's sedge hat that he had bought along the way. Both of us wore filthy robes that reeked of sweat. I urged K to give up the idea of meeting the priest, but he stubbornly persisted, declaring that if I didn't like it, I could wait outside. Since there was no arguing with him, I reluctantly went along as far as the temple's entrance hall. I was privately convinced we would be turned away, but priests are surprisingly civil people, and we were immediately shown into a fine large room to meet him.

I was far from sharing K's religious interests back then, so I didn't pay much attention to what they said to each other, but I gathered that K was asking a great deal about Nichiren. I do remember the dismissive look on his face when the priest remarked that Nichiren was renowned for his excellent cursive writing style—K's own writing was far from good. He was after more profound information. I don't know that the priest was able to satisfy him, but once we left the temple grounds, K began to talk fervently to me about Nichiren. I was hot and exhausted and in no mood to listen to all this, so my responses were minimal. After a while even this became too much of an effort, so I simply remained silent and let him talk.

It must have been the following evening, when we had arrived at our night's lodging, eaten, and were on the point of turning in, that things suddenly grew difficult between us. K was unhappy with the fact that I had not really listened to what he'd said to me about Nichiren the previous day. Anyone without spiritual aspirations is a fool, he declared, and he attacked me for what he obviously saw as my frivolity. For my part, the question of Ojōsan of course complicated my feelings, and I couldn't simply laugh off his contemptuous accusations. I set about defending myself.

CHAPTER 85

In those days I was in the habit of using the adjective *human*. K maintained that this favorite expression of mine was actually a cover for all my personal weaknesses. Thinking back on it now, I can see his point. But I had originally begun to use the word out of resistance to K, in order to convince him of his lack of human feelings, so I was not in a position to consider the question objectively. I stuck to my guns and reiterated my argument.

K then demanded to know just what it was in him that I believed lacked this quality. "You're perfectly human, indeed you're even too human" was my response. "It's just that when you talk, the things you say lack humanity. And the same goes for your behavior." K offered no refutation, except to say that if he appeared that way, it was because he had not yet attained a sufficient level of spiritual discipline.

This did not so much take the wind out of my sails as arouse my pity. I immediately stopped arguing, and he too soon grew calmer.

If only I shared his knowledge of the lives of the ancients, he remarked mournfully, I wouldn't be attacking him in this way. When K spoke of "the ancients," of course, he was not referring to men of legendary daring and courage. His heroes were the fierce ascetics of old, those mortifiers of the flesh who lashed themselves for the sake of spiritual attainment. He was sorry, K declared, that I had no understanding of what anguish he suffered from his own shortcomings.

With this, we both went to sleep. The following morning we returned to business as usual and set off again to plod on our sweaty way. But my mind kept going back over the previous night's events. I burned with regret—why had I passed up the perfect opportunity to say at last what was on my mind? Rather than employ an abstraction such as *human*, I should have made a clean and direct confession to K.

And truly it was my feelings for Ojōsan that had prompted me to start using this word in the first place, so it would have been more to the point to reveal to K the facts that lay behind my argument rather than belabor him with its theoretical distillation. Our relationship was so firmly defined by lofty scholarly exchange, I must admit, that I lacked the courage to break through it. I could explain this failing as that of affectation, or as the result of vanity, although what I mean by these words is not quite their normal interpretation. I only hope you will understand what I am saying here.

We arrived back in Tokyo burned black by the sun. By this time I was in yet another frame of mind. Concepts such as "human" and other futile abstractions had all but vanished from my head. K, for his part, showed no more traces of the religious ascetic; he too, I am sure, was no longer troubling himself with the question of the spirit and the flesh.

We gaped about us at the swirling life of Tokyo, like two visitors from another world. Then we set off for the Ryōkoku district,[1] where we had a chicken dinner. So fortified, K suggested we walk back home to Koishikawa. I was physically the stronger, so I readily agreed.

Okusan was taken aback at our appearance when we arrived. Not only were we black from the sun, we were gaunt from the long, exhausting walk. She nevertheless congratulated us on looking so much stronger, and Ojōsan laughed at her inconsistency. No doubt it was the combination of the circumstance and the pleasure of hearing her laughter again, but in that moment I was happy, freed of the anger that had plagued me before the trip.

CHAPTER 86

But there was more. Something had changed in Ojōsan's attitude, I noticed. Both Okusan and Ojōsan set about providing us with the female care and attention that we needed to regain normalcy after our journey, but it seemed to me that Ojōsan was far more attentive to me than to K. If it had been blatant, it might have made me uncomfortable, even irritated. But I was delighted at how decorously she behaved. She devoted the greater part of her innate kindness to me in a way that only I would notice. K therefore remained oblivious and unconcerned. A gleeful song of victory sang in my heart.

Summer ended at last, and mid-September arrived, the time when lectures would resume. Our schedules meant that once more we came and went from the house at different hours. Three times a week I returned later than K, but I never detected any sign of Ojōsan's presence in his room. K went back to turning as I entered and remarking, "Just back, are you?" and I answered with my usual mechanical and meaningless response.

It would have been the middle of October. I had overslept and rushed off to classes without changing out of the Japanese clothing I wore around the house; rather than waste time with laced shoes, I hastily slipped on a pair of straw sandals. Our schedules meant that I would get back home before K did.

When I arrived, I flung open the lattice door, assuming he wouldn't be there—and caught the sound of his voice within. I also heard Ojōsan's laughter. Not needing to spend time unlacing my shoes at the door as usual, I stepped straight out of my sandals and into the house and opened the sliding doors to our rooms. My eyes took in the sight of K, seated as usual at his desk. Ojōsan, however, was no longer in the room. All I caught was a glimpse of her retreating form, obviously making a hasty exit.

I asked K why he had returned early. He had stayed home that day because he felt unwell, he replied.

No sooner was I back in my room and seated than Ojōsan appeared with tea, and now at last she greeted me. I was not the sort of person who could ask with an easy laugh why she had run away just then; instead, the matter nagged at my mind. She stood up and went off down the veranda, but she paused a moment before K's room and exchanged a few words with him. They seemed to be a continuation of their previous talk, but as I had not heard what had gone before, I could make no sense of them.

Over time Ojōsan grew increasingly nonchalant. Even when we were both at home, she would go to K's room via the veranda and call his name. Then she would go in and make herself at home. Sometimes, of course, she was bringing him mail or delivering his washing, the kind of interaction that could only be considered normal for those living under the same roof, but my fierce and single-minded desire to have her all to myself drove me to read more into it. At times I felt she was going out of her way to avoid my room and visit only his.

So why, you may ask, did I not ask K to leave the house? But that would have defeated the very purpose for bringing him there in the first place. It was beyond me to do it.

CHAPTER 87

It was a cold, rainy day in November. Sodden in my overcoat, I made my way as usual past the fierce Enma image that stands in Genkaku Temple[1] and up the hill to the house. K's room was deserted, but his charcoal brazier was newly lit. I hurriedly opened the doors through to my room, eager to warm my chilled hands at my own glowing charcoal. But my brazier held only the cold white ash of its earlier fire; even the embers were dead. My mood quickly shifted to one of displeasure.

Okusan had heard me arrive and came to greet me. Seeing me standing silent in the middle of the room, she sympathetically helped me out of my coat and into my casual household kimono. I complained of the cold, and she obligingly carried in K's brazier from next door. Was K home yet? I asked. He had returned and then gone out again, she told me. This puzzled me, as it was a day when his class schedule meant he came home later than I. He probably had some business to attend to, Okusan said.

I sat for a while reading. The house was still and hushed, there was no sound of any voice, and after a while the early winter chill, combined with the desolate silence, began to penetrate me. Seized by a sudden urge to be among a bustling throng of people, I put my book down and rose to my feet. The rain seemed to have lifted at last, but the sky still hung heavily chill and leaden, so to be on the safe side, as I went out I slung an oil-paper umbrella over my shoulder. I set off east down the hill, following the earthen wall that ran along the rear of the Arsenal.

In those days the roads were not yet improved, and the slope was a lot steeper than it is today. The street was narrower and not straight as now. As you descended into the valley, high buildings blocked the sun, and because drainage was poor, it was damp and muddy underfoot. The worst section was between the narrow stone bridge and the street of Yanagi-chō. Even in high rain clogs or rubber boots, you had to tread carefully to avoid the mud. Everyone was forced to pick their way gingerly along the long thin rut that had formed in the middle of the road. It was a mere foot or two wide, so it was a bit like walking along a kimono sash that had been casually unrolled down the center of the road. People made their way cautiously, in single file.

I was negotiating this narrow strip when I ran abruptly into K. Concentrating on where I was putting my feet, I was unaware of him until we were face-to-face. Only when I raised my eyes on impulse to see what was suddenly blocking my way did I discover him there.

Where had he been? I asked. He had just stepped out for a bit, he said. His reply was typically brief and unresponsive. We maneuvered past each other on the narrow strip of navigable road, and as we did, I saw that a young woman was behind him. Short-sighted as I was, I had not seen her until now, but once K had passed me, my eyes fell on her face, and I was astonished to discover that it was Ojōsan.

She greeted me, her cheeks slightly flushed. In those days, fashionable girls wore their hair swept straight back from the forehead and coiled on top of the head. For a long moment I stared blankly at this twist of hair. Then I became conscious of the fact that one of us would have to make way for the other. Resolutely, I stepped aside, putting one foot into the mud and so leaving a space for her to pass me with relative ease.

When I arrived at Yanagi-chō, I could not think where to go. All possibilities now felt equally bleak. For a while I tramped despairingly along through the sludge, oblivious to the splashes, then went home again.

CHAPTER 88

I asked K if he and Ojōsan had left the house together. No, he replied. They had come across each other in Masago-chō,[1] he explained, so they came home together. I could not really question him further, but over dinner I felt an urge to ask Ojōsan the same question. Her response was to laugh in that way I so disliked, then to challenge me to guess where she'd been. In those days I had a quick temper, and I felt a sudden surge of anger at being treated so flippantly. Okusan was the only person at the table to notice, however. K remained oblivious.

I was uncertain whether Ojōsan was being intentionally teasing or only innocently playful. As young women went, she was very astute, but I had to admit that certain aspects of her were typical of the things about other girls that annoyed me. It was since K's arrival in the house that I had begun to notice these irritating traits. I was unsure whether to put this down to my own jealousy of K or to her artfulness in relation to me. I am not inclined even now to dismiss my jealousy. As I have said many times, I was well aware that jealousy was at work below my love for Ojōsan. The smallest trifle, something that would be quite insignificant to anyone else, could set it off.

To digress for a moment, it seems to me that this kind of jealousy is perhaps a necessary part of love. Since my marriage, I have been aware that my jealous impulses have slowly faded; at the same time, I no longer feel that early fierce passion of love.

Hesitant as my heart had been, I now knew I had to gather my courage and fling it down before her. By *her* I mean Okusan, not Ojōsan. My plan was to set marriage discussions in motion by coming straight out and asking for Ojōsan's hand. Yet though my decision was made, I still held back from day to day. I know this makes me seem terribly irresolute—I don't mind that it does. But my inability to act did not stem from lack of willpower. Before K had appeared on the scene, any move I felt the urge to make was blocked by my abhorrence of falling into a trap as I had done once before; after K's arrival, my suspicion that she might be more attracted to him held me back. If she did indeed favor him, I had decided, then there was no value in declaring my own love.

It was not so much that the thought of the shame was painful to me; it was rather that, no matter how I loved her, I hated the thought of marrying a woman who secretly longed for another. Many men are perfectly happy to marry the girl they love whether she returns the feelings or not, but in those days I considered such men to be more worldly and cynical than we were, or else more obtuse to the workings of love. I was much too ardent to have any truck with the notion that once you marry you somehow simply settle down. In a word, I had a romantic faith in the nobility of love, while simultaneously practicing a devious form of it.

Naturally, during all our long time together there had been occasions when I could have confessed myself directly to Ojōsan and asked for her hand, but I had purposely chosen not to. I was very conscious of the fact that Japanese convention forbade such things, but it was not really this alone that restrained me. I assumed that in such a situation Japanese, and particularly Japanese girls, lacked the courage to be frank and honest, so I could not hope for a candid response from her.

CHAPTER 89

Thus I found myself at a standstill, unable to move in either direction. Maybe you know the feeling of lying there snoozing, perhaps when you are ill, and suddenly you find that your limbs are paralyzed, although you are perfectly aware of everything around you. This was how it sometimes felt to me then, unknown to those around me.

The year ended, and spring came. One day Okusan suggested to K that he invite some friends over so we could play the New Year game of poem cards.[1] She was astonished when K responded that he had no friends. Indeed it was true, no one in K's life really fit the description. He had a number of acquaintances who would pass the time of day with him when they came across each other, but they were hardly the kind of people to ask over for a game of cards. Okusan then turned to me and asked if I knew of anyone to invite, but I was not in the mood for such jolly games, so I gave a noncommittal reply.

When evening came, however, Ojōsan dragged us both off to play. With just the four of us, it was a very subdued game. Unused to such frivolities as he was, moreover, K remained reserved and standoffish. I demanded to know whether he even knew the *Hyakunin isshū* poems. "Not really," he replied. Ojōsan apparently took my words to be contemptuous, for she then began to lend him her obvious support, and in the end the two of them were more or less aligned against me. With any encouragement the situation could easily have escalated into a quarrel as far as I was concerned, but luckily K steadfastly maintained his earlier aloof indifference. I could detect not the slightest hint of triumph in him, so I managed to finish the game without incident.

It would have been two or three days later that Okusan and Ojōsan set off in the morning to visit some relatives in Ichigaya. Classes had not yet started, so K and I were in effect left to look after the house for the day. I felt no urge either to read or to take a walk and instead settled beside the brazier, chin propped on elbow, daydreaming. Next door K was equally quiet. Such silence reigned that for each of us, the other could as well not have been there. There was nothing unusual in this silence, of course, and I paid it no particular attention.

Around ten o'clock K suddenly opened the doors between our rooms and stood in the doorway. What was I thinking? he asked. I had not really been thinking anything, or if I had, then I was probably mulling over the usual problem of Ojōsan. Okusan was a necessary part of my conundrum, of course, but lately K's inseparable involvement had complicated it further. He had been vaguely present in my mind as a kind of obstacle, but now that I was face-to-face with him, I couldn't come out and say so. I simply looked at him silently. K then strode into my room and sat down in front of my brazier. I took my elbows off the edge and pushed the brazier slightly toward him.

K began to talk in a way that was quite out of character. To which part of Ichigaya had Okusan and Ojōsan gone? he asked. I said I believed they went to the aunt's house. Who is she? he asked. I told him she was the wife of a military officer. Why had they gone out so early in the year, when the round of New Year visits traditionally did not begin for women until after the fifteenth of January? I could only reply that I did not know.

CHAPTER 90

K persisted with his questions about Okusan and Ojōsan. Eventually he began to ask the kind of personal question that I had no way of answering. I was not so much annoyed as astonished. There was a glaring contrast between his indifference whenever I had brought up the subject of these two on previous occasions, and his very different attitude now. Finally I asked why he was suddenly so obsessed with the subject today. He instantly fell silent, but his closed mouth twitched tremulously. He never spoke much, and when he did, he had the habit of first working his mouth around. The weight of his utterances was no doubt evidenced in the way the lips resisted his will and opened only reluctantly. The voice that finally broke through was twice as strong as that of an average man.

Seeing his mouth working now, I knew that something was coming, but I had no clue what was in store. You can imagine my amazement when K launched into a ponderous confession of his agonized love for Ojōsan. I froze, as if his words were a magic wand that turned me instantly to stone. My mouth failed to so much as twitch in an effort to respond.

My whole being was reduced to a single concentrated point—of terror, of pain. I stiffened instantaneously from head to foot, like stone or steel. So rigid was I that I almost lost the power of breath. Luckily, however, this state quickly passed. A moment later I had returned to human feelings. And now a bitter regret swept over me. He had beaten me to it.

I had no idea what my next move should be, however. I was too distressed, I suppose, to think coherently. I simply remained frozen, uncomfortably aware of the nasty sweat that was soaking the armpits of my shirt. K, meanwhile, was continuing the faltering confession of his love, pausing from time to time to grope for words. I was in agony. My distress must have been written on my face as blatantly as some advertising poster, I thought. Even K must surely notice it. But it seemed in fact that his attention was too deeply focused on himself to register my expression. His confession never varied in tone. There was a heavy dullness to it, it seemed to me, and a kind of unyielding inertia. While part of me listened to this faltering declaration, my heart was seething with the question *What shall I do, oh, what shall I do?* so that I scarcely comprehended the details of what K was saying. The overall tone of his words, however, struck me to the core. So my pain was now mixed with a kind of terror—the beginnings of a horrified recognition that he was stronger than I.

When K finished, I could say nothing. I was not struck dumb by any internal debate about whether it would be wiser to make the same confession to him or to keep my secret to myself. It was simply that I could not speak. Nor did I wish to.

At lunch K and I faced each other across the table. Served by the maid, we ate what seemed to me an unusually tasteless meal. We spoke barely a word during the meal. We had no idea when Okusan and Ojōsan would return.

CHAPTER 91

We returned to our separate rooms and did not see each other again. K was as silent as he'd been that morning. I too sat quietly, deep in thought.

It seemed clear to me that I should reveal my heart to K, but I also felt that my chance had already passed. My silence had been a terrible mistake, it seemed to me now; I should have cut across his words with a counteroffensive; at the very least, I would have been wiser to follow his confession by frankly telling him my own feelings. At this stage, no matter how I looked at it, with K's confession over and done with it would be awkward to come back to the subject and express my own feelings. I could see no way to bring it up naturally. I felt dizzy with remorse.

If only he would open the sliding doors that separated us and charge into the room again, I thought. Earlier, he had caught me off guard, quite unprepared to cope with him. My underlying impulse now was to somehow regain the advantage I had lost that morning. From time to time I raised my eyes expectantly to the sliding doors. But the doors stayed closed. And beyond them K remained quiet.

After a while this hush started to unnerve me. What would he be thinking in there? No sooner had the question entered my head than it began to obsess me. It was perfectly normal for us to maintain separate silences on either side of the doors, and usually the quieter K was, the more likely I was to forget he was there. In my present state, however, I was clearly a bit mad. Yet despite my urgent need to confront him, I could not take the offensive and open the doors myself. Having missed my chance to speak, I now could only wait for his next move.

At length I could stay still no more. The longer I forced myself to remain motionless, the more urgently I longed to leap up and burst into K's room. There was nothing for it but to get up and go out onto the veranda. From there I moved on into the sitting room, where I absently poured myself a cup of hot water from the kettle and drank it. Then I went out to the entrance hall, and from there, having carefully avoided K's room, I found myself out in the road. Needless to say, I had no destination in mind. I simply needed to keep moving. I wandered aimlessly through streets that were bright with New Year decorations. Walk as I might, K continued to fill my mind. In fact, I was not even attempting to rid myself of such thoughts by walking. As I prowled the streets, my mind was intent on chewing over and digesting the image of him that hung before me.

Above all, he puzzled me. Why should he have unburdened himself to me out of the blue like that? Why had his passion reached such a pitch that he felt he must confess it to me? And where had his normal self disappeared to? I could find no answers. I knew how strong he was, and how intensely earnest. I was convinced that there was a lot more I needed to know before I could decide on my own attitude. On the other hand, the thought of having anything more to do with him was strangely repugnant. As I strode about the town in a daze, K's face, as he sat quietly in his room, was constantly before my eyes, while a voice seemed to be telling me that no matter how I walked, he would remain impervious to me. In short, I had begun to feel an almost magical power in him. Perhaps, I even found myself thinking, he had cast an evil spell that would last the rest of my life.

When at length I came home, exhausted, there was still no sound of life from K's room.

CHAPTER 92

Soon after I returned, I heard a rickshaw approaching. In those days the wheels were not yet lined with rubber, and you could hear the noisy clatter from quite a distance. The vehicle eventually pulled up in front of the gate.

About thirty minutes later I was summoned for the evening meal. The room next door was still scattered with the bright disorder of the formal visiting kimonos that the two ladies had just taken off. They apologized to us for being late. They had hurried home, Okusan said, to be in time to prepare supper. This thoughtfulness, however, was quite lost on both K and me. At the table my responses were brief and curt, as if begrudging each word. K was even more taciturn. The two ladies were still in fine high spirits from their rare excursion together, so our black mood was starkly evident in contrast.

Okusan asked me what had happened. I said I wasn't feeling very well. This was no more than the truth. Then Ojōsan addressed the same question to K. He gave a different reply. He simply said he didn't feel like talking. Why not? she demanded. On a sudden impulse, I raised my reluctant eyes to his face, curious to know how he would respond. K's lips were trembling in that way he had. Anyone who did not know him would judge that he was lost for an answer. Ojōsan laughed and said he must be thinking those difficult thoughts of his again. He reddened slightly.

That evening I went to bed earlier than usual. Concerned at my statement that I was feeling unwell, Okusan arrived around ten with some buckwheat soup. My room was already dark, however. She slid the door open a fraction and peered in, in consternation. As she did so, the lamplight from K's desk cast a soft diagonal beam into my room. It seemed he was still up. Okusan came in and sat at my pillow, setting the bowl down beside me. "Do have this," she said. "It will warm you up. You must have caught cold." Grudgingly I drank the glutinous liquid, while she sat watching.

I lay in the dark thinking until late in the night. What this amounted to, of course, was fruitlessly going over and over the same problem without arriving at any conclusion. At one point I suddenly wondered what K was doing right then in the room next door. "Hey," I called out, only half aware of what I was doing. "Hey," he immediately responded. He was still up. "Haven't you gone to bed yet?" I asked through the doors. He was just about to, he replied. "What are you doing?" I asked. This time there was no reply. Instead, five or six minutes later, I heard as clearly as if it were happening beside me the rasp of a cupboard being opened and the dull thump of bedding being laid on the floor. "What time is it?" I asked. "Twenty past one," he replied. Then I heard him softly blow out the flame of his lamp, and blackness and silence fell upon the house.

As I lay in the dark, my staring eyes only grew clearer. Again without really thinking, I called to K once more. Once more he responded. At length, I brought myself to say I wanted to talk more about what he had told me that morning. "Is it okay to talk now?" I asked. I did not, of course, intend to have this conversation through closed doors. I was just hoping for a simple answer. But although K had responded willingly enough to my earlier calls, he now resisted. "Mm, well," he muttered softly. Another shock of fear ran through me.

CHAPTER 93

K's evasive response was unmistakably echoed in his attitude the next day and the day after. He showed not the least inclination to broach the subject at issue between us. Granted, he had no opportunity to do so. We could not take our time and discuss things calmly unless both Okusan and Ojōsan had left the house for the day. I knew this perfectly well. Yet it still riled me. I had prepared myself in wait for K to make the next move, but now I changed my mind and decided that I would be the one to speak first if a chance presented itself.

I was also silently watchful of Okusan and Ojōsan. However, I detected nothing in either of them that was in the least different from usual. If their behavior had not visibly changed since K's confession, I felt, then he'd clearly confessed himself to me alone. He had yet to broach it with either Ojōsan or her guardian. This thought brought me some small comfort. In that case, I decided, it was better to lie in wait for a moment when I could naturally bring up the subject rather than make it obvious that I was purposely creating one. I would lay the topic aside for the moment and let things be.

Put this way, the decision sounds terribly simple. But the process I went through to reach it involved surges of thought and emotion, high and low, that swept through my heart like tides. I observed K's stolid immobility, and imputed various meanings to it. I kept a close watch on all that Okusan and Ojōsan did and spoke, and questioned whether what I saw truly reflected what was in their hearts. Could that delicate and complex instrument that lies in the human breast ever really produce a reading that was absolutely clear and truthful, like a clock's hands pointing to numbers on its dial? I wondered. In other words, only after a convoluted process of interpreting everything now one way and now another did I finally settle on my decision—although strictly speaking the word *settle* is singularly inappropriate for my state of mind at the time.

Lectures began again. On days when our schedule coincided, we set off together, and if it was convenient for us both, we came home together. To an outsider, we would have appeared just as friendly as before. Yet each of us within his heart was most certainly thinking his separate thoughts. One day as we were walking along together, I chose my moment and suddenly took the offensive. I began by asking whether he had made his recent confession only to me or whether he had spoken also to Okusan and Ojōsan. His reply would indicate the approach I should take, I'd decided. He declared that he had not yet spoken of it to anyone else. This privately delighted me, as it confirmed my assumption. I was well aware that he was more daring than I, and that I was no match for his courage. Yet I also had a strange faith that he was telling the truth. Despite his three-year deception of his adoptive family over the matter of school fees, he had never been in the least deceitful with me. I was in fact all the more inclined to trust him on this evidence. Thus, suspicious though I was by nature, I had no reason to doubt his unhesitating answer.

What did he plan to do about this love? I then asked. Was it simply something he had confessed to me in private, or did he intend to take practical steps to get what he wanted? But now he did not reply. Head down, he strode along in silence. "Don't hide anything from me," I said. "Tell me all that's on your mind." He declared that he had no need to hide anything—but he made absolutely no attempt to answer my question. I could hardly pause in the street and have the matter out with him then and there. I left it at that.

CHAPTER 94

One day I paid a rare visit to the university library. My supervisor had instructed me to check on something related to my field of study for the following week. Settling myself at a corner of one of the large desks, where the sunlight from the nearby window fell across me, I flipped through recently arrived foreign journals. I could not find what I wanted, however, so I had to keep going back to the shelves. Finally I came across the article I was after and set about avidly reading. At this point someone on the other side of the desk softly called my name. Raising my eyes, I discovered K standing there. He leaned forward over the desk toward me, his face close to mine. It is library etiquette not to disturb nearby readers, so K's action was perfectly reasonable, but on this occasion it strangely unnerved me.

"Are you studying?" he asked in a low voice.

"I have to look something up," I replied.

His face still hovered close to mine. In the same low voice he asked if I would come out for a walk.

Yes, I replied, if he would wait just a little.

"I'll wait," he said, and sank down on the chair directly in front of me.

This had the effect of distracting me so much that I found it impossible to concentrate anymore. The conviction seized me that he had something up his sleeve and had come to discuss things with me. I was driven to lay down my journal and rise.

"Finished?" K serenely inquired, seeing me begin to get to my feet.

"It's not important," I answered. I returned the journal, and we left the library together.

We had no particular destination in mind, so we walked through Tatsuoka-chō to Ikenohata and on into Ueno Park. There K suddenly broached the subject that lay between us. All things considered, it seemed obvious that he had invited me out for a walk for this purpose. But he still showed no evidence of moving toward a plan of action. "What do you think?" he asked. What he wanted to know was how I saw him, knowing the depths of love to which he had succumbed. He was, in other words, seeking a critical evaluation of his present state.

I could tell from this how unlike his usual self he was. Let me remind you that he had none of that weakness of character that makes most people concerned with what others are thinking. He had the kind of daring and courage that would simply press ahead once he'd decided something. I had all too vivid memories of this characteristic from the time of his family troubles, so the difference in his present behavior was quite clear to me.

Why was my opinion so important now? I asked him. The fact was, he was ashamed of his weakness, he replied in an unusually dejected voice. He was at a loss, no longer had a clear sense of things, so all he could do was seek a fair assessment from me. I cut in with a question—what did he mean by "at a loss"? He didn't know whether to proceed or retreat, he explained. I pressed in another step, and asked whether he thought himself capable of retreat, if that was what he decided. Words now failed him. "It's agony" was all he managed. And indeed he looked racked. If the person at issue had not been Ojōsan, I could have poured such a balm of soothing reassurances upon those poor tortured features. I flatter myself that I was born with a compassionate sympathy for others. Just then, however, I was a different person.

CHAPTER 95

I watched K's every move, vigilant as a man pitting himself against someone trained in a different school of combat. My eyes, my heart, my body, every atom of my being, was focused on him with unwavering intent. In his innocence, K was completely unwary. He was not so much poorly defended as utterly vulnerable. It was as if I could lift from his very hands the map of a fortress that was in his charge and take all the time I wanted to examine it as he watched.

Now I understood that he had lost his way in a labyrinth between his ideals and reality, I felt with conviction that I could knock him down with a single blow. My eyes fixed on this purpose, I stepped straight into the breach. I grew instantly solemn. It was part of my strategy, but in fact I was tense enough for it to feel perfectly natural, so I was in no position to notice that I was behaving shamefully, even comically.

I began by tossing back at him the statement "anyone without spiritual aspirations is a fool," the words he had used against me on our journey around Bōshū I threw them at him in precisely the tone he had used to me then. I didn't do it vindictively, however. I confess that I had a crueler aim than mere revenge. I wanted with these words to block K's way to love.

K had been born into the Pure Land sect, which encourages its priests to marry, but once he reached his teenage years, he developed beliefs that were somewhat different. I am poorly qualified to speak on this, I know, as I lack much understanding of sectarian differences, but I was certainly aware of how he felt about relations between the sexes. K had always loved the expression "spiritual austerity," which I understood to contain the idea of control over the passions.

Later I had discovered that those words held a still more rigorous meaning for him. His prime article of faith was the necessity to sacrifice everything in pursuit of "the true Way." Following the path was not only a question of self-denial and abstinence—even selfless love, beyond the realms of desire, was conceived as a stumbling block. I had often heard him declaim about this in the days when he was self-supporting. I was already in love with Ojōsan back then, so naturally I threw myself into defending the realms of desire. He had looked at me pityingly, with much more contempt than sympathy in his eyes.

Now, with all that lay between us, the words I had just thrown back at K would certainly have struck home painfully. But as I have said, I was not using them to strike at the philosophy he had so rigorously cultivated. I wanted instead for him to stay true to his old convictions. Whether he attained his spiritual aspirations was beside the point—he could reach enlightenment itself, for all I cared. My single fear was that he would change the direction he had chosen for his life and thereby come into conflict with my own interests. In other words, blatant self-interest lay behind my words.

"Anyone without spiritual aspirations is a fool," I repeated, watching to see what effect these words would have on K.

"A fool," K responded at length. "I'm a fool."

He came to an instantaneous halt and stood rooted to the spot, staring at the ground. This startled me. He seemed to me like a cornered thief who will suddenly turn threatening. Then I realized that he presented no danger; all the power had left his voice. I longed to read his eyes, but they remained averted. Then, slowly, he set off walking once more.

CHAPTER 96

I walked along beside him, ready, or perhaps better to say lying in wait, for what he would say next. I felt quite prepared to spring an underhanded attack on him if need be. But I also had the conscience that education had instilled in me. If someone had appeared at my side and whispered "Coward!" I would surely have come to myself with a start. And if that man had been K, I would have blushed before him. But K was far too honest to reproach me, far too pure-hearted, too good. In the blind urgency of the moment, however, I failed to honor this in him. Instead I struck home. I used his own virtue to defeat him.

After a while K spoke my name and turned to look at me. This time it was I who stopped in my tracks. K halted too. At last I was able to I look him directly in the eye. His superior height forced me to look up at him, but I did so with the heart of a wolf crouching before an innocent lamb.

"Let's not talk about it anymore," he said. There was a strange grief both in his voice and in the expression in his eyes. I could say nothing in reply. "Please stop," he said again, pleading now.

My answer was cruel. I leaped like a wolf upon the lamb's throat. "I wasn't the one who brought it up, you know. You began it. If you want to stop, that's fine by me. But there's no point in just shutting up. You have to resolve to put a stop to it in your heart as well. What about all those fine principles of yours? Where's your moral fiber?"

At these words, his tall frame seemed to shrink and dwindle before my eyes. He was, as I have said, incredibly obstinate and headstrong, yet he was also far too honest to be able to shrug it off if his own inconsistency was forcefully brought home to him. Seeing him cowed, I at last breathed a sigh of relief. Then he said suddenly, "Resolve?" Before I could respond, he went on, "Resolve—well, I'm not without resolve." He spoke as if to himself, or as if in a trance.

Our conversation came to a halt, and we turned toward home. It was a fairly warm and windless day, but nevertheless it was winter, and the leafless park felt desolate. I turned once to look back at the russet shapes of the frost-burned cedars, their tips neatly aligned against the gloomy sky, and felt the cold sink its teeth into my back. We hurried on in the dusk over Hongō Hill and dipped into the valley below Koishikawa. Only now did I at last feel the beginnings of a glow of warmth inside my overcoat.

We barely spoke on our way home, though our haste might explain this silence. When we were back and seated at the dinner table, Okusan asked why we had been late. I replied that K had invited me out, and we had gone to Ueno. On such a cold day? said Okusan in surprise. Ojōsan wondered what had taken us there. Nothing, I replied simply, we had just gone for a walk. Always taciturn, K now spoke even less than usual. He failed to make the slightest response to Okusan's cajolings and Ojōsan's smiles. He gulped down his food, and retired to his room while I was still at the table.

CHAPTER 97

These were the days before "the new awakening" or "the new way of life," as modern slogans have it. But if K failed to toss away his old self and throw himself into becoming a new man, it was not for want of such concepts. Rather, it was because he could not bear to reject a self and a past that had been so noble and exalted. One might even say that it had been his reason for living. So his failure to rush headlong in pursuit of love must not be read as proof that his love was lukewarm. No matter how fierce was the passion that gripped him, the fact is he was paralyzed, transfixed by the contemplation of his own past. Only something so momentous as to drive from his consciousness all thoughts of before and after could have propelled him forward. And with his eyes fixed on the past, he had no choice but to continue along its trajectory. Also, there was in K a kind of obduracy and power of endurance lacking in modern men. In this respect I was confident that I knew him well.

For me, that evening was relatively peaceful. I followed K to his room, settled myself beside his desk, and deliberately chattered on for a while about nothing in particular. He looked annoyed. No doubt a light of victory glinted in my eye, and my voice held a note of triumph. After I'd spent some time warming my hands over his brazier, I returned to my room. Just for that moment I felt that, though K was in every way superior to me, for once I had nothing to fear from him.

Soon I drifted into a calm sleep. But I was awakened by the sudden sound of my name. Turning to look, I saw that the sliding doors were partly open, and K's dark shape was standing there. The desk lamp still glowed in the room beyond. Stunned by the sudden change in my world, for a long moment I could only lie there, speechless and staring.

"Are you in bed already?" K asked. He always stayed up late.

"What is it?" I said, addressing K's shadowy phantom shape.

"Nothing really," he replied. "I just dropped in on my way back from the bathroom to check if you were asleep yet." With the lamplight behind him, I could make out nothing of his expression. His voice, however, was if anything calmer than usual.

After a moment he slid the doors carefully closed. Darkness instantly returned to my room. I closed my eyes again, to shut out the blackness and dream in peace. I remember nothing more. But the next morning when I recalled the incident, it struck me as somehow strange. Had I perhaps dreamed it? I wondered.

Over breakfast I asked him about it. Yes, he said, he had opened the doors and called my name.

"Why did you do that?" I asked, but he gave only a vague reply.

We lapsed into silence. Then he abruptly asked if I was sleeping well lately. The question struck me as rather odd.

That day our lectures would begin at the same time, so we set off together. The previous night's incident had been bothering me all morning, and I brought up the subject again as we walked. He still gave no satisfactory answer, however. "Did you want to continue our earlier conversation?" I asked.

He vehemently denied it. This firm response seemed like a curt reminder that he had said he wouldn't talk about it anymore. He always had a fierce pride in his own consistency, I reminded myself. Then I found myself recalling how he had spoken of "resolve." Suddenly this simple word, until that moment quite insignificant, began strangely to oppress me.

CHAPTER 98

I was well aware that K usually acted decisively, but I could also see perfectly well why he was being so astonishingly irresolute now. I proudly believed, in other words, that my knowledge of the norm gave me a clear grasp of the present exception. But as I slowly digested this word *resolve,* my confident pride teetered and finally began to crumble. Perhaps he was not behaving so out of character after all. Perhaps, in fact, he held carefully tucked away within his breast the means by which to solve at a stroke all his doubts, anguish, and torment. When I considered the word *resolve* in this fresh light, a shock ran through me. I would probably have been wiser to turn this astonishment to good account and coolly reconsider just what this resolve might constitute. Sadly, however, I was blinded by my own single-minded preoccupation. The only interpretation I could imagine was that he was resolved to act in relation to Ojōsan. I leaped to the conclusion that his decisiveness would be exercised in the pursuit of love.

A voice whispered in my ear that it was time for me too to be decisive, and I unhesitatingly complied. I gathered my courage for a final resolve. I must act before K did, and without his knowledge, I decided. Silently I awaited my chance. Two or three days passed, however, and no opportunity presented itself. I was waiting for a time when K was out and Ojōsan had also left the house, when I could approach Okusan in private. But day after day either he or she was always there to stymie my plan. The longed-for moment never arrived. I seethed with impatience.

A week later I could finally wait no longer, and I faked illness to attain my end. I lay in bed until around ten, grunting a vague response when Okusan, Ojōsan, and K himself told me it was time to get up. When K and Ojōsan had both left and a hush had fallen on the house, I finally left my bed. "What's the matter?" Okusan asked when she saw me appear. She urged me to go back to bed and said she would bring me something to eat. But I was in no mood to sleep further, being in fact perfectly well. I washed my face and ate in the sitting room as usual, while Okusan served me from the other side of the brazier. As I sat there, bowl in hand, eating what could be either breakfast or lunch, I was agonizing over how to broach the subject of Ojōsan, so no doubt I looked every bit the part of a suffering invalid.

I finished the meal and lit a cigarette. Okusan could not leave until I rose, so she sat on beside the brazier. The maid was called in to remove the dishes, while Okusan kept me company, busying herself with topping up the kettle or wiping the rim of the brazier as she sat there.

"Is there something you ought to be doing?" I asked.

"No," she said, then inquired why I wanted to know.

"Actually," I replied, "I have something I'd like to discuss."

"What is it?" she said casually, her eyes on my face. She was treating the moment lightly, apparently unreceptive to my mood, and I faltered over how to proceed. After beating about the bush for a while, I finally asked whether K had recently said anything to her.

"What about?" she asked, startled. Then, before I could answer, she said, "Did he say something to you?"

CHAPTER 99

"No," I replied, having no intention of telling Okusan what K had confessed to me. But the lie immediately made me unhappy. I awkwardly backed away from it by saying that K hadn't asked me to say anything on his behalf that I could recall, and my present business had nothing to do with him.

"I see," she said, and waited for more.

There was nothing for it but to broach the subject at last. "Okusan," I said abruptly, "I wish to marry Ojōsan."

She took this more calmly than I had anticipated, although she stared at me in silence, apparently at a loss how to respond.

But I had gone too far now to let her gaze disconcert me. "Please, Okusan. Please let me marry her," I said. "Let me make her my wife."

Okusan's mature years lent her far greater calm than I could muster. "That's all very well," she replied, "but isn't this rather hasty?"

"It's now I want to marry her," I said, which made her laugh.

"Have you thought this through properly?" she went on.

I earnestly assured her that although the request was sudden, the impulse behind it was anything but.

A few more questions followed, which I have forgotten. Okusan had quite a masculine clarity and directness that made her far easier to talk to than the usual woman in this kind of situation.

"Very good," she finally said. "You may have her. Or rather," she corrected herself, "since I'm not in a position to speak so patronizingly, let me say, 'Please take her for your wife.' As you know, the poor girl has no father to give her away."

And so the question was settled, straightforwardly and without fuss. It would have taken no more than fifteen minutes from beginning to end. Okusan demanded no conditions. It would not be necessary to consult the relatives, she maintained. All she had to do was inform them of the decision. She even stated that there was no need to consult the wishes of Ojōsan herself.

Here I balked—educated man though I was, I was apparently the more conventional in such matters. As for the relatives, I said, I would leave that up to her, but surely the right thing to do next was to gain the girl's consent.

"Please don't worry," Okusan replied. "I wouldn't make her marry anyone she didn't want to."

Once back in my room, I felt somewhat unnerved at how remarkably smoothly the discussion had gone. I even found myself almost doubting that it could all really be as safely settled as it seemed. At the same time, however, my whole being was swept with a sense of renewal at the thought that the future was now decided.

Around noon I went into the living room and asked Okusan when she planned to tell Ojōsan the news of our conversation. Since she had already agreed, she said, it didn't matter when she told her daughter. I turned to go back to my room with the uncomfortable feeling that she was playing the male far better than I was in all this, but Okusan held me back. If I wished, she said, she would tell her daughter right away, as soon as she came back from her lessons that day.

That would be best, I agreed, and returned to my room. But the idea of sitting mutely at my desk listening as the two of them murmured together in the distance made me jittery. At length I put on my hat and went out.

And now once again, on the road below the house, I crossed paths with Ojōsan coming up. Quite innocent of all that had happened, she looked surprised to see me.

"You're back, are you?" I said politely, raising my hat.

"Are you better now?" she asked in a rather puzzled tone.

"Yes, yes, much better, thanks," I replied, and stepped briskly around the corner toward Suidō Bridge.

CHAPTER 100

I walked through Sarugaku-chō, out onto the main street of Shinbōchō, and turned toward Ogawamachi. This was the route I usually took when I wanted to browse among the secondhand bookshops, but today I could not summon any interest in tattered old volumes. As I strode along, it was the house I had left that filled my thoughts. I thought of what Okusan had said that morning, and I imagined what would follow once Ojōsan arrived back. My legs seemed propelled forward by these two thoughts. From time to time, I found myself halting in the middle of the road at the thought that Okusan would at this moment be talking to Ojōsan. Then my feet would pause again when it struck me that by now the conversation would probably be over.

At length I crossed the Mansei Bridge, climbed the hill to Kanda Myōjin Shrine, then from Hongō Hill made my way down Kikusaka to the foot of the road leading up to Koishikawa. Throughout this long walk, in essence a kind of elliptical course through three city wards,[1] I had scarcely thought once of K. Looking back now, I ask myself why, but there are no answers. I can only marvel that it was so. I could simply say that my heart was so intensely focused on the scene at home that it drove him from my mind, but it astonishes me to think that my conscience could let that happen.

My conscience sprang to life again the moment I opened the lattice door at the entrance and stepped into the house, to follow my usual course through K's room into mine. He was, as always, seated at his desk reading. As always, he raised his eyes from the book and looked at me. But he did not say the habitual words, "Just back, are you?" Instead he said, "Are you better now? Have you been to the doctor?"

In that instant I had the urge to kneel before him and ask his pardon. Nor was this some mere feeble impulse. I believe that if K and I had been standing in the wilderness together just then, I would have followed the dictates of my conscience and begged his forgiveness. But there were others in the house. My natural instinct was quickly curbed. And to my sorrow, it never returned.

We saw each other again over the evening meal. Innocent of what had happened, K was merely subdued. He cast no suspicious glance my way. Okusan, of course, understood nothing of how things stood and was markedly cheerful. Only I knew everything. The food was lead in my mouth.

Ojōsan did not join us at the table as she usually did. "I won't be long," she called from the next room when Okusan urged her to join us.

K looked surprised and finally asked Okusan what was wrong.

"She's probably feeling shy," replied Okusan, sending a glance in my direction.

"Why should she?" K persisted, increasingly puzzled.

Okusan looked at me again, with a little smile.

As soon as I came to the table, I had been able to guess from Okusan's face more or less what had transpired. But the thought of sitting there while everything was explained to K was intolerable. Okusan was the kind of person who could all too easily do this without a second thought, and I was cold with trepidation. Luckily, however, K sank back into silence, and Okusan, though more jovial than usual, did not after all move the conversation in the direction I dreaded. With a sigh of relief, I returned to my room.

But I was haunted with worry over how to deal with K. I prepared an arsenal of justifications for my defense, but none would hold up when I was face-to-face with him. Coward that I was, I had no stomach for the explanation I would have to give.

CHAPTER 101

Two or three days passed, and still I said nothing. All that time, needless to say, constant anxiety about K weighed me down. I must at least make some sort of move just to ease my conscience, I told myself. Okusan's high spirits and Ojōsan's manner with me were a further painful goad to action. In her forthright and unreserved way, Okusan might all too easily let something slip at the dinner table at any moment. I could never be sure, either, that K's heart would not find cause for suspicion in the way Ojōsan had begun to behave toward me, which seemed to me worryingly obvious. All told, it was imperative to let K know how matters now stood between me and the family. Yet making such a move felt next to impossible—I was all too aware what shaky moral ground I stood on.

Perhaps there was nothing for it, I thought, but to ask Okusan to reveal the situation to K, needless to say at a time when I was out. But simply having the facts told to him indirectly would do nothing to alter my shame. On the other hand, if I asked her to tell him some made-up story, she would certainly demand an explanation. And if I were to confess the whole thing to her, I would be choosing to reveal my failings to the girl I loved and her mother. I was an earnest young man, and it seemed to me that such a confession would compromise the trust that marriage depended on. I could not bear the thought of losing so much as a particle of my beloved's belief in me before we had even married.

In short, I was a fool whose foot had slipped from the straight and narrow path of honesty that I had set myself to walk. Or perhaps I was really just cunning. For now, only heaven and my own heart understood the truth. But I was cornered; in the very act of regaining my integrity, I would have to reveal to those around me that I had lost it. I was desperate to cover my deceitfulness, yet it was imperative that I act. I was paralyzed, transfixed by my dilemma.

Five or six days later, Okusan suddenly inquired whether I had told K about it. Not yet, I replied. Why not? she asked reproachfully. I froze. The shock of her next words has seared them into my memory.

"So that's why he looked so odd when I mentioned it. Don't you think it was wrong of you to keep quiet and pretend nothing had happened, to such a close friend?"

I asked if K had said anything in response. Not really, she replied. But I could not resist pressing her for more detailed information. Okusan, of course, had no reason to hide anything.

"There really is nothing worth telling," she said, then launched into a thorough description of how he had taken the news. All in all, I saw that K had taken this final blow extremely calmly. His first reaction to the news of my new relationship with Ojōsan had been simply to say "Is that so?" "I hope you'll rejoice with us," Okusan had said, and at this he looked her in the eye for the first time. "Congratulations," he said with a little smile, and stood up. Before he opened the door to leave the sitting room, he turned to her again and asked when the wedding would be. "I wish I could give them a wedding gift," he apparently said, "but I'm afraid I haven't the money."

As I sat before her hearing these words, my heart clenched tight with pain.

CHAPTER 102

I realized that two days or more had passed since Okusan had told K about our engagement. Nothing in K's manner toward me had hinted that he knew anything, so I had remained unaware of it. I was now filled with respect for his composure, even though it was no doubt only superficial. By any standard, he was by far the better man. *Though I've won through cunning, the real victory is his* was the thought that spun in my head. *How he must despise me!* I said to myself, and I blushed with shame. Yet it mortified me to imagine going to K after all this and submitting to the inevitable humiliation.

Floundering in indecision, I finally put off the question of what to do until the next day. This was Saturday evening.

That night, however, K killed himself.

I still shudder at the memory of finding him there. I usually slept with my head facing east, but for some reason—fate, perhaps—that evening I had laid out my bedding to face the opposite direction.[1] I was awakened in the night by a chill draft blowing in on my face. Opening my eyes, I saw that the sliding doors between our two rooms, which were normally closed, stood slightly ajar, just as they had when he appeared there some nights earlier.

This time, however, K's dark figure was not standing in the doorway. As if with a sudden presentiment, I propped myself on one elbow and peered tensely into his room. The lamp had burned low. The bedding was laid out. But the edge of the quilt was thrown back. And there was K, slumped forward with his back to me.

I called out to him. There was no response. "Is something wrong?" I called again. But his body remained motionless. I leaped up and went to the doorway. Standing there, I surveyed his room by the lamp's faint light.

My first feeling was almost the same as the initial shock his sudden confession of love had given me. I took in the room with a single sweeping glance, and then my gaze froze—my eyeballs stared in their sockets as if made of glass. I stood rooted to the spot. When this first gale of shock had blown through me, my next thought was *Oh god, it's all over*. The knowledge that this was irredeemable shot its black blaze through my future and for an instant lit with terrifying clarity all the life that lay before me. Then I began to tremble.

But even in this extremity I could not forget about myself. My eyes fell on a letter lying on the desk. It was addressed to me, as I had guessed. Frantically, I tore open the seal. But I was not prepared for what I read there. I had assumed that this letter would say things deeply painful for me to read, and I was terrified at how Okusan and Ojōsan would despise me if they saw it. A quick glance instantly relieved me, however. *Saved!* I thought. (In fact, of course, it was only my reputation that was saved, but how others saw me was a matter of immense importance just then.)

The letter was simple and contained nothing specific. He was committing suicide, he wrote, because he was weak and infirm of purpose, and because the future held nothing for him. With a few brief words he thanked me for all I had done for him. As a final request, he asked me to see to his affairs after his death. He also asked me to apologize to Okusan for the trouble he was causing her and to inform his family. The letter was a series of simple statements of essential matters; the only thing missing was any mention of Ojōsan. I read it to the end and understood that K had deliberately avoided mentioning her.

But it was the letter's final words that pierced my heart most keenly. With the last of the brush's ink, he had added that he should have died sooner and did not know why he had lived so long.

I folded the letter with trembling hands and slid it back into its envelope. I replaced it carefully on the desk so that it would be clearly visible to the others. Then I turned and at last I saw the blood that had spurted over the sliding doors.

CHAPTER 103

Impulsively I lifted K's head a little, cradling it in both hands. I wanted to take in for a moment the sight of his dead face. But when I peered up at the face that hung there, I instantly released him. It was not simply horror at the sight. His head felt appallingly heavy. I stared down for a while at the cold ears I had touched, and at the closely cropped head of thick hair, so normal and familiar. I had not the least urge to cry. My only feeling was fear. This was not simply a commonplace fright stimulated by the scene before my eyes. What I felt was a deep terror of my fate, a fate that spoke to me from the abrupt chill of my friend's body.

I returned to my room in a stupor and began to pace. *Pointless though it is,* my brain instructed me, *for now you must just keep moving.* I had to do something, I thought, and simultaneously I was thinking, *There's nothing I can do.* I could only turn and turn in the room, like a caged bear.

A few times I had the impulse to go in and wake Okusan. But this was quickly checked by the thought that it would be wrong to show a woman such a horrifying sight. I was paralyzed by a fierce resolve that I must not shock either her or, above all, her daughter. And so I would return to my pacing and circling.

At some point I lit my lamp, and from time to time I glanced at the clock. Nothing was more tediously slow than that clock. I had no idea exactly when I had woken, but it was definitely sometime close to daybreak. As I turned and turned in the room, waiting desperately for dawn to come, I was tortured by the sensation that this black night might never end.

We were in the habit of rising before seven, since many of our lectures began at eight. This meant that the maid got up around six. It was not yet six when I went to wake her that day. My footsteps woke Okusan, who pointed out to me that it was Sunday. "If you're awake," I said to Okusan, "perhaps you could come to my room a moment." She followed me, a kimono coat draped over her nightdress. I quickly closed the far doors to K's room. Then I said in a low voice, "Something dreadful has happened."

"What is it?" she asked.

"Don't be shocked," I said, indicating the next-door room with my chin. She turned pale. "K has committed suicide."

Okusan stood as though paralyzed, staring mutely at me. I suddenly found myself sinking to my knees before her, head lowered in contrition. "I'm so sorry. It's all my fault," I said. "Now this unforgivable thing has happened to you and Ojōsan."

I had had no thought of saying any such thing before I faced her—only when I saw her expression did the words spring to my lips, unbidden. Consider it an apology directed to the two ladies, but it was really meant for K, whom it could no longer reach. Those impulsive words of remorse were spoken beyond my will, directly from my natural being.

Fortunately for me, Okusan did not read my words so deeply. Though ashen, she said comfortingly, "What could you possibly have done about something so unforeseen?" But her face was carved deep with shock and dread, the muscles rigid.

CHAPTER 104

Though I pitied Okusan, I now stood again and opened the sliding doors that I had so recently closed. K's lamp had burned out, and the room was sunk in almost total darkness. I went back and picked up my own lamp, then turned at the doorway to look at her. Cowering behind me, she peered into the little room beyond. But she made no move to enter. "Leave things as they are," she said, "and open the shutters."

And now Okusan became the levelheaded, practical officer's wife. She sent me to the doctor's home, then to the police. She gave all the orders, and allowed no one into the room until the correct procedure was completed.

K had slit his carotid artery with a small knife and died immediately. It was his only wound. The blood on the paper doors, which I had glimpsed by the dreamlike half-light of his lamp, had spurted from his neck. Now I gazed at it again, in the clarity of daylight. I was stunned at the violent force that pulses the blood through us.

The two of us set to work and cleaned up his room with all the skill and efficiency we could muster. Luckily, most of his blood had been absorbed by the bedding and the floor matting was not much harmed, so our task was relatively easy. Together we carried his corpse into my room and laid it out on its side in a natural sleeping position. I then went off and sent a telegram to his family.

When I returned, incense was burning beside the pillow. As I entered the room, that funereal scent assailed my nose, and I discovered mother and daughter sitting there wreathed in its smoke. This was the first time I had seen Ojōsan since the night before. She was weeping. Okusan's eyes too were red. I had had no thought of tears until that moment, but now at last I was able to let a sensation of sorrow pervade me. Words cannot express what a comfort that was. Thanks to this grief, a touch of balm momentarily soothed my poor heart, which had been clenched tight around its fear and pain.

Wordlessly, I seated myself beside them. Okusan urged me to offer incense before the corpse. I did so, then returned to sit quietly again. Ojōsan did not speak to me. Occasionally she exchanged a few words with her mother, but they concerned only the immediate situation. She did not yet have the where-withal to speak of K as he had been in life. I was glad at least that she had been spared the horrible scene of the night before. I trembled to imagine how such a terrible sight could destroy the loveliness of one so young and beautiful. This thought haunted me, even when my own fear raised the very hairs on my head. It brought the kind of shudder one would feel in setting merci-lessly upon a beautiful, innocent flower with a whip.

When K's father and brother arrived, I told them my own views on where I thought he should be buried. K and I had often walked around the Zōshigaya cemetery together, and he was extremely fond of the place. I had once promised him half-jokingly that if he died, I would bury him there. I did ask myself what good it would do me to fulfill this pledge to him now. But I wanted him buried close by, for I was determined to return to his grave every month for the rest of my life and kneel before it in renewed penitence and shame. They let me have my way, no doubt acknowledging the important role I had played in the care of their estranged brother and son.

CHAPTER 105

On the way back from K's funeral, one of his friends asked me why I thought he had killed himself. This question had been dogging me ever since his suicide. Okusan, Ojōsan, K's father and brother, acquaintances whom I had informed, even unknown newspaper reporters—all had asked me the same thing. Every time someone asked, my conscience smarted painfully, and I heard behind the words a voice say, *Quick, confess that it was you who killed him.*

My answer to everyone was the same. I simply repeated the words of his final letter to me and made no further statement. The fellow who had asked me on our way back from the funeral, and received the same answer, now took from his pocket a newspaper cutting and handed it to me. I read the piece he indicated as we walked on. It said that K had killed himself from despair at being disinherited. I folded the page and returned it to him without comment. He told me that another paper had reported that K had gone mad and killed himself. I had been too preoccupied to look at newspapers and so was quite ignorant of all this, although I had all along been concerned about what they might write. Above all, I feared that something unpleasant or disturbing for Okusan and Ojōsan might appear there. It particularly tortured me to think that Ojōsan might be so much as mentioned in passing. I asked this friend if anything else had been written in the papers. These two references were all he had seen, he told me.

Soon after this I moved into the house where I still live. Both Okusan and Ojōsan disliked the thought of staying in their old house, while every evening I found myself reliving the memory of that night. After some discussion, therefore, we decided to find somewhere else.

After two months I graduated from the university. Six months later Ojōsan and I finally married. On the face of things I could congratulate myself on all having gone according to plan. Both Okusan and Ojōsan seemed wonderfully happy, and so indeed was I. But a black shadow hovered behind my happiness. This very happiness, it seemed to me, could well be a fuse that drew the flame of my life toward a bitter fate.

Once married, Ojōsan—but I should now begin to call her "my wife"—my wife for some reason suggested that we visit K's grave together. This jolted me. Why had she suddenly come up with such an idea? I inquired. She replied that it would surely please K if we visited him together. I stared hard at her guileless face, until she asked why I was looking at her like that.

I agreed to her request, and together we went to Zōshigaya. I poured water over K's fresh grave and washed it. My wife placed incense and flowers before it. We both bowed our heads and placed our hands together in prayer. No doubt she wished to receive K's blessing from beyond the grave by conveying to him the news of our marriage. As for me, the words *I was to blame, I was to blame* were going around and around in my head.

My wife stroked K's headstone and declared it a fine one. It was not particularly impressive, but she probably felt the need to praise it because I had personally gone to the stonemason and chosen it. Privately, I balanced in my mind the images of this new grave, my new wife, and K's new white bones lying buried at my feet, and a sense of the cold mockery of fate crept over me. I vowed then that I would never come here with her again.

CHAPTER 106

My feelings toward my dead friend remained unchanged. I had feared all along that this would be so. Even my wedding, that longed-for event, was not without a secret disquiet. We humans cannot know what lies ahead, however, and I hoped that our marriage might perhaps be the key to a change in my state of mind that would lead to a new life. But as I faced my wife day after day, my fragile hope crumbled in the face of cold reality. When I was with her, K would suddenly loom threateningly in my mind. She stood between us, in effect, and her very presence bound K and me indissolubly together. She was everything I could have wanted, yet because of this unwitting role she played, I found myself withdrawing from her. She, of course, immediately registered this. She felt it but could not understand it. From time to time she would demand to know why I was so morose, or whether I was somehow displeased with her. As a rule, I managed to reassure her by dismissing her doubts with a laugh, but occasionally it led to some outburst. "You hate me, don't you?" she would cry, or I would have to suffer reproachful accusations of hiding something from her. This was always torture for me.

Again and again I would decide to summon my courage and confess everything to her. But at the last minute some power not my own would always press me back. You know me well enough to need no explanation, I believe, but I will write here what must be said. I had not the slightest urge in those days to present myself to her in a false light. If I had confessed to her with the same sincerity and humility of heart with which I confessed to my dead friend, I know she would have wept tears of joy and forgiven all. So it was not sheer self-interest that kept me mute. No, I failed to confess for the simple reason that I could not bring myself to contaminate her memory of the past with the tiniest hint of darkness. It was agony for me to contemplate this pure creature sullied in any way, you understand.

A year passed, and still I could not forget. My heart was in a constant state of agitation. To escape it, I plunged into my books. I began to study with ferocious energy. One day, I thought hopefully, I would produce the fruits of this learning for the world to see. But it was no use—I could take no pleasure in deceiving myself like this, in creating some artificial goal and forcing myself to anticipate its achievement. After a while, I could no longer bury my heart in books. Once more I found myself surveying the world from a distance, arms folded.

My wife apparently interpreted my state of mind as a kind of ennui, a slackness of spirit that came from not having to worry about day-to-day survival. This was understandable. Her mother had enough money to allow them both to make do, and my own financial situation meant I had no need to work. I had always taken money for granted, I admit. But the main reason for my immobility lay quite elsewhere. True enough, my uncle's betrayal had made me fiercely determined never to be beholden to anyone again—but back then my distrust of others had only reinforced my sense of self. The world might be rotten, I felt, but I at least am a man of integrity. But this faith in myself had been shattered on account of K. I suddenly understood that I was no different from my uncle, and the knowledge made me reel. What could I do? Others were already repulsive to me, and now I was repulsive even to myself.

CHAPTER 107

No longer able to forget myself in a living tomb of books, I tried instead to drown my soul in drink. I cannot say I like alcohol, but I am someone who can drink if I choose to, and I set about obliterating my heart by drinking all I could. This was a puerile way out, of course, and it very quickly led to an even greater despair with the world. In the midst of a drunken stupor, I would come to my senses and realize what an idiot I was to try to fool myself like this. Then my vision and understanding grew clear, and I sat shivering and sober. There were desolate times when even the poor disguise of drunkenness failed to work, no matter how I drank. And each time I sought pleasure in drink, I emerged more depressed than ever. My darling wife and her mother were unavoidably witness to all this and naturally did their best to make sense of it as they could.

I gathered that my wife's mother sometimes said some rather unpleasant things about me to her, although she never passed them on to me. My wife could not resist being critical herself, however. She never spoke strongly, of course, and I very rarely became provoked to the point where I lost my temper. She would simply ask me from time to time to tell her honestly if there was something about her that bothered me. "Stop drinking," she would say, "you'll ruin yourself." Sometimes she wept and declared, "You've become a changed person." But worst of all was when she added, "You wouldn't have changed like this if K were still alive." I agreed that that might well be true, but I was filled with sorrow at the gulf that lay between our separate understandings of this remark. And yet I still felt no urge to explain everything to her.

Sometimes I apologized to her, the morning after I had come home late and drunk. She would laugh, or else fall silent, and occasionally she wept. Whatever her reaction, I hated myself. In apologizing to her, I was actually apologizing to myself. Finally I gave up drinking, less because of my wife's admonishments than because of self-disgust.

I gave up drink, but I remained disinclined to do anything else. I resorted to books again, to pass the time. But my reading was aimless—I simply read each book and tossed it aside. Whenever my wife asked what the point of my study was, I responded with a bitter smile. In my heart, though, I was saddened that the person I loved and trusted most in the world could not understand me. *But it's within your power to help her understand,* I thought, *and yet you're too cowardly to do so,* and I grew still sadder. Desolation filled me. There were many times when I felt I lived utterly alone, remote and cut off from the world around me.

All this time the cause of K's death continued to obsess me. At the time it happened, the single thought of love had engrossed me, and no doubt this preoccupation influenced my simplistic understanding of the event. I had immediately concluded that K killed himself because of a broken heart. But once I could look back on it in a calmer frame of mind, it struck me that his motive was surely not so simple and straightforward. Had it resulted from a fatal collision between reality and ideals? Perhaps—but this was still not quite it. Eventually, I began to wonder whether it was not the same unbearable loneliness that I now felt that had brought K to his decision. I shuddered. Like a chill wind, the presentiment that I might be treading the same path as K had walked began from time to time to send shivers through me.

CHAPTER 108

Time passed, and my wife's mother became ill. The doctor who examined her told us it was incurable. I nursed her devotedly, both for her own sake and for the sake of the wife I loved. In larger terms, however, I did so also for the sake of humanity itself. I had long felt an urgent need to act in some way, but I remained at an impasse, sitting idle as the years passed. Isolated as I was from the human world, I felt for the first time that I was doing something of real worth. I was sustained by what I can only describe as a sense of atonement for past sin.

In due course my wife's mother died, leaving my wife and me alone together. I was all she had left in life to trust and depend on, she said to me. At these words, tears filled my eyes to think that she had to trust someone who had forfeited all trust in himself. *Poor thing,* I thought, and I even said as much to her. "Why?" she asked, uncomprehending. But I could not explain. She cried then. "You're always so cynical and watchful of me," she said bitterly. "That's why you say such things."

After her mother's death, I did my best to be kind and gentle to her, and not simply because I loved her. No, behind my solicitous attention lay something larger, something that transcended the individual. My heart was stirring, just as it had when I nursed her mother. This change seemed to make her happy. Yet behind her happiness I sensed a vague uneasiness that sprang from puzzlement. Even if she had understood, however, she would hardly have felt reassured. It seems to me that women are more inclined than men to respond to the sort of kindness that focuses exclusively on themselves, even if it is morally questionable from a stricter perspective, and that they are less able to fully appreciate the kind of love that derives from the larger claims of humanity.

Once she wondered aloud to me whether a man's heart and a woman's could ever really become one. I replied evasively that they probably can when you are young. She seemed then to be gazing back at her own past, and at length she gave a tiny sigh.

From around this time, a horrible darkness would occasionally grip me. At first the force that would suddenly overwhelm me seemed external, but as time went by, my heart began to stir of its own accord in response to this fearful shadow. In the end I came to feel that it was no external thing but something secretly nurtured all along deep within my own breast. Whenever the sensation came upon me, I questioned my own sanity. But I had no inclination to consult a doctor, or anybody else for that matter.

What this feeling produced was, quite simply, a keen awareness of the nature of human sin. That is what sent me back each month to K's grave. It is also what lay behind the nursing of my dying mother-in-law, and what bade me treat my wife so tenderly. There were even times when I longed for some stranger to come along and flog me as I deserved. At some stage this feeling transformed into a conviction that it should be I who hurt myself. And then the thought struck me that I should not just hurt myself but kill myself. At all events, I resolved that I must live my life as if I were already dead.

How many years has it been since I made that decision? My wife and I have lived in peace together all that time. We have in no way been unhappy, quite the opposite. But this one thing in me, this thing that for me is so vital, has always been for my wife a place of incomprehensible darkness. The thought fills me with pity for her.

CHAPTER 109

Though I had resolved to live as if I were dead, some external stimulus would occasionally set my heart dancing. But the moment I felt the urge to break through my deathly impasse and act, a terrible force would rise up out of nowhere and press me fiercely back into immobility. A voice would bear down on me with the words *You have no right*, and I would instantly wilt and go limp. When a little later I tried to rise again, again this force would press me back. I ground my teeth in impotent rage. "Why do you stand in my way like this?" I would cry. The strange force would laugh coldly back at me and reply, *You know very well why*. And again my will would collapse.

You must understand that during all these long years of seemingly uneventful and monotonous peace, this grueling battle has been raging endlessly inside me. If my wife was vexed by my state, I was far, far more mortified by it myself. Eventually, when I could no longer bear to be immobilized inside this prison, and all my desperate attempts to break its bars proved futile, I began to feel that my easiest option really was suicide. "But why?" I hear you ask in astonished disbelief. The fact is, this strange and terrifying force within me had paralyzed my heart with its iron grip, blocking every exit route bar one—the way to death alone lay open and free for the taking. If I were to break this deadlock and move in any way, my steps could only carry me down that path.

Two or three times before now I have been poised to set off along the road to death that my destiny has laid before me so beguilingly. But each time my wife held my heart back. Needless to say, I have not had the courage to take her with me—I have been too cowardly even to confess my story to her, heaven knows, and the merest thought of inflicting double suicide on her and making her a cruel sacrifice to my own fate filled me with horror. My karma is my own, after all, and hers is hers. To cast our two lives into the flames together would not only be against nature, it would break the heart.

And yet it filled me with pity to think of her alone after I was gone. Those words she had spoken after her mother's death— that I was all she had left in life to trust and depend on—were seared into my breast. I hung in a constant state of indecision. Sometimes, seeing her face, I felt glad that I had not acted. Then I would quail and cower again. From time to time she would turn on me a look that bespoke sorrowing disappointment.

Remember, this is how my life has been lived. My state of mind was much the same the day we first met at Kamakura and that day we walked together beyond the town. A black shadow was constantly at my back. I was dragging out my life on this earth for the sake of my wife. That evening after you graduated was no different. I meant it when I promised to meet you again come September. I fully intended to see you once more. Autumn ended, winter came, and even as spring drew in, I was still looking forward to our next meeting.

And then, at the height of the summer, Emperor Meiji passed away.[1] I felt then that as the spirit of the Meiji era had begun with him, so it had ended with his death. I was struck with an overwhelming sense that my generation, we who had felt Meiji's influence most deeply, were doomed to linger on simply as anachronisms as long as we remained alive. When I said this in so many words to my wife, she laughed it off. But then for some reason she added teasingly, "Well, then, you could follow the old style and die with your lord, couldn't you."

CHAPTER 110

I had almost forgotten the expression "to die with your lord." It's not a phrase that is used in normal life these days. It must have lain there deep in my memory all these years, decaying slowly. Reminded of it by my wife's jest, I replied that if I were to die a loyal follower's death, the lord I was following to the grave would be the spirit of the Meiji era itself. I was joking too, of course, but as I spoke it seemed to me that this old, disused expression had somehow gained a new meaning.

About a month passed. On the night of the cremation, I sat as usual in my study. As the imperial coffin emerged from the palace, I heard the boom of the funeral cannon. To me it sounded the Meiji era's end. Later I read in the newspaper that it also signaled the end of General Nogi.[1] When my eyes fell on this news, I seized the paper and waved it at my wife. "He died with his lord!" I found myself exclaiming.

There I read the letter that the general had written before he died. He had been longing all this time, he wrote, to die in expiation for his failure in the Satsuma Rebellion.[2] I paused to count on my fingers the years he must have lived with this resolution in his heart. Thirty-five years had passed since the Satsuma Rebellion. By his own account, General Nogi had spent those thirty-five long years yearning to die without finding the moment to do so. Which had been more excruciating for him, I wondered—those thirty-five years of life, or the moment when he thrust the sword into his belly?

Two or three days later I finally decided to kill myself. I would guess that my reasons will be as hard for you to fully grasp as I found General Nogi's reasons to be. If so, it must simply be put down to the different eras we belong to, I think. Or perhaps, after all, our differences spring from the individual natures we were born with. At any rate, I have done my best in these pages to explain to you my own strange nature.

I will be leaving my wife behind, but fortunately she will not want for the necessities of life. I do not want her to witness any horror. I intend to die in such a way that she will not have to see blood. I will leave the world quietly, without her knowing. I would like to have her believe that I died instantaneously. I would be content if she decided I had gone mad.

It is now ten days since I decided to die. You should know that I have spent most of that time writing this long memoir to leave for you. I was planning to see you again and tell you all this in person, but having written it, I am now glad I chose this method, since it has allowed me to describe myself more clearly to you. I have not written from mere personal whim. My past, which made me what I am, is an aspect of human experience that only I can describe. My effort to write as honestly as possible will not be in vain, I feel, since it will help both you and others who read it to understand humanity better. Just recently, I heard that Watanabe Kazan chose to postpone his suicide for a week while he painted *Kantan*.[3] Some will find this decision ridiculous, but no doubt his heart had its own reasons that made it imperative for him. This labor of mine is not simply a way of fulfilling my promise to you. It is for the greater part the result of a need I have felt within myself.

But now I have answered that need. There is nothing left for me to do. When this letter reaches your hands, I will no longer be in this world. I will be long dead. Ten days ago my wife went to her aunt's place over in Ichigaya. Her aunt was ill and help was short, so I urged her to go. I wrote most of this long letter while she was absent. I hastily hid it whenever she returned to the house.

My aim has been to present both the good and bad in my life, for others to learn from. I must make clear to you, however, that my wife is the sole exception. I want her told nothing. My one request is that her memory of my life be preserved as untarnished as possible. While she remains alive, I therefore ask that you keep all this to yourself, a secret intended for your eyes alone.

Notes

CHAPTER 1

1 *Kamakura:* This former capital of Japan had recently established itself as a summer resort convenient to Tokyo, where visitors could indulge in the fashionable pastime of sea bathing.

CHAPTER 60

1 *the basic exchange of marriage cups:* Marriage formally took place with a simple ceremony involving drinking sake from the same cup.

CHAPTER 64

1 *Hongō Hill . . . Denzūin Temple:* An area of present-day Tokyo's Bunkyō ward, where Tokyo University is located. Denzūin Temple is a Pure Land Buddhist temple.
2 *the Sino-Japanese War:* 1894–95.

CHAPTER 65

1 *koto:* A traditional zitherlike Japanese instrument with thirteen strings.
2 *Ojōsan:* The daughter is referred to throughout by this polite title for an unmarried girl.

CHAPTER 72

1 *adopt a son-in-law . . . marry out as a bride:* Although the wife traditionally joined her husband's family register, formal adoption of a husband into the wife's family was not uncommon in cases where the family had no son to receive an inheritance.

CHAPTER 74

1 *the Komagome area:* part of Tokyo's present-day Bunkyō ward.

CHAPTER 81

1 *Swedenborg:* Emanuel Swedenborg (1688–1772), Swedish philosopher and mystic.
2 *the Bōshū Peninsula:* In present-day southern Chiba Prefecture.

CHAPTER 84

1 *Chōshi:* A fishing-port town in present-day Chiba Prefecture.
2 *the famous Buddhist priest Nichiren:* Nichiren (1222–82) founded the Nichiren sect, which places ultimate faith in the Lotus Sutra.

CHAPTER 85

1 *the Ryōkoku district:* A busy district centered around the Ryōkoku Bridge in Tokyo.

CHAPTER 87

1 *the fierce Enma image that stands in Genkaku Temple:* Genkaku Temple is in the Tokyo district of Koishikawa, close to where Sōseki imagines Okusan's house to stand. Enma is the ruler of the realms of the dead.

CHAPTER 88

1 *Masago-chō:* An area in present-day Bunkyō ward, near Tokyo
   University.

CHAPTER 89

1 *the New Year game of poem cards:* A traditional game in which
   cards containing the second half of famous poems are turned
   faceup, and the participants must match each to the appropriate
   card containing the poem's first half. The poems are those in the
   anthology *Hyakunin isshū,* "One Hundred Poems of One Hundred Poets," a title usually referring to the collection made by
   Fujiwara no Teika (1162–1241).

CHAPTER 100

1 *elliptical course . . . three city wards:* Koishikawa, Kanda, and
   Hongō wards.

CHAPTER 102

1 *I had laid out my bedding . . . opposite direction:* It is considered
   unlucky to lie facing west, which is the realm of the dead.

CHAPTER 109

1 *Emperor Meiji passed away:* See Introduction.

CHAPTER 110

1 *the end of General Nogi:* See Introduction.
2 *his failure in the Satsuma Rebellion:* In the civil war of 1877,
   forces loyal to the emperor clashed with those of the rebellious
   Satsuma province. The imperial forces won, but as regimental
   commander, General Nogi felt responsible for the enemy's cap-
   ture of the symbolic regimental colors.

3 *Watanabe Kazan . . . while he painted* Kantan: Watanabe Kazan
   (1793–1841), artist and scholar, painted the famous *Kantan*. It
   depicts the Chinese legend of a young man in the village of that
   name, who gains enlightenment when a dream reveals to him the
   transience of fame and glory. Kazan committed ritual suicide.

ALSO AVAILABLE FROM PENGUIN CLASSICS

Kusamakura

Translated with an Introduction and Notes by Meredith McKinney

ISBN 978-0-14-310519-0

Natsume Sōseki's *Kusamakura* follows its nameless young artist-narrator on a meandering walking tour of the mountains, where he has a series of mysterious encounters with a lovely young woman. Written at a time when Japan was opening its doors to the world, *Kusamakura* turns inward to the pristine mountain idyll and the taciturn lyricism of its courtship scenes, enshrining the essence of old Japan in a work of enchanting literary nostalgia.

PENGUIN
CLASSICS

ALSO AVAILABLE FROM
PENGUIN CLASSICS

Sanshiro

Translated by Jay Rubin
Introduction by Haruki Murakami

Sōseki's only coming-of-age novel, *Sanshiro* depicts the eponymous twenty-three-year-old protagonist as he leaves the sleepy countryside to attend a university in the constantly moving "real world" of Tokyo. Baffled and excited by the traffic, the academics, and—most of all—the women, Sanshirō must find a way among the sophisticates that fill his new life.

ISBN 978-0-14-045562-5

PENGUIN
CLASSICS